LET THE WRONG LIGHT IN

AVON GALE

REAMSPINNER
PRESS

Published by
DREAMSPINNER PRESS

5032 Capital Circle SW, Suite 2, PMB# 279, Tallahassee, FL 32305-7886 USA
http://www.dreamspinnerpress.com/

Let the Wrong Light In
© 2015 Avon Gale.

Cover Art
© 2015 Aaron Anderson.
aaronbydesign55@gmail.com
Cover content is for illustrative purposes only and any person depicted on the cover is a model.

ISBN: 978-1-63476-315-8
Digital ISBN: 978-1-63476-316-5
Library of Congress Control Number: 2015945836
First Edition September 2015

Printed in the United States of America
∞
This paper meets the requirements of
ANSI/NISO Z39.48-1992 (Permanence of Paper).

To my mom, who encouraged me to tell stories long before I learned how to write them down.

To Eric, Robin, Kristen and Jen, for somehow always knowing when to be an anchor and when to be a thunderstorm. And to Morgan and Eileen, who gave me back houses to build when I thought I'd forgotten how to draw. The constant support and encouragement from all of you means more to me than I can say. As does your patience with my overuse of metaphors. Love you guys!!<3

CHAPTER 1

THE UMPTEENTH proposal that ends up back on his desk, complete with a tersely written note that basically says *no chance in hell*, is the proverbial sustainable-living and eco-friendly straw that breaks Avery Hextall's back.

He's been at Ratcliff and Roberts architectural firm for two years, patiently working his way up the ranks to junior associate. When he found himself with an ergonomically designed desk and his very own *voice mail*, he thought his first project couldn't be far behind. Unfortunately he was saddled with a project manager who put the "cad" in AutoCAD and took a vicious glee in rejecting every single design Avery put in front of him.

He has no idea what he's done to piss off Malin Lacroix, but whatever it is, he's apparently a lot better at doing that than he is at designing buildings. Fuck. Think of all the student loan debt he could have saved himself if he'd only known that ahead of time.

His latest design, though—he was really proud of it, and he was *sure* it would at least make it past Project Manager Prissypants' desk. He'd spent three weeks of his life on it, living on coffee spiked with two of those five-hour energy supplement things and eating nothing but Frosted Flakes. He was pretty sure he was designing the goddamn thing in his *sleep*—if he'd actually slept. He still wasn't sure about that.

What he *was* sure about was that he'd pored over blueprints of every building he ever loved and every graduate-school design he ever did. Hell, he even looked at the shit he drew in his fifth-grade art class and asked his mom if his Lego creations struck her as particularly innovative and sustainable. She told him very calmly to get some sleep and then hung up. Avery took that as a *no*.

When it was finished, he sent the whole thing to his friend from graduate school, Blake Everett, himself an architect at an award-winning firm in Seattle. Then he paced around his living room, smoking cigarettes some chick left at his apartment a month or two before, and waited for Everett to respond.

Everett's e-mail came a few hours later—*fuck you, you brilliant goddamn bastard*—and Avery gave a fist bump to his cat—or pillow. Whatever. He was really tired. And then he promptly went to sleep despite it being two in the afternoon on a Saturday. He spent the next day feverishly preparing the design for submission and drank two beers. He hit *send* on the e-mail to Lacroix when it was uploaded, watched some girl-on-girl porn on the Spice Channel, and then fell asleep on his couch.

He strolled into work on Monday morning convinced he'd finally done it, that he would *finally* see an Avery Hextall design on something other than a computer screen. He was high as a fucking kite for the next two weeks, right up until two minutes before, when he got back from lunch.

There it is, his proposal, sitting in the exact center of his desk with Lacroix's crisp handwriting inked in red across the top page. Lacroix uses red ink because he's some kind of sadistic bastard. Or maybe he has a recurrent high school calculus-teacher fantasy. Whichever. Avery knows what it means before he even reads it, and it feels like a thundercloud has just unleashed a storm on his kite and tangled the damn thing up in a tree.

Or something like that. Fuck it. He's too angry for appropriate metaphors.

He is *pissed.* And he's going to get some goddamn answers. Namely what the hell Lacroix's note—*too complicated given the parameters*—means. Fuck. Avery designs commercial-use buildings, not Playmobil toy sets. Lacroix is going to have to explain himself, because this is personal—just like the fourth *Jaws* movie—only this makes even less sense.

THE PROBLEM with barging into Lacroix's office, Avery quickly discovers, is the reality is far more anticlimactic than he imagined. It starts out promisingly enough. He storms in without knocking, and that's pretty great. Then he yells for five minutes and even pounds his fist on Lacroix's desk for added dramatic effect.

Lacroix just *looks* at him. "Is there a problem, Mr. Hextall?"

Avery gives his desk a cursory glance, looking for the red pen. Fuck that red pen, man. And fuck Lacroix. Fuck him and his classy suits, his icy eyes, his hands that look more like a violinist's than a project manager's. They're nice hands, actually... and wait, what is he doing? He's here to yell at Lacroix, not think about his hands.

"Yeah, there's a problem," Avery huffs, ready to shout so loud that the glass panes in the window behind Lacroix will shatter into pieces. Maybe the son of a bitch will get sucked outside—à la every action movie Avery's ever seen. "The problem is you're a prick with no soul."

"Please have a seat." Lacroix waves at the chair in front of his desk, the chair Avery is holding on to with both hands. He's thinking about swinging it at Lacroix's head.

Avery yanks the chair out and sits down, realizes he's just obeyed Lacroix, and then stands up again. "No."

Lacroix shrugs, in that effortless, annoying way of his that's number sixty-five on Avery's "Reasons I Irrationally Hate Malin Lacroix" list. He has another list of rational reasons. Avery is a believer in the power of lists.

"Suit yourself," Lacroix says, watching him with those pale eyes of his. "I assume you are here because I rejected your proposal?"

There's the slightest hint of amusement in Lacroix's voice. At least, Avery thinks he hears it. Or maybe he just wants an excuse to pick up the dumb glass paperweight on Lacroix's desk and hurl it at something, which is exactly the next step of his spur-of-the-moment plan.

The glass is cold in his fingers—smooth—and the architect in him appreciates the form of it, even as the rest of him wants to smash it into Lacroix's face. "*Yes.* Do you know how hard I worked on that?"

Lacroix has his fingers around Avery's wrist. They're warm, surprisingly strong, and his grasp is starting to hurt.

"Hextall." Lacroix's voice is just as firm as his grip, and there's something in his tone that takes Avery's breath away completely. "Put that down, and then sit. I'm not going to tell you again."

Lacroix says that like Avery is his dog—or a junior associate, same thing. And it should be infuriating. It *is*, but that's exactly what Avery does. He flexes his hand with a petulant mutter and then collapses in the seat with as much grace as a fallen angel sauntering into a whorehouse.

"There." Lacroix sounds pleased, but Avery can't tell for sure because he refuses to look at the motherfucker. "Now I know you're upset that I did not select your design, and I am perfectly willing to give you feedback. Provided you stop sulking."

"I know why you did it." Avery's starting to feel kind of… maybe not *embarrassed*. He's still really pissed, but he's sort of wishing he thought this through. As usual that doesn't make him stop talking. "You want to crush my hopes and dreams. That's why."

"I'm sure you are aware that I reject most of the junior designers' submissions—all of them, not just yours. But I assure you it's for the benefit of this firm, not personal enjoyment." Lacroix pauses. "Well, maybe I find it a little enjoyable in your case." Now he's *definitely* amused. Avery doesn't need to look up from his intense concentration on the threads of his dress pants to see that.

"And all of you think the same thing—that I am failing to appreciate your genius, that I'm too rigid and don't understand how brilliant you are. Or if I *only knew* how you stayed up for days on end, living on coffee and cigarettes, running purely on fumes from the *fires of creation*—then I would understand that this is more to you than just a building. Does that sound familiar?"

It does. And it also sounds like his life resembles one of the songs from *Rent*. He finally looks up, wary, and meets Lacroix's gaze. Probably responding with jazz hands and *La Vie Boheme* isn't the best thing to do, even if it would be fucking funny as hell. So he doesn't say anything at all.

"I thought so. And I myself am a designer, Mr. Hextall. I understand the simple elements of a good design. But my job is to select a proposal that has a chance of winning the bid for a certain project. And so, yes, they *are* just buildings to me. I'm not here to inflate your ego with constant praise. You're no longer in graduate school."

"Wait. They do that in graduate school? Someone should call Columbia University and tell them that, then." Avery leans forward, eyes narrowed. "That was a goddamn good design and you know it." Maybe if Lacroix agrees, he can leave, and they can both pretend he didn't just do this.

There's an angry flash in Lacroix's eyes, and his mouth sets into a hard line. "I'm going to assume you need longer than the average person to absorb information, and simply remind you that my job is not to select proposals based entirely on their design but their functionality, cost effectiveness, and adherence to the client's wishes. Do you understand that, or shall I draw you a diagram explaining how architecture firms work?"

Avery glares at him. "I understand. Yeah. I knew there would be soulless corporate types, just not soulless architects. Is that why you're in project management, because all your designs are stuffy and boring?"

"No. I'm in project management because I'm very good at convincing clients to select our firm's proposals. Which, by the way, I accomplish without shouting at them and suggesting they're idiots." Lacroix sighs. "Even though most of them are. I'm able to adapt our designs so that they *actually get built*, Hextall. So you might want to rethink which one of us is so rigid, hmm?"

"I designed that building according to the specifications we were given." Avery's voice is less angry now, and he's fidgety, unable to sit still. "If there were other ones, you should have told me."

"I don't *have* to do anything," Lacroix snaps. Then he closes his eyes like he's counting to ten. Or… whatever the fuck ten is in French. Avery is pretty sure that's Lacroix's nationality. "Let me show you something."

Lacroix turns his computer screen so Avery can see it, and what's on the monitor doesn't make a whole lot of sense to him at first. He leans forward, squints, grabs his glasses from his front pocket out of instinct, and puts them on. "Fascinating. Are these the things called 'spreadsheets' I've heard so much about?"

"Were you this annoying in all your classes, Hextall?"

"Oh yeah." Avery doesn't look away from the screen. "It's a good thing this place only needed two reference letters, or I'd be in trouble."

There's a huff that might be a laugh, and then Lacroix continues. "This is the schematic of the job for which your proposal was rejected." He starts clicking with the mouse, pulling up screens comprised of bar graphs and a lot of boring math. "It was a brilliant design. Your talent is only very rarely in question."

Avery is too shocked by the first actual word of praise he's ever heard from Lacroix to do anything but gape like a drunken fish

5

with black-rimmed glasses. Did he fall asleep? Because no way did that just happen....

Wait. Does he really want to fall asleep and dream about Lacroix? Absolutely not. The praise, though. He could get used to that.

"Mr. Hextall?"

"Oh. Uh. What?" Avery adjusts his glasses and tries for his scowl, but he can't quite manage it. Besides, he's interested in what's on the screen. There are a lot of words about soil composition and weather patterns, right next to things like *bid tabulation* and *schedule of values.*

"I have to take every single proposal that meets my expectations and filter them through the requirements of the client, and then through the company and our available resources. At the end of the day, I select the proposal that comes closest to satisfying both." He finishes clicking buttons, and there's a screen with Avery's initials and some more graphs—as well as a lot of numbers. "Here is the breakdown of your design."

Avery studies the screen, and he's not entirely sure what he's reading, but he has a pretty good idea based on the frightening amount of numbers in red.

"It was too expensive?"

"That was one issue. Yes."

"For us or for them?" Avery looks at him, his temper flaring, though it is solely on behalf of his artistic soul this time. "And what do you mean, one issue? What are the others? Because sometimes you have to pay more for quality—"

"Hextall, be quiet. Look at the screen and listen to me." Lacroix has that same tone in his voice he did when he told Avery to sit. "You're thinking like an architect, not a businessman. There are more things to consider than a brief cost analysis and environmental impact survey." Lacroix waves his hand dismissively. "Did you know that the insurance required for this particular company to have a—what did you call it, a free-standing atrium—would likely cost a thousand people their jobs, just to pay for it?"

"They said they wanted open spaces with plenty of light. That's what I was designing. How was I supposed to know that other stuff?"

Lacroix sighs, and turns his computer screen away from Avery. "You're not. I am. There were issues with some of the soil composites and water runoff from a nearby lake. I imagine you didn't know there was a lake nearby either. And that impacted it as well."

Avery takes his glasses off and rubs the lenses with his shirt. "I could have fixed that. All of it. If someone had told me."

"I'm sure you could have. But you are a junior associate in a firm, and Thomas's design was far better suited for the environment and the cost."

Brandon Thomas. Ugh. Of course. The shining golden boy who was nice to just about everyone and also really genuine about it. He also was impossible to hate. And oh, had Avery ever tried. Including right this moment, learning Brandon's design had been chosen instead of his.

"So you didn't hate it." Avery falls back in his chair, stares up at the ceiling, and tries to figure out how to say "I'm sorry" without actually having to say it. In hindsight, this entire thing was a terrible idea. At least he didn't throw the paperweight. "My design, I mean."

"This one? No. I've hated a few of them because I find your adherence to sustainability affects your form, on occasion. I'm beginning to think your trademark is unnecessarily complicated."

That surprises him enough to prompt him to look at Lacroix again. "You better not be talking about the passive solar-heating coil that I integrated into the curvature of the staircase, because that was fucking brilliant."

"Passive solar heating... you mean a *window?*"

"It's not my fault you hate the Earth." Avery expels a breath. He probably just fucked himself six ways to Sunday, and if he gets a reputation for being a prima donna, he'll end up designing condos for retirees in Virginia Beach or something equally horrible. He just can't bring himself to apologize, even though he knows he should. It probably won't do any good... but still.

Avery remains obstinately silent. All he has left here is his pride and a fucking killer staircase design.

"I assume this little chat addresses all your questions, Mr. Hextall?" Lacroix is still staring at him. Avery thinks he looks like a hawk. Does that make Avery a bunny rabbit if he can't look away?

He nods as grudgingly as possible.

"Good. You are more than welcome to schedule a meeting with me about your designs, but don't you ever barge in here and act like I

7

owe you any answers for doing my job. Or like I'm carrying out some personal crusade to end your professional career. Consider it a new rule that you don't enter my office without my express permission." Lacroix's winter voice feels like ice sliding down Avery's spine.

No wonder he didn't like that staircase of mine. He's way too cold for solar anything. It's a sign of maturity that he doesn't allow that thought to become actual words.

"I would suggest taking a few days off. Expend some of this energy of yours on something other than nearly losing your job."

Avery stands up, nods, and shoves his hands into his pockets before he can do something dumb, like try to shake Lacroix's hand.

"Yeah. Okay." He heads toward the door and says, without looking back, "I didn't know. That other stuff."

Lacroix is quiet for a moment. "And now you do. And you won't act that way again."

It's not a question, which is a good thing because Avery doesn't want to make promises he can't keep. And promising he won't make impulsive decisions is like promising he can keep the sun from rising.

It's also a clear assertion of who has the control, who holds the power over whom. And instead of infuriating Avery like it should, it does something just as maddening.

Avery walks out of Lacroix's office, heads back to his desk, and grabs his cell phone. There is only one thing to do after the double gut punch of rejection and forced humility.

It's time to get drunk.

CHAPTER 2

"YOU STORMED into Malin Lacroix's office and called him a prick?" Harlan starts laughing. "Oh man, Avery. Half the contractors in the city are terrified of him. And you still have a job?"

"Yeah." Avery is drinking a gin and tonic, and it's his third or fourth one since he showed up to meet Harlan for dinner. Which they haven't had yet, technically, unless edamame counts. The way his head feels suggests it doesn't. "Don't think he likes me, though."

"I can't imagine why." Harlan points at him with his cocktail straw. "You do get a little shortsighted about your designs. You always have."

"Oh my god. You can't side with him. You're my friend. You're—" Avery leans forward, his voice dramatic and whispery. "You're my fuck *buddy*." From the corner of his eye, Avery sees a girl at the next table look over at the two of them. Avery grins at her and winks. "Fucking good job, me. Right?"

"Shh," Harlan says, but he's laughing. Harlan is the hardest guy in the world to piss off, which is why they're still friends. He shakes his head fondly at Avery. "Don't curse in front of a lady."

Avery groans, puts his head on the table, and bangs his forehead against it a few times. "You would be so much easier to deal with if you weren't so pretty, Harlan." Avery is sure Harlan's screwed more straight dudes than that guy with the camcorder and the go gay for cash website. He's got perfect abs. His jeans always look like they were made just for him, and he has hair that looks like it's sun kissed and isn't even highlighted at a salon. His Southern accent, rather than sounding like he should be on *Duck Dynasty*, is as charming as everything else about him.

Avery once tried to mimic it to pick up a girl at a party. Harlan told him he should stop because he sounded like the kind of Southerner who puts up a Confederate flag in his garage and drives a gas-guzzling truck. Harlan, on the other hand, sounds like a Southern gentleman who

9

doesn't curse in front of ladies and takes public transportation. Which is exactly what he is.

"We all have our crosses to bear, Avery." Harlan pats him on the shoulder. "And I'm only saying that because, as a contractor, I know how impossible you creative people are. So I sort of understand that aspect of Lacroix's position. That's all."

"No. Stop. You're not supposed to understand. You're supposed to say, 'Avery, that man is a horrible human being with no taste, and he wouldn't know a good design if it walked up and introduced itself and asked Lacroix if he wanted a blowjob for twenty-five bucks.'"

"Ah, Avery—"

"I mean, Jesus, Harlan. I know you're a contractor, but you can lay drywall. And like, drywall-ers, you know?" This isn't making sense, but that's never stopped Avery before. "That's exciting and sexy. It's not bar graphs and math, which is all Lacroix does." Avery adopts an obnoxious French accent when he says his boss's name. "He's boring. He has one thing on his desk, and it's a paperweight. So that's interesting. I bet his house is all white walls and like, nonefficiency appliances."

"Avery, maybe you should sit up—"

"No." Avery keeps his head on his arms, but he turns so Harlan can still hear him, because the shit he's saying is important. "He's prolly got one of those dishwashers that uses sixty-four gallons of water. And I bet he doesn't separate the recycling out of his trash."

Harlan coughs. "He's very drunk."

"Huh?" Avery lifts his head and looks blearily at Harlan. "Lacroix? Nuh-uh. Closet alcoholism would make him interesting and maybe have a personality." It takes Avery about three seconds to realize Harlan isn't talking to him. He's talking about him. He turns his head, sees who is standing next to the table, and groans. "Fuck me. I hate everything. Of course it's you."

Why in the name of hell is Lacroix standing there? He must be cursed. There is no other explanation. Avery puts his head on his arms again. "Go away. I'm on vacation. I don't have to be nice to you."

"I don't have a dishwasher," Lacroix says flatly.

"Great. Washing dishes by hand wastes even more water. I bet you leave the faucet running and take twenty-five minute steaming-hot showers in the morning." He might have been wrong about that being three drinks. It might have been more. He was definitely not wrong about edamame being a shitty excuse for dinner. Holy fuck is he drunk.

"Hi. I'm Harlan Pearce." Harlan introduces himself to Lacroix before Avery finishes what he started and destroys his career in a single bound. The Superman of Fuckups. Great.

"Malin Lacroix."

Avery is imagining them shaking hands, and he feels betrayed.

"Avery is, ah. Venting… letting off some steam. He's called me terrible names before too."

"Colonel Sanders is not that bad. It's better than that Looney Tunes rooster," Avery mutters, the words muffled against the table—or they would be if the universe didn't hate him.

"I'm certain he is. Rejection is always difficult, isn't it, Avery?"

"If you don't want me to barge in your office and ask you shit in a loud voice, don't saunter up to my… drinking office… and ask me hypothetical questions. And don't use my first name," he adds, finally looking up at his boss. He's in his dress shirt, his tie loosened and his shirtsleeves rolled up. "You look different."

Lacroix smiles down at him—that tiny smile that Avery doesn't like because it's stupid. "Do I?"

"Yup." Avery looks over at Harlan, who is signaling with his eyes for Avery to be quiet. Avery just makes a kissing motion at him and turns back to Lacroix. "You look a lot less stuffy. Like a normal person."

"And you look… defeated." Lacroix's smile is sharper, and it's strange. It's a loud restaurant, but Avery can't seem to hear anything else, notice anything else, who isn't his boss. "Much like you did earlier, when you were aware you should apologize and were angry about it."

That kills all of Avery's ire, and all he feels is incredibly tired. And drunk. Lacroix is clearly enjoying himself at Avery's expense, which is making him feel weird, and he doesn't like it. "Go away. Fire me when I get back. I don't care. Why are you even here? I thought you lived in Mordor."

"Sorry to disappoint you," Lacroix says in a smooth voice, and Avery is pretty sure the reference just sailed way over his head. "I'm here to meet a friend."

"What? You have friends? Are they boring math people too?" Avery grins at him, meanly, like he's picking on a kid at the bus stop. An older kid who could run him over with a car. "Hey, is it Thomas? Is he going to give you a twenty-five dollar blowjob?" The instant he says that, Avery is well aware he's gone too far.

How does he still have a job, and why is he doing his level best not to? Something about Lacroix's insufferable smugness makes Avery want to rile him up. And he's always been the type to push and push, just to see what he can get away with. But he rarely does it like this. What the hell does he want? Lacroix to lose his cool and punch him in the mouth? Jesus, he's acting like a twelve-year-old boy with a crush on a—

Oh no. No, no, no. A horrible suspicion is planted in Avery's brain, and he starts sucking on the ice in his watery gin and tonic, desperate for more liquor to burn it out of there.

"I don't think you want me to answer that, Avery," Lacroix says, and it is so strange to hear him use his first name, strange and something else. And oh, Avery is fucked. He is so, so fucked. "I'll see you at work in a few days, and we'll pretend this never happened. Won't we."

It's yet another question that isn't really a question, but this time Avery nods. "Sure thing, Malin," he responds, trying for his usual bravado. He's never used Lacroix's first name before. It's weird.

Lacroix responds by correcting his pronunciation, nodding politely at Harlan, and then walking away. Avery is envious. It would be nice to make such an obvious fuck-you statement without implying your coworkers suck cock for money.

Harlan is staring at him with an expression that often means he's going to say something Avery doesn't want to hear. All he does, though, is signal for their check (and get the waitress's phone number—the rascal) and pay the tab. He also takes Avery home with him, but instead of taking him to bed, he puts a glass of water next to the guest bed and resists Avery's sloppy attempts to seduce him. Which is a good thing because as soon as his head hits the pillow, his days of no sleep and the combination of stress, alcohol, and no substantial food catch up with him, and he's out like a light.

12

AVERY CONVINCES himself he's not nervous about going to work and seeing Lacroix again, and he decides the best way to prove that is by avoiding him.

It works. Mostly because they don't spend much time together. Avery sees him in passing every so often, and they exchange a cool nod. Then Avery looks away first because Lacroix seems to expect it.

He's also mildly miffed at Harlan. The day after his embarrassing gin-and-tonic-fueled babblefest, Harlan *still* told him no when he tried to get some. He let Avery stay at his place, made him dinner, and even rented a dumb horror movie. But he absolutely refused to fall prey to any of Avery's patented seduction moves, such as "climb on your lap" and "offer to wash your back in the shower."

When those things didn't work as expected, he tried getting Harlan drunk. That didn't end with sex, but it did end with Harlan's drawl sounding a lot less Southern gentleman and more rowdy redneck, which Avery thought was awesome and also hilarious. He lied and said it was hot, just to see if that'd work, but Harlan hit him with a pillow and told him to knock it off.

Finally he resorted to asking *why* they weren't fucking, given neither of them are in a relationship and they've been screwing around since they met. Avery was a junior in college and took a summer job helping out at a construction site to understand what it was like to "build things" and "touch the materials." He ended up touching a lot of material that summer, mainly cotton shirts he was pulling off Harlan.

He learned two things. When you design buildings, you can be in air-conditioning and smoke while doing it. And he likes cock sometimes. It was mildly surprising, but when he told his mother—in less specific terms—she said, "Well, of course you like boys, honey. Did you really not know that? Your father and I thought.... Well, I'm glad you finally figured it out." Then his mother and father joined PFLAG, and his mom made cookies for their bake sale.

His parents were pretty fucking great, actually.

Harlan, however, was not so great. He could actually resist Avery's incessant questioning, and all he'd say was "I just don't think it's a good idea."

Avery wanted to know *why* it was a bad idea. Harlan told him he'd figure it out in time. Avery reminded him it took him nineteen years to figure out the whole "I like cock" thing. Harlan helped him out with that, so why couldn't he just lend a hand again? Or a mouth. Anything really. They didn't have to fuck if Harlan didn't want—

That's when Harlan took Avery's shoulders in both of his hands and firmly told Avery he should get home because he had to feed the cat. He did not appreciate Avery's joke. "Oh, I see. You don't want to fuck me because you're worried about the pussy."

So instead he called Harlan Foghorn Leghorn—he'd been trying to think of that fucking rooster's name since that night at the bar—and left his wet towel on the guest bed. Ha! It was the little things. It really was.

Harlan would tell him eventually. He was like Avery's wise, all-knowing sage—with a Southern accent and a perfect blowjob mouth—and Avery always appreciated his friend's ability to think rationally and form coherent thoughts. He just needed to start sharing them, was all.

But Harlan isn't returning any of Avery's four thousand text messages saying *no srsly what did u mean??* And the nagging thought that he's *missing* something is driving him just as crazy as the not-getting-laid part.

One night it gets a little too much. Sure he's a devotee of the Spice Channel and adult magazines and the Internet and whatever else, but goddamn. He wants an actual *person*. So Thursday night after work, he goes to the gym, showers, and heads to a bar he sometimes frequents when he's in the mood for a guy and his usual hookup buddy isn't around. Or is being an evasive weirdo.

Avery might be high-strung and have a temper, but he's also charming and determined, and he doesn't foresee a problem finding himself a dance partner for the evening. Except it becomes painfully obvious, about an hour or so after he gets there, he left his dance card at home, hidden under a pile of magazines and past-due bills on his kitchen counter. It's not that there aren't people there who are hot and even interested. It's just that none of them are pinging his "yeah, take me home and fuck me" radar.

This only serves to make him *more* determined. So now he's one of those creeper guys, circling around like a greyhound after a rabbit.

Or however that would work for a bisexual dude looking for meaningless sex, but being unusually picky about it.

He's about to give up and go home to his laptop and his right hand when he sees someone at the end of the bar who looks familiar. His heart jumps into his throat and makes him taste restless lust and sudden fear. The man is a few inches over six feet tall, is well dressed, and has white-blond hair. For half a second, Avery is certain the man is Lacroix.

He tries to tell himself that it doesn't really matter. If Lacroix's here, he's *here*. It's not like a bar named Just John isn't obviously a gay bar, so "I didn't know" is really no excuse. But he can't stop thinking about it, about that man really being Lacroix. It's making him twitchy, even though he's not sure why. This is more attention than he's paid to anyone else tonight, even though he tells himself it's for different reasons.

Sometimes when he was in school and designing something, he'd stare at his plans and they wouldn't make any *sense*. It would be a mess of jumbled elements and half-thought ideas without any structure. Then there would be one simple thing—an element or a color or even just a spare doodle—that would make the entire thing snap into focus.

That's exactly what happens when the man turns around enough for Avery to see it *isn't* Lacroix, and for him to recognize what he's feeling isn't relief. It's disappointment.

Oh. Fuck no.

Avery finishes his drink, gets enough money out of his wallet to cover his tab, and shoves it across at the bartender. His ears are ringing, and he's fumbling with the money despite only having one drink. It's enough that the bartender asks if he's okay. Avery laughs a little wildly and shakes his head. Then he heads for the door. Maybe some fresh air will clear his head, even if that's never worked before.

It doesn't work this time either. Avery gets home, and he's barely aware of the walk he took to get there, of the sights and sounds around him as he heads back to his apartment. He does somehow manage to send a text message to Harlan that says *no* and feels like a lie, which makes him throw his phone across the room hard enough to hit the wall.

He goes into his bedroom and lies on his bed in the darkness—he doesn't need a spotlight on his shame, thanks—and unbuttons his pants.

There's almost a grim resolve about the way he slides his hand inside and rubs it over himself. He's hard. Of course he is. But he's been in a low-level state of sexual frustration since last week. And not because Harlan constantly denied him, though it certainly didn't help.

It was because of Lacroix.

Avery throws one arm up and over his eyes. He breathes slowly, his hand easy on himself, and tries to think about anything else, anyone else—even Brandon Fucking Thomas—which should make him mad. But instead, he thinks about twenty-five dollar blowjobs and the man at the bar. It gets all confused until the image in his head is of him on his knees. Lacroix's hand is heavy on his shoulder, and he's looking at him with a cold stare and telling Avery how to pronounce his name. And making him say it until he gets it right.

And smacking Avery in the mouth when he doesn't.

Avery groans. He moves his hand faster, and he makes himself stop. He flails a hand out for the remote so he can turn on the television and do this with something else, anything else. He doesn't care. Whatever it is it has to be better than thinking about sucking off his boss. The best part of being bisexual is it doubles the number of hot people to jerk off to.

Except he turns the television on and the show is *Hoarders*. That's too weird for even him, so he turns it off again and closes his eyes, panting. He's trying to think about the last time with Harlan, or the hot girls he had a hell of a threesome with a few weeks ago, or even the pro athlete he met in an airport bar and gave a hurried hand job to.

It doesn't matter. Every time he gets close, his guard slips, and whoever's in his head is suddenly Malin Fucking Lacroix. Avery tries to stop, and it's so frustrating he finally punches the mattress in frustration and mutters, "Fine, fuck it," to himself. He's half-convinced he's worked himself into a tizzy over this, and now he just has to do this once, and it'll be fine.

Yeah. He should just get the idea out, and then it'll be gone. Maybe he's just mixing up work with everything else in his life right now. It's been so all-consuming lately. That's probably all it is. Right? Right. And hey, he's heard it a million times. You shouldn't feel guilty about things you fantasize about. It's not that you really want them.

16

So he lets himself think about it—what would happen if that were really Lacroix in the bar. He would probably be mad Avery saw him. So he'd stand up and....

"Come on," Lacroix says in a terse voice, tosses back his drink, and puts the glass on the table. He doesn't look back at Avery, but he doesn't have to.

Avery follows him away from the bar and into the back. There's a hallway, and he knows it because he's been there before a few times.

Then Lacroix shoves him up against the wall, gets in front of him, and puts his hands on either side of his head. "You're not going to ever tell anyone you saw me here, are you."

Avery leans back against the wall, cocky as usual, and grins at him. "Everyone. Gonna put it in the department newsletter. Maybe on Facebook. I know. I'll tweet it. I bet you don't even know what that means, do you. You're a Twidiot. Ha."

"You have a smart mouth, Avery. Unfortunately that's the most intelligent thing about you."

Avery is pretty sure he's heard that line in a movie or read it somewhere, but he's not writing a fucking screenplay. He's trying to get off, and whether or not he made that up or stole it from someone, the next thing Lacroix does is smack him across the mouth. Fuck. Why does he keep thinking about that?

"Don't speak until I tell you to, Avery." Lacroix's eyes are brutally cold. He grabs Avery's shoulders and pushes—hard—shoving Avery to his knees right there in the hallway. "Let's see if Thomas is better than you at sucking cock too."

Wait, the fuck is that about? There is no fucking way Lacroix is sleeping with Brandon Thomas. He just said that about the blowjobs to be a dick. It's not real or anything.

But what if it were? a voice in his head whispers, since that's who is in charge at the moment.

Avery tilts his head up—challenging and wanting to say something—but he never gets the chance. When he opens his mouth, Lacroix smacks him across the face, hard. He works at his belt with his other hand. "Not a word, Avery."

17

Avery takes it. His head echoes and rings with the slap. He narrows his eyes, but he's watching Lacroix's fingers as he finishes with his belt and moves down to the button and zipper on his pants.

"That what happens when I disobey the rules? You smack me around?"

"No." Lacroix gets his hand in Avery's short hair, and pulls his head back. "This is." With that, Lacroix shoves his cock in Avery's mouth. It's too deep, and he chokes immediately. He can't breathe, and Lacroix doesn't stop. He just keeps going, and fucks his mouth harder—

Avery comes before he gets through that little fantasy. When he finally catches his breath, he can't decide if he's relieved or disappointed not to see what else he might have come up with.

No pun intended.

He lies there for a long time, feeling his racing heartbeat settle down and staring up at the darkened ceiling of his bedroom. He tells himself a lot of people have fantasies about people they'd never sleep with. It happens all the time. And okay, maybe that's usually because they're, like, celebrities or whatever. But hey, this has to count. Right?

A voice tries to tell him it totally doesn't. But Avery is finished listening to that voice, because it's just got him off thinking about his *boss* manhandling him and shoving his cock in his mouth.

"Shut up," Avery says out loud, as if that's going to help. He doesn't hear any more helpful suggestions from his subconscious. Every time he thinks about Lacroix pushing him to his knees and smacking him in the face, he forces the image to change to someone—anyone—else. If he's going to have really hot imaginary sex, he's going to pick someone a lot better than Malin Lacroix.

Like Don Draper. Or that hot girl who ends up in the elevator with him sometimes—a redhead who wears tiny shorts and has an adorable smile. Definitely not a humorless Frenchman with cold eyes and a voice that sounds like he just put an ice cube down the back of his shirt.

Definitely… not.

ME: *HEY everett u ever want 2 sleep w/your boss?*
   Everett: *what?*
   Me: *like do you want to fuck him?*

Everett: *no?*
Me: *wait do you like him*
Everett: *sure hes fine hes like 68 though*
Me: *fine. u ever want 2 sleep w/someone u really dont like?*
Everett: *you mean like a republican?*
Me: *sure whatever, just someone you cant stand*
Everett: *who likes 2 fuck people they dont like? not even u r that weird haha*

Blake Everett is the least helpful friend in the history of ever. Jesus Fucking *Christ*.

CHAPTER 3

ALL OF the lies Avery has been telling himself start to fall to pieces around him, like a house of cards hit by a tornado. Or his favorite hockey team around the playoffs. It's very dramatic, and it all happens in way too short a time period. When it's over he feels like he needs to drink himself into a coma.

The first disillusionment happens at approximately nine thirty in the morning on a Monday, in the sleek, stylish breakroom.

Avery's fixing himself some coffee when Brandon comes up to him, looking a little nervous and rubbing at the back of his neck. He looks disheveled and sheepish, just like a sitcom character. "Hey, Avery, can I talk to you for a sec?"

The lack of a laugh track when Brandon speaks is a disappointment. Avery shrugs and leans against the counter. "Sure, what's up?"

Brandon looks around and pitches his voice low. Which is dumb. There's no one around to hear anyway. "Maybe not... maybe not here? We could go out for lunch or something."

"A lunch date. I'm so flattered, Thomas." Avery grins around his coffee mug, and there's a bite to his words he doesn't necessarily mean. He sips his coffee and tells himself to calm down. "That's fine. I'll meet you at the elevators."

Brandon nods, squares his shoulders, and says, "We'll have to go somewhere healthy. I'm training for a half marathon."

Of course he is. "Yeah. Definitely. I'm training for a three-fourths one, so I'll have to eat one-fourth healthier than you."

Brandon tilts his head like a curious cocker spaniel. "You... what?"

Avery sighs. "A joke, Thomas."

"Is that math even correct? I don't think it was."

"A joke," Avery says, but he catches a slight smile. Golden Boy has a sense of humor, maybe. About fractions. But still it's a start.

THEY GO to lunch at a restaurant a few blocks away, and it's warm enough they can sit outside. Brandon does order something disgustingly healthy, but he looks kind of miserable about eating it, which Avery finds mildly gratifying. They talk about work, of course, until Brandon does his best General Patton impression and says in a flat voice, "Look, I'm not going to apologize to you that Lacroix liked my design for the Byrne project. I'm an architect, and I'm here to do my job. So I'd appreciate if you would stop glaring at me all the time."

Avery stares at him, a piece of his designer pizza—goat cheese and fancy crust, costs $17.50, and you don't even get a salad—raised halfway to his mouth. There's an ominous gust of wind blowing through the figurative landscape of his mind. As usual Avery's brain pulls on an imaginary windbreaker and ignores it completely.

"Why would I want you to apologize? It's not you, dude. It's just that my design was awesome, and Lacroix is a fucker."

Brandon smiles his infuriatingly genuine smile at Avery. "I loved the solar staircase on your proposal."

"Thank you," Avery says, hitting the table with the flat of his hand. "Someone should appreciate it."

Brandon puts his lettuce-wrapped… thing… down on his plate and looks at it with an expression of such loathing Avery pushes his pizza plate toward him. Brandon picks up a piece, clearly grateful. "It's kind of weird they gave you Lacroix to work with, though. I mean, your stuff is edgy, and he's not that way. But I'm sure it's frustrating to get turned down so much."

"Yes, Thomas. It really is." Avery gives him a completely serious look. "Thank you for reminding me."

Brandon returns the look flawlessly. "You're welcome. If you're sick to your stomach, I'll finish your pizza." He smiles winningly.

Avery figures he's been wrong about Brandon from the beginning, and it's refreshing. Though with his all-American good looks and remarkably perfect hair, it's like having lunch with a Disney prince. Avery nods toward the plate. "Go ahead. You can take your lettuce thing with you and give it to the birds that obviously follow you around, singing little songs." He starts whistling, but it inexplicably turns from "Zip-A-Dee-Do-Dah" to an Alice in Chains song. Oops.

"You're very weird." Brandon takes another piece of his pizza. "So could you stop glaring at me? Sometimes I think you're doodling elaborate death machines on your notes during staff meetings."

"Don't be dumb, Thomas. I don't take notes at staff meetings. And I'm not glaring at you," Avery protests.

That's a lie. He really has been shooting Brandon some death glares. But it has nothing to do with the proposal and everything to do with Lacroix. How can Avery tell him that? *Sorry, I made this inappropriate comment about you sucking off Lacroix, then got off thinking about him smacking me and telling me to do it better than you.*

Brandon looks skeptical. "You are, though. You're doing it right now."

"No, look. I was disappointed, okay? I worked hard on that proposal, and I am tired of Lacroix rejecting my designs. But I can't stress enough that it's not why I'm glaring at you. If I am. Which I'm not," he adds. Because Avery is terrible at lying, he immediately follows up with "At least on purpose."

Brandon's expression tightens, and his mouth settles into a hard line. He doesn't look quite so young or innocent anymore. "So there's some other reason."

Avery stares at him. There's no way this is happening. He is not going to say anything about that comment. Although, fuck. What if Lacroix told him? What if ol' Mal is playing games with them, scheming and pulling strings, like they're puppets, just to see what they'll do? If that's true, then Avery needs to own up to saying it, but if it's not true, he's going to make Brandon mad at him.

Now he can't design buildings or make friends. His entire life is a lie, goddammit.

"You're doing it again." Brandon looks downright unfriendly, and Avery stares up at the umbrella, which is tilted at a jaunty angle over their table. Before he can think of something to say, Brandon says flatly, "So you probably know, and you don't approve."

"Wait. What?" Avery's attention snaps back to him immediately. He can't mean that. He can't. Brandon Thomas is not about to tell him he's having an affair with Malin Lacroix. Avery is way too irrational to be right about this kind of stuff.

"Look, I don't broadcast these things, but my personal life is my own business." Brandon has his wallet out. He's trying to find money to pay for his lunch. They don't have a check yet, and Brandon keeps dropping things. It's entirely unlike him.

Holy fuck. It's true.

"I made that up, though," Avery says, wide-eyed. He watches Brandon and notices how uncomfortable he is. Maybe Lacroix is blackmailing him. A Disney prince should not date a Disney villain. This is madness. "I was drunk. Did he tell you that I was drunk?"

Brandon's gaze settles on him. Everything about him is rigid, like the umbrella on the table, but decidedly less jaunty. "Did who tell me what?"

"Okay. Wait. Wait." Avery waves at the chair. "I'll get a dessert and let you have some. But I don't think we're talking about the same thing. I made an off-color comment to Lacroix when I was drunk a few weeks ago. I didn't mean it."

"What was it?"

Shit. "I was implying that you were sleeping with our boss." Avery closes his eyes and scrubs a hand across his face. "Well, that he was sleeping with you—" Avery opens his eyes, looks at Brandon's face, and immediately stops talking. "Are you giggling? You are. Jesus Christ. That's not... I told him you were doing it for money. How's that?"

"Was it a lot?" Brandon looks delighted. Avery is convinced they're on a hidden-camera show. This is just too weird.

"Um. Actually. No."

"How much?" Brandon is grinning, and then he throws a napkin at him and cheerfully takes another slice of pizza off Avery's plate. "Out with it, Avery. How much do I charge the boss to fuck me?"

"I'm not sure, but you charge him twenty-five bucks for a blowjob. Maybe you do it for the thrill, not the cash? I don't know. I was drunk."

Brandon chokes on the pizza, which serves him right. "Twenty-five dollars? I should be glaring at *you* in staff meetings. That's insulting." Brandon is General Patton again, giving him the "Rommel, you magnificent bastard, I read your book" look. "They're definitely worth more than that. So I've been told."

"Okay. But I wasn't trying to insult you. It was a paying-your-employees-for-sex insult aimed at our boss, Brandon." This time, Avery looks around to make sure Lacroix's not going to suddenly pop up next to their table. "So I was trying to imply he was a cheap john, not that you were a... ah... cheap whore." Avery winces. "I know how that sounds, I'm sorry."

"I don't know if you heard me. I said they'd be worth a lot more than twenty-five dollars."

Avery gives him a quizzical look and takes the last piece of pizza before Brandon can steal it. "Yeah. Next time I suggest people pay you for a blowjob, I'll make sure to raise the rate so I don't imply you're cheap."

Brandon studies him for a minute. "That's all?"

"What, do you want to work out a price with me, so you're not insulted? I think you're being a little too anal about this." There's a joke there, but Avery wisely doesn't make it.

"It doesn't bother you that I...?" Brandon's voice is soft, and he's looking down at the table. Avery is honestly clueless until he realizes what just happened. Brandon really does give blowjobs—meaning he likes guys. And he's worried Avery cares about that?

"Oh my God. You thought I was glaring at you because you're gay? Is that it?"

Brandon nods. Avery rolls his eyes, picks up the menu, and tosses it to him.

"No. Wow. I could care less who you sleep with, Brandon," he says. "Now pick a dessert so I can make up for suggesting you give cheap head to our boss, okay?"

Brandon is watching him carefully, like he doesn't believe it.

"I'm so okay with you blowing whoever you want," Avery assures him. Except maybe Lacroix. But that's only because he cares about his new friend and wants him to have a happy relationship.

"Thanks, Avery." Brandon sounds very sincere. "I appreciate that. And now you can order me this brownie thing with extra caramel." Brandon leans back in his chair, and he looks much more relaxed than Avery's ever seen him. And then suddenly he starts to look very smug. "So you were glaring at me 'cause you thought I was sleeping with the boss, huh? Jealous?"

"No sundae for you," Avery says immediately, closing the menu.

"Come on, Avery. I'm hardly going to go around and tell everyone. That'd be a dick move." Brandon chuckles. "Anyway, I thought—you brought a girl to the Christmas party."

"Yeah, so?" Avery shrugs. "Bisexuals exist, Brandon. I like hot people and having sex with them and then forgetting their names and never calling them again. I guess I assume everyone's the same. Or maybe I just hope they are."

"Including our boss." Brandon shakes his head. "I have never gone to bed with Lacroix. He's all yours. I've got a boyfriend, anyway."

It's Avery's turn to throw something, but the only thing on the table that would work is his glass of water—overkill—and the lettuce thing on Brandon's plate—underwhelming. "I don't—look, it's not—it was one time I thought about it, and... can we not talk about this?" Avery doesn't mean that—he *would* like to talk about it to someone—but he's just not sure this is a good time or place. They've had enough bonding for the day.

"Yeah, okay. We should get back. But you know. If you want to talk, I can meet you out for a drink after work." Brandon waves his hand in a careless gesture, and then his smile turns into a grin, and he starts laughing. "Thanks for lunch. I'll see if Lacroix can give me a raise, and next time it's on me."

"Ha-ha."

"Hey, Avery? I really do appreciate that you... y'know. Don't care. I don't even know if it would be a big deal or not, if everyone at the office knew."

Avery pats him on the shoulder. "It would. Only because architects are severely overworked, and everyone would be resentful you were getting laid at all."

Brandon's grin is so smug it almost makes Avery want to trip him. As does the sincerity on his face when he says, "Want some advice on how to get a design approved by Lacroix?"

"What? Like you're an expert now? You've gotten one design approved, Brandon."

"And that's one more than you," Brandon points out. Avery hits him in the shoulder, but he can't help the laugh.

"I think I liked it better when I didn't want to like you," Avery says. "But okay. Sure, oh wise one. What's your advice?"

"Think of Lacroix more as his own, separate set of specs than the project manager. That's finally what I did. Like he's the client's representative, not ours. It's easier somehow to change your design that way."

Avery isn't sure he needed to think more about Lacroix, but it's good advice. "The client before the client, you mean?" Avery thinks about that for a minute, which is an eternity in Avery time. Then he asks, "That's what you did?"

Brandon nods. "A friend gave me that advice, and I really kept it in mind for the last design."

"Geez, Brandon, you're telling me to either be a suck-up or—"

"One more blowjob joke, and I'll kick you in the shins. I know how. I have a black belt in jujitsu."

Avery isn't sure he believes that, but maybe it's safer to pretend he does.

As they walk back, Avery thinks maybe he got out of this one okay. It's easy to focus on that, and with Brandon's easy conversation and the sun warm on his face, he can ignore the distant rumble of figurative thunder booming away in his mind, tighten that mental windbreaker, and just keep walking.

CHAPTER 4

AVERY THOUGHT if he jerked off thinking about Lacroix, he would stop *wanting* to jerk off thinking about Lacroix. It didn't work out quite so well. Finally he gives up thinking about anyone else and has weird sex fantasies involving his boss and smacking and bending into all kinds of uncomfortable positions. Apparently that's what he's into for the moment.

It's been a long time since this has happened, since he's wanted someone quite this badly. Relationships have always been on fast-forward—the chase takes place at the bar or wherever else, the courtship in his apartment, and the nasty breakup is an awkward good-bye in the morning, or an "I'll call you" that sometimes he means and most times he doesn't.

He's always been focused on his career. When he's focused on one thing, it's very hard to get his mind onto something else, which is clearly why he's driving himself crazy. His mind is suddenly fixed on the subject of sex with Lacroix and doesn't want to get off. Until Avery does.

Avery comes up with about a half-dozen crazy schemes to seduce Lacroix, but the potential obstacles all outweigh the possible rewards by a million—the part where he doesn't see his boss all that often, and the part where Lacroix and he loathe each other.

He doesn't think sprawling naked in Lacroix's chair is going to work. Especially because, thanks to the little impromptu visit after his last proposal was declined, there's now a rule about scheduling an appointment with Lacroix's assistant before barging into his office.

Luckily there's a new bid out there, and Avery jumps into design as a way to stop thinking about his stupid boss. And that's helpful even if he's less manic about it than last time. He doesn't want to throw his heart and soul into it again, but he's never learned how not to do things that way. So his design keeps him working long hours, and it's mentally taxing, though he makes sure to get more sleep and eat something other than caffeine.

Maybe it's because he's able to keep a bit of a distance this time. Maybe it's because he's not hyperfocused on perfection and innovation, but he designs something subtle. There are sharp angles that give the suggestion they could bend into a curve or snap into a straight line at any moment—an uncertainty that is very deliberate, almost like a tease. Decidedly not Avery, but he likes it.

It's a departure for him, but it feels right, and he actually researches soil quality and composition, even drives to the site and watches the sun until it falls beneath the horizon. The light is perfect, and he immediately comes up with an elaborate, beautiful series of windows that would break it up into a dramatic clash of light and color. But instead, he thinks about the people inside the building, how they might end up with the sun in their eyes and how annoying that would be.

Or how irritated he would be, as the designer, if it were actually constructed and some cretin put up fucking vertical blinds and tore the artistry out of his soul forever.

Yeah. Definitely need to scale that back. Besides, it's a performing-arts center, so all the attention should be on the artistry inside. Right? The building is more like a frame, or a stage.

Or a window....

The finished product is simple—for him. It's a square design with strong lines and sharp delineations between metal, brick, and glass. The slight curvature in the glass of the main entranceway breaks up the rigidity of the facade, and the two cylindrical glass structures on either side are whimsical enough to soften the otherwise stark angles.

And at night, lit up, the building would glow—almost as if it trapped all the light from the sun during the day, just so it would shine brightest at night.

He keeps Brandon's advice in mind the whole time he's working on it, and even though he hates to admit it, Lacroix's feedback from his last design. He thinks about the building in terms of its functionality, as more than just a design, and he tries to keep things as eco-friendly as he can, but sometimes he has to adjust for cost or the sake of complexity.

Who said he couldn't learn?

Avery stares at the rendering and wonders why no one's ever told him he's so fucking obvious before. Because all of that about the framework and the practicalities may be true, but what he's looking at is more than that. It's unforgiving stone set in uncompromising lines, clashing with the sudden, unexpected curve of the glass that won't entirely conform to the rules—a union of formality and inflexibility with aggression and dissent.

Great. He's designed the *Kama Sutra* of performing-arts centers. This isn't just a building or a spotlight on a stage. It's a very fucking obvious message that says, "Hey, Lacroix, I'm like glass, and it'd be great if you wanted to put your uncompromising angles all over me." Fucking hell.

Until this very moment, Avery has never noticed how much he uses glass as a design element. Glass lit from within so nothing behind it has a place to hide. Glass, which is forged in fire but still breaks far too easily.

Fuck. Can't he be a little quicker on figuring out his own shit? Jaime, the only girlfriend with whom he's ever stayed friends, is a psychologist. He once told her he was an open book because he didn't want people to reach the end and be disappointed. *I'd rather have it all there in the open, for whomever to see.*

Apparently his designs feel the same way. It's hard to find flaws when everything is so… exposed.

Jesus. How did he not notice this?

Because this is the most self-aware you've ever been as a designer. You boiled things down to their simplest forms, and it says you're a transparent, moody bitch who wants to bang his boss.

He should tell Jaime that. She'd have a field day.

Avery thinks about throwing the design out and resubmitting his (really awesome) design for some luxury lofts Lacroix had rejected with the note, *Would you live here?*

He also thinks about not submitting anything because this isn't graduate school, and he's allowed to do that—pass on projects that don't speak to him.

Avery spends a long time sitting quietly at his desk in the darkened building, chewing on a pen. It's a good design. He knows that. It might show Lacroix he did listen to his feedback, though part of him rebels at the idea of doing anything Lacroix says, just on principle. Or at the very least, without Lacroix making him do it.

Is this worth it? Just to have a building he can drive past and point at and say, "See that? That started in my mind, and now it's right here. I can touch it, and look, the light does exactly what I thought it would."

Wait. What the hell? Of course it's worth it. Besides, it's not like Lacroix will look at the plans and go, "Obviously you want me. Look at the lines and the half-circle glass thingy there. It's so frightfully clear, Mr. Hextall." In Avery's head, Lacroix uses words like "glass thingy" as if he were not also an architect, and words like "frightfully," as if he were a character on *Downton Abbey*. Squares and half circles are not entirely new concepts he's dreamed up on his own, and the design does fit the specifications and make sense in a very succinct way.

I designed a spotlight and a stage in one. I know, right? I'm so meta it hurts. There. If anyone asks, he'll just say that.

Avery hits *submit* on the program before he can talk himself out of it and promptly has second, third, and fourth thoughts before he even gets to the elevator. He tells himself it's too late to do anything about it. Computer espionage is not on his list of marketable skills. Besides, if the old axiom (or is it a Dr. Phil saying? Avery can't ever remember) that the best predictor of future behavior is past behavior is true, he's free to go home, have a drink, become horribly bored by *Mistee's Muffalicious Vacation III*, and jerk off thinking about his boss fucking him over his desk, mouth next to his ear saying, "Pay attention, Avery."

Because there is no way in hell Lacroix will choose his design. And then maybe Avery will hate him even more, and that will cure whatever this is, and everything will be just great.

A WEEK later Avery is woken up in the middle of the night by a storm and thunder so loud it rattles the windows hard enough he's worried they'll shatter. His cat paws daintily on his dresser, knocking off some loose change and a set of keys because cats are seriously the worst.

"It's not my fault it's storming," Avery tells her and tries to pick her up. Unfortunately there's a loud crack of thunder, and she vaults off him like she has springs in all her limbs. She scratches the hell out of his arm and hides under the bed.

"I could get you declawed. I could. Or I could get a dog. Just keep that in mind," Avery grumbles, pulling the covers over his head.

The next morning Avery arrives to an e-mail from Lacroix's assistant, Ford O'Keefe, in his inbox.

> *Hextall,*
> *Mr. Lacroix would like to meet with you at ten this morning. Please be on time, and remember you're not supposed to go in his office until I buzz him to let him know you're there.*
> *If you have any conflicting obligations, reschedule them.*

For the next hour or so, Avery sits at his desk and stares at Ford's e-mail. He has no idea what to think of it or what it might mean, but nervousness claws at his stomach and makes him want to throw up his coffee and cinnamon Pop-Tarts.

Brandon sends an e-mail to his personal account, asking if he's hungover. Avery shakes his head "no" when he reads it because typing is too hard. He wants to tell Brandon about the e-mail from Ford and see if Brandon got one before he was awarded the Byrne project.

He doesn't because he's not sure he wants to know the answer. And no way is he telling Brandon he's tired because his cat woke him up. Lame.

Brandon responds to his nod with an e-mail.

you sure? you look kinda terrible dude.

Brandon acts like a frat boy more than Avery thought he would, so he responds in kind.

sorry, guess your mom kept me up too late last night.

Then he pretends to be very busy, which involves him clicking through websites and occasionally looking down at his phone, as if he actually performs any of these activities at work. Ever.

When it's finally time to go to Lacroix's office, he stops by the restroom and splashes water on his face, grips hard at the white porcelain sink, and stares at himself in the mirror. He honestly has no idea what is going to happen. He takes a few deep breaths and heads toward Lacroix's office, and tries to look nonchalant.

Avery stops in front of Lacroix's assistant's desk. His smile is more of a grimace than anything. "Hi."

Ford's return expression is the same, but he's not nervous. He just hates Avery. "I should have been here. Before."

Avery blinks at him, confused and too wound up to find even a little bit of tact. "What the hell does that mean?"

"You step out for ten minutes, and a crazy junior associate barges in your boss's office. Ten minutes."

"Oh. Um. Sorry?" Avery shrugs, unsure what to say. He's not really sorry, and an idiot could tell that.

"Crazy," Ford says flatly. Then he picks up his phone and hits a button. "Hextall is here. He looks nervous."

"Hey!"

Ford nods, hangs up the phone, and waves a hand toward the door. "You can go in." He sounds almost disappointed.

"Thanks." Avery would normally give him a smirk or something, but he doesn't. He just opens the door and walks in, and he can't do anything but wait, eyes sharp on Lacroix, standing behind his desk.

Lacroix's expression is inscrutable—lines of stone—and Avery isn't thinking about his proposal or his nerves anymore. He can't concentrate on a thing but the heat and aggression he immediately feels when their eyes meet.

"Sit down."

Avery stays where he is for a few long seconds, just to be ornery. But nerves get the better of him eventually, so he takes a seat in front of Lacroix's desk. The paperweight is still there, the inside frosted and twisted with red glass. It's impossible to see through.

Someone needs to save me from my own metaphors.

Lacroix messes with something in front of him and shifts papers around very intently. Avery hasn't ever seen him fidget like that before.

"The Knight Performing Arts Center," Lacroix says. He tosses something at Avery. Not his proposal with that damnable red pen, but a neatly organized stack of papers fixed together with a clip. "These are the preliminary questions the investors sent back about your design. We'll go over them in detail at three, so it would be a good idea for you to take a look at them beforehand. I'm confident that they will select our bid, so clear your schedule for the foreseeable future."

Avery looks at the paper in his hand, and then he looks up at Lacroix. "You're kidding."

Lacroix's smile isn't as chilly as Avery expected when this moment came. The fact does weird things to his insides. "Three o'clock, Avery. Don't be late."

"Yeah. Okay." It's not gracious, and this moment is nothing like he thought it would be, but it fucking finally happened. Holy shit. Avery grins. "Oh man. This must be killing you, huh."

Lacroix looks pointedly at the door. "I don't need you to still be in here."

Avery is too wound up to laugh. His hands are shaking. He wants to call his mom. And the kid who lived across the street from him in fifth grade who told him drawing buildings was stupid and threw rocks at him. And Harlan. And holy shit, Everett—

"Hextall."

Lacroix's voice grabs his attention like a bucket full of cold water. Or a slap to the face.

"Yeah?" Fuck. That was the last thing he wanted to think about.

"Congratulations."

It's the least congratulatory-sounding congratulations in the history of ever, but Avery doesn't care. Actually it kind of makes the whole thing better.

On his way past Ford's desk, he makes finger guns at him and says, "See you at three." Then laughs all the way back to his office.

Plenty of time to worry himself to death later. For now, he's going to enjoy the moment.

CHAPTER 5

AVERY IS meandering his way through the Friday night crowd at Madison's.

"Hey, Avery. Over here." Brandon stands up, waves, and gestures toward their table near the back.

Avery raises his beer bottle in acknowledgement and soldiers on, murmuring his apologies as he ducks around people standing four deep at the bar. His nerves are frayed, and he just wants to sit down, have a few beers, and then go home and sleep.

He has a site visit in the morning. On a Saturday. At seven in the morning on a Saturday. If that isn't bad enough, he has to go with Lacroix. Fuck. What kind of a weekend is that?

"Man, did you just leave work?" Brandon moves over when Avery gets to the table and gives him a sympathetic look. "I should be glad the only project managing Lacroix did for the Byrne job was to introduce me to their contractor. All he literally does is sign things."

Avery takes a long drink of his beer. "It's not nice to brag, Brandon."

Brandon grins, shrugs, and then nods toward the other man at the table. "Avery, this is Justin. Justin, this is my friend Avery, from work."

"Your gay work friend." Justin, who looks oddly familiar, stands up and extends his hand. "Hi. Nice to meet you."

Avery shakes it easily. "Half-gay. And wow, Brandon. Way to out a guy. There's a code, you know." He takes his seat, settles in, and lets the noise and energy of the crowd wash over him. That always helps perk him up, and God knows he could use it.

"Oh yeah? Is 'don't suggest my boyfriend gives cheap blowjobs' on there?"

Avery raises his eyebrows at that, and then grins. He likes Justin already. "Yeah. Probably."

"Justin. Be nice." Brandon sounds like he couldn't possibly mean that any less.

"Nah. He's got a point." Avery takes another drink and studies Justin with frank interest. He's too tired to try and disguise it, and besides, he sucks at that anyway. "You look familiar. Have we met before?"

What he really means by that is "we haven't hooked up before, have we?" Awkward city.

Justin glances at Brandon. "Ooh. He doesn't know."

Brandon rolls his eyes. "No. Why would he? You're being dramatic." Brandon leans over and punches Justin on the arm. "It's not the Hatfield and McCoys, man."

Avery looks back and forth between them. "Wow. That... I have no idea what that reference means."

"Justin looks familiar because he's an architect."

As far as an explanation goes, that one is pretty terrible. "Yes. And we all know each other through The Gay Architects Association. I forgot. Were you at the potluck last month?"

"Yup. I brought the pasta salad," Justin answers, without missing a beat.

Avery salutes him with his beer bottle. "It was really good. I liked the bacon."

"It was real too. Only straight architects put bacon bits in their pasta salad." Justin smiles. "I'm in it for the real meat."

"Aren't we all?" Avery laughs and clinks his beer bottle with Justin's.

"Oh, this was a good idea," Brandon says and sighs. "Introducing you two. And Avery, you remember that contract for that sports arena in New Jersey? The really big deal project that was going on a few years ago?"

Avery nods. Of course he does. It consumed their entire organization for months, what with every designer and sports fan at Ratcliff and Roberts dying to say they had a hand in the new arena. Even if it is in New Jersey.

They made it all the way to the final round and then lost out to Durham and Sikes, a rival firm that absconded with more than a few contracts on which Ratcliff and Roberts bid.

Suddenly the Hatfield and McCoy comment makes a little more sense. "So you're with Durham, I take it?"

Justin nods. "Yup."

"That must have been hell on your home life." Avery watches as Brandon and Justin exchange a look, and he gets it. "Wait. Is that how you two *met*?"

Brandon rubs the back of his neck sheepishly. "He was on their design team. Yeah."

"Brandon, you are really full of surprises. Here I thought you were like, some kind of angel. And you're dating enemy architects who are guys. Wow. Was I ever wrong. Next you're going to tell me you tie guys up and whip them and shit in bed."

Justin chokes on his drink, and Brandon turns a faint shade of red and gives his boyfriend a clear don't-say-a-word look, which is hot.

"Wait. Were you sent to spy on him? Was it, like, sexy architect espionage?" Avery leans forward, elbows on the table. "Tell me all about it. This is better than the Spice Channel."

"Oh man. Anything is better than the Spice Channel," Justin interjects.

"I can cancel it. I just thought you might like some porn with girls in it, on occasion," Brandon mutters defensively. "You'd think most people would appreciate their boyfriend's dedication to their bisexuality."

"Bran, we have the Internet and a smart TV. We don't need a channel. And no, there was no sexy espionage. But that's a good one, isn't it?" Justin grins slowly at his boyfriend. "Let's tell people that's what was going on."

Brandon rolls his eyes again. "No. It wasn't espionage. We actually met at—somewhere else. It didn't have anything to do with architecture. Anyway Justin here was a card-carrying member of the In Denial About Being a Gay Architect Society or whatever you're calling it."

"This part of the story is boring because I sound dumb in it," Justin announces.

"What about the part where you met at some secret other place that you're not telling me about? I've found the most interesting part of a story is the part you try to gloss over. So let's have it."

"Oh." Justin studies his beer bottle very carefully, and then looks over at Brandon. It's a clear sign he's waiting for something, and it takes Avery a minute to figure out what it is.

Permission.

Brandon clearly isn't giving it, and there's a moment between them that's heated, tense, and also really, really hot. Avery doesn't say anything because he doesn't want to interrupt, and also because he's kind of getting off watching it. It's been a long week. "Hey, you really don't have to tell me. I'm just being an ass."

"We hooked up not knowing much of anything about each other," Brandon explains, even though that is the definition of every hookup ever. Or at least, that's the definition when Avery does it. "Then there was that meeting for all the firms that advanced to the final round? And we saw each other, and... yeah. Surprise."

"And now you subscribe to the Spice Channel and own a smart TV, and it's love." Avery smiles at both of them and bats his eyelashes. "That's really romantic. It's like—"

"If you make a *Fountainhead* joke, I will punch you in the face."

Avery makes an affronted noise. "I wasn't going to." He was totally going to. "Anyway that's pretty great. Good for you two. I mean it."

The waitress comes back to take their orders, and they settle on a pitcher of some locally brewed IPA. When they all have a fresh round, Justin turns to Avery and says brightly, "So Avery. Brandon says you have a thing for your boss."

"Oh he does, does he?"

"Mmmhmm. Hot. Or it would be if.... Well, we all have our types." Justin pats him on the arm. "Mine is hot and blond. Yours is... older French assholes?"

"Justin isn't a fan of Lacroix."

"I wasn't picking up on that." Avery studies Justin carefully. "Why not?"

"Lacroix is really good at what he does. He's been in the industry a long time, but he's notoriously hard to work with." Justin shrugs and pushes his glass back and forth, from hand to hand. It's oddly mesmerizing. "He's always on these committees and finds some way to stop progress or introduce a million different restrictions for the hell of it. Or so it seems."

"Ah yes. Vague business clichés." Avery nods understandingly. "I bet he's also stepped on some feet on his climb up the corporate ladder. Thrown some people under a bus along the way. Pitched a great many persons off the peak of the pinnacle of success. That sort of thing. It's all very clear now."

"See. I told you," Brandon says, nodding at Avery. "Cute but annoying."

"You think I'm cute? Aw, Brandon. Thanks. But I only like you as a friend." Avery takes a sip of his beer. It's maybe a little nice to hear someone call him cute. Fuck. He needs to get laid.

Justin shrugs. "I just don't know if you want a long list of specifics. But... yeah. He's really good at overcomplicating things for no reason. Even projects that have nothing to do with him. We figure it's out of spite, but who knows."

Avery is finding himself in the weird position of agreeing with Justin, and being completely unable to say so. "Huh," is about all he can manage.

"I respect the guy, but I wish he'd join some other firm nowhere near here. West Coast maybe. But we're not talking about work. We're talking about you wanting to sex him up." Justin does a terrible dance move with his arms. "It sounds to me like you don't like him. You just want to sleep with him."

"Yes!" Avery puts his beer glass down so firmly some of his IPA spills. "God. Okay. I keep asking people if that's weird, and they say it is." He means he sent one text message to Everett and didn't really explain himself, but whatever.

"Because it is. I mean, no offense, Avery. You can fuck whoever you want. But yeah, someone you work with, who you don't even like? I just don't get why you'd want to." Brandon peers at him from those bright blue eyes.

Justin pours himself some more beer. "I get it. Come on, Brandon." Justin is giving Brandon what is supposed to be a Very Significant Look. "It's how you know me and Avery will never, ever sleep together. But he'd totally bang you if he could. Which he can't," Justin adds firmly.

"Why is this suddenly the plot to a gay Lifetime movie?" But Avery understands what Justin is telling him. Though he's not sure he sees Brandon quite the same way. He seems too... nice. Which *apparently* is not Avery's type. "I'm not really into that whole cheating thing. I can't lie to save my fucking life. Also Brandon's my coworker. What if I need to blackmail him someday? I can't get involved."

"You make a compelling argument, Avery."

"Thank you. And besides, I like you." Avery has always been very easy with his friendship and his affection, and he tends to give it relatively quickly after meeting someone. He does like Justin, and he genuinely *is* happy, if not a little envious, of what they have together. "But yeah. I guess. Still I've never wanted to fuck Ratcliff. Or Roberts."

"Have you met them, though?" Brandon makes a face. "They're old. Older than Lacroix, even. Although one time I heard Ratcliff yelling at....What's his name, the guy who's about to make partner?"

"Dabney?"

"Yeah. Him." Brandon leans in conspiratorially. "He was mad about the appetizers at the Christmas party. So if you like jerks, you might blow him. I think he's got a scary wife, though. So maybe not while she's home."

Avery very nearly chokes on his beer. "Brandon, are you drunk? You are, aren't you? We've had like two beers. That's disgraceful."

"This is what happens when you only eat lettuce wraps." Justin fills his glass, then does the same for Brandon. "Drink more, though. You're handsy when you're drunk. So, do you think you've got a shot? Tell me your sordid tales, Hextall. I'm in a committed, monogamous relationship, and this sounds like one of the videos Brandon has on our smart TV."

"Oh, that one with the businessman and the hot salesman who needs to get his sales up." Brandon clears his throat. "I'm drunk. What? Fuck it." He pours himself some more beer. "That's a good video. I don't care."

"There's nothing to tell. I don't—I guess maybe I'm attracted to him." That's the first time he's said that out loud, and it's not... too awful, but the beer could be helping with that. "But he drives me fucking crazy. He argues about things for no reason. He won't let me finish a sentence. He changes things because I say I like them. It's like that Katy Perry song, y'know the one?"

Brandon sings a few lines of that "Hot N Cold" song, off-key and in a terrible, terrible falsetto.

Justin and Avery stare at him, until Brandon glares at the both of them, defensive. "What? It's on my running playlist. Shut up. Besides you two knew it."

"Yeah, but you run marathons and eat lettuce wraps," Justin points out. "You're more of a Mumford and Sons guy."

"I only downloaded two of their songs," Brandon protests, then points at Avery. "We're talking about Avery's crush on our boss. Who I gave cheap blowjobs to."

Justin raises his eyebrows. "Those weren't just cheap, babe. Those were, like, the outlet mall price of blowjobs."

Avery is going to have to remember that one.

"Talk about Avery some more," Brandon demands, pointing at him. "Leave my blowjobs out of this."

"Haha. Okay. So do we know if Lacroix has a card for the Gay Architects Club?"

"He was married once," Brandon points out. "I think it ended pretty badly. Or messily. Maybe? Or else I'm making that up." He pushes his beer glass toward Justin. "I need some more of that."

"You really don't, but okay." Justin pours it for him and shakes his head. "It's like eight o'clock, you loser. And that doesn't matter. Maybe they got divorced 'cause he likes cock. Or something. I'm just saying it doesn't kick him out of the club."

"In my world, everyone is bisexual," Avery says, and Justin clinks his beer glass against Avery's.

Brandon takes the glass Justin pushes at him and then fixes Avery with a very serious look. "Don't sleep with Lacroix, Avery. It'll end badly, and then you'll have to get a new job. And I like you, 'cause you're half-gay and you let me have your pizza."

"You're very important to me too, Brandon." Avery finishes his glass of beer, and despite the fact he kind of wants to stick around and drink more—it's not like he'd say no to a drunken threesome—he should really get home. He's hungry, he can feel the exhaustion pressing at the back of his eyes, and he has to be in top form to deal with Lacroix in the morning.

Avery stands up, stretches, and rubs at his eyes with the heel of his hand. "I should go. But this was fun. It was good to meet you," he says to Justin sincerely, holding his hand out. "I have some great blackmail material on Brandon, *and* you're pretty cool."

"Win-win. And hey, Avery, if you fuck your boss and it turns into a *Melrose Place* episode, you can come work with me." Justin shakes his hand. He's got a good, firm handshake.

Fuck. Why can't he ever fall for nice guys like Justin? Or Brandon, who is actually more his type, with the being kind of bossy?

And why the fuck did he just think that? Fall for? No. Fuck everything. He's tired, and that's his excuse for right now. He doesn't even like Lacroix. He's wanted to punch him about sixteen times in the last twenty-four hours.

Yeah. And how many times did you want to get on your knees for him?

Okay. It's not fair that his inner voice doesn't get as tired as he does. Avery ignores that and thanks Justin for the almost job offer. Then he gets some cash out of his wallet. "I'll see you Monday," he says to Brandon, who is sprawled in the chair, running his finger along the edge of his beer glass and giving Justin a look he shouldn't in public.

"I'll walk you out," Brandon says, like they're at Brandon's house and this is his living room. And it's 1953.

"I can find the front door," Avery says dryly. "I'm not as drunk as you."

Behind him, Justin is sneakily switching Brandon's glass with his own, emptier one. He puts a finger to his mouth when he catches Avery watching him.

"S'okay. I'm gonna find the bathroom anyway. Be back, babe," he says to Justin. "Don't do that thing where you switch our glasses and think I won't notice. Because I'll notice."

"I never do that. What?" Justin sips at Brandon's beer, eyes wide.

Brandon walks with Avery toward the front of the bar, then slings an arm around him and leans in—time for the drunk conspiratorial talk, apparently—and says, "M'glad that you don't care about Justin and me. Also, fuck. Why am I drunk? I don't do this... not usually."

"I didn't think so. But man, I am learning a lot about you, Brandon. You get drunk after work. You give blowjobs that are worth a lot of money. You're dating a guy you met at some kinky get-together where there were probably a lot of women going by mistress and dudes in gimp suits."

"Hey, wait. Who told you that? Was it Justin? Because that was so awful, it was awkward. Ugh. I don't even know where you get all that latex stuff. And we weren't going to talk about that. I can't believe he told you."

"He didn't," Avery says, grinning. "You did."

"Huh?" Brandon blinks at him, at sea. "I did? When?"

"Just now. Don't worry. That's pretty weird, but who the hell would I tell? You've got shit on me too. And I think wanting to bang Lacroix is a lot worse."

"Oh. Right." Brandon nods. "Okay then. But don't... just... if you think you're into that, man, there are websites. Start with those before you go to something called Total Domination Tuesdays."

"Oh my God, Brandon. It's almost a shame that I like you now." Avery pats him on the back again. "Get back to Justin before he drinks all your beer."

"See. I knew he did that. I knew it. But okay. Have a good weekend." Brandon narrows his eyes suddenly. "Don't blow him over the weekend. Stay strong, Avery."

Avery scowls. "You get to tell Justin what to do, not me." His scowl turns into a grimace. "But thanks. Yeah. I won't. This will go away."

"Probably yeah." Brandon clears his throat. "Of course I thought that about Justin. So. But I'm sure that won't happen with you." He pats Avery on the arm, reassuring. "At least I hope it doesn't. See you Monday."

Avery really, really has got to get some friends who are better at lying than he is, not worse.

AVERY MANAGES to get through his site visit with Lacroix without blowing him, but it doesn't get any better.

The problem is the more the guy pisses him off, the more Avery wants to shove him against a wall and get on his knees. And the more he wants that, the more contrary it makes him. And that's generally what makes Lacroix get mad at him.

It's also annoying because Avery is starting to have a grudging respect for how good Lacroix is at his job. Avery loses his patience with people other than Lacroix, like the contractors and the builders who seem to want to finish the damn project in five days or something absurd. It's not a goddamn *Extreme Home Makeover* show, and yet they seem to want to rush everything. Probably to save money, but fuck that noise. It's not about money. It's about the fucking building. Ugh.

Of course, he's not the one paying to have it built. Still, goddammit, they could have some more respect for his design and not suggest dumb things like "can we just use colored stone instead of brick?" Don't they get what the slight material change is supposed to symbolize? Smooth, cold stone into roughened, angry brick? God they're stupid.

So when Avery loses his temper, he paces angrily and lets Lacroix deal with them. And gradually he starts to appreciate that because, for once, it's not him Lacroix is shutting down. Unfortunately he finds it really attractive.

The hours are getting longer, and the threads of Avery's temper are dangerously frayed. He's tense and he can't seem to relax. When he's not at work, he's thinking about work, and the only time he ever takes a deep breath is at night, in bed, after he's gotten off thinking about his fucking boss.

He's holding on, though, because there's also the elation of having his first project come to life. It's getting built no matter what the pedestrian, evil contractors and businessmen try to do. And he is grateful to Lacroix for dealing with them almost exclusively, though sometimes he concedes on a few points Avery really wishes he wouldn't. He's learning—grudgingly—it's just part of the process. It might be a very fascinating procedure—despite the occasional flare-up of his temper and the smothering of his artistic soul—if he weren't flailing in the fires of lust over Lacroix.

There's a hellish week where suddenly the investors are saying a lot of things about "capital expenses" and "zoning privileges" and "capacity studies"—things he understands in theory from his business classes but that don't seem to be making Lacroix happy. It involves an exhausting amount of e-mails. Avery nearly falls asleep at his desk and feels like AutoCAD is organically linked to his brain. He can't remember the last time he left work when it was light outside.

Or got there when it was light outside, for that matter.

Avery is in Lacroix's office. And it's late—almost nine thirty. He lost track of what day it is about a week ago, but he thinks it might be a Tuesday. Or Thursday? He's sure there's a T in there, anyway. He's sitting in the chair that's usually across from Lacroix's desk, and as usual he's turned it so he can put his feet in the other chair, or even on Lacroix's desk—though admittedly he doesn't keep them there for long. This time he's just slouched in the chair, bone tired, watching Lacroix make his seventy-fifth phone call of the day. He can't even find the energy to stretch.

Lacroix is clearly not happy with whomever he's speaking with. He's not yelling. He rarely raises his voice, rarely displays any temper at all unless it happens to be Avery making him mad. But he's so tense he looks as if his jaw is going to crack while he's on the phone. All he's saying is "Yes, I see. Yes. Of course we will. Yes, that is perfectly understandable." Yet he looks like he wants to tell them they're fucking idiots and throw his phone at something.

Avery wishes he would do that, just for the novelty.

When he gets off the call, Avery leans his head against the chair and fights back a yawn. "They being dicks again, or what?" It's benign. He's too tired to be contrary or annoying on purpose.

Lacroix says something back—all harsh, angry syllables. For a second, Avery is worried he's gone insane because he has absolutely no idea what the words mean. And it takes him a few to realize that's because whatever it was Lacroix just said, it wasn't in English.

Avery's never, *ever* heard Lacroix speak in anything but English. In fact, on their last drive out to the Knight site, Avery kept asking him to teach him insulting phrases in French so he could yell them at people when he got mad. Lacroix refused because he hates fun. So Avery just yelled them in English and got a lecture about professionalism. There was really no pleasing the guy.

And Avery doesn't know French at all, except for that "Voulez-Vous Coucher Avec Moi" song, but even Avery can tell that's what Lacroix just spoke to him in. And that's what gets at Avery, digs in beneath the exhaustion and nerves and defensiveness he wears around Lacroix like armor. It wasn't on purpose. He meant to answer Avery in English. Avery is sure of it.

Lacroix gets angry, irritated, frustrated quite often. Sometimes it's not even Avery's fault. But never once has he gotten so worked up that he's forgotten English, and there is something so hot about that Avery can't even stand it. His breath is caught in his throat, and he can't stop staring. He wants to hear Lacroix do that again.

"What?" His own voice is soft and quiet. It may not even be audible.

Except Lacroix has supersonic hearing. "I said of course. Yes. Are they ever anything else?" Lacroix's eyes narrow suspiciously. "What's the matter with you?"

I want you really fucking bad. That's what's the matter with me. And I can't fucking take it anymore. Avery stands up and moves around the desk slowly, his eyes still locked on Lacroix's. He stops when they're mere inches apart. He can see Lacroix getting angry, but he doesn't give ground or take so much as a single step back from Avery.

That's also really hot, goddammit.

And there's a long moment where they just stare at each other. There's tension there. Avery might be tired and a little crazy, but he knows he's not the only one that feels it. It's good in the same way horror movies and roller coasters are—breathless anticipation while you wait for the bad guy to jump out from behind the curtain, the flutter of nerves in your stomach before that very first drop.

Avery might have let it alone, might have sucker-punched him as Lacroix is so obviously expecting. But then Lacroix tilts his chin up. His mouth curves in something too cold to be a smile, and he does it again—says something under his breath in French and jerks his chin at him. The French he doesn't understand, but the gesture is pretty clear in any language. Avery gets that.

That was an invitation, so this is your fault, Lacroix.

"Fuck." Avery grabs him, and there's an electricity when he touches Lacroix that races up his spine and turns everything into heat. He shoves Lacroix back—hard—and Lacroix shoves right back in return. That just makes him want more, so he ducks his head, throws his shoulder out, catches Lacroix in the chest, and knocks him backward.

Lacroix's very close to throwing a punch. Avery's been at the receiving end of one or two, so he can tell. And fuck, no. That's not what this is about.

"No, goddamn it. Just—" He gets Lacroix's back against the glass window behind the desk, mostly by accident, and when Lacroix tries to fight him, he drops to knees.

Lacroix goes still immediately. "What in the hell are you doing?" It's English, but Avery's never heard his voice so heavily accented before. Lacroix grabs him by the hair and pulls his head up. That's so close to what he's wanted for so long that Avery moans.

"Figure it out." He starts undoing Lacroix's belt without pause. His fingers are shaking. He half expects Lacroix to stop him. The way he's looking at him, the way he's breathing—it's like he still wants to fight, like the last thing he wants is Avery's mouth anywhere near him.

But Lacroix doesn't stop him. He stares down while Avery fumbles his way through getting Lacroix's belt off and unbuttoning his pants. Lacroix's hand is still in Avery's hair. He hasn't made a sound.

He's not hard, but Avery wouldn't have expected him to be, not with the way this started. There's a strange exhilaration in being on his knees for someone and having to make them want it—like it's some kind of challenge. And that's not anything he's used to when it comes to sex, at least not by the time he's got someone's cock in his mouth. But nothing about this is normal.

At first, it seems like Lacroix is just letting Avery make a fool of himself because not much is happening, and also because that seems like something he'd do. There's a momentary twinge of panic as Avery considers that possibility, but he doesn't stop or slow. Because Avery is very, very good at this, and if Lacroix is playing some game with him…. Well, he's not going to win it. Avery knows just about every trick there is to this—even has one or two named after him—and he's goddamn determined to make Lacroix want it.

For most of his really good tricks, he's going to need Lacroix to cooperate a little more. But luckily he's a got a few reliable standbys. He slowly moves his mouth up and down, and then, on a whim, gently drags his teeth up the length of him when he pulls back.

That gets a noise out of Lacroix, for the first time, a soft inhalation of breath that should no way be as hot as it is. Avery does it again, slower this time. Lacroix's hips push forward the slightest bit and his cock hardens in Avery's mouth. Avery resists the urge to smirk, and does it a few more times, using his teeth a little harder than he'd like it personally—but whatever works.

He moves on to the things he's really good at. He drops his hand and takes Lacroix as deep as he can, takes it slow and easy at first and gradually increasing the speed and the pressure until he's hitting the back of Avery's throat. Avery doesn't choke, though he usually makes himself when he does this because the kind of guys he picks up are usually into that.

But he doesn't make himself do anything this time. He teases at it and waits for what he wants, which is for Lacroix to make him, obviously. But Lacroix is either not getting the message or is just being contrary.

Avery finally pulls off, glares up at him, and uses his hand a little too rough out of frustration. He notices what that does to Lacroix and files it away for future consideration. "Oh come on." His voice is almost unrecognizable—heat and want all tangled up together. "You know you've wanted to choke me since you met me. Just fucking do it."

Thinking about being on his knees and asking Lacroix to fuck his throat is a little too much for Avery. He reaches down with one hand and rubs at his cock through his pants. That feels good and distracts him enough that he's barely aware of Lacroix tightening his fingers in his hair and doesn't expect the sudden, savage forward thrust of his hips that drives his cock in deep.

There's definitely nothing showy at all about the way he's choking on Lacroix's cock. Holy fuck. Avery relaxes his jaw and lets him. It's uncomfortable, but he can handle it. He tries to breathe as best he can. That works right up until Lacroix releases his hair, grabs the back of his neck, and then pulls Avery's head toward him as he thrusts in forcefully and doesn't let go.

Avery suddenly feels a lot less in control of this entire thing than he did a moment ago. He tries to wait it out and just take it, but the longer he chokes, the less determined he is. His eyes are watering and he's struggling. Lacroix holds it just a shade past too long, enough for Avery to feel a few sharp stings of instinctual panic. His body wants some air and isn't getting it. Avery hits him in the thigh, pulls hard against the hand on his neck, and finally, finally Lacroix lets him move.

"The fuck is the matter with you?" Avery pants, leaning back for a minute and glaring up at Lacroix. And wow, if he thought his voice sounded rough before....

"Finish it. Now."

That's the first thing Lacroix's said during all of this. He's barely even made a noise, and he's snapping an order at Avery—and Avery nearly comes right there. His chest is still heaving as he fights for air. His eyes are watering, but he gets back up on his knees. "Yeah. Okay." He takes a deep breath and looks up at Lacroix. "Do it again."

Lacroix says something under his breath that may or not may not be in French. Avery is a little too distracted by Lacroix grabbing his neck to tell for sure. He tenses up when Lacroix thrusts in again—ready to be choked—but Lacroix fucks his mouth, instead. He's definitely into it now. His breath escapes in short, heavy pants, moving his hips in a steady, even rhythm. Avery takes the opportunity to undo his belt and get his pants open—which is a relief, given how fucking hard he is.

Avery isn't stupid. He knows Lacroix wants to surprise him with it. He doesn't want him to be able to get ready or anticipate it. And that makes Avery tilt his head up to look at Lacroix. Their gazes clash together, and he tries to tell Lacroix he can take it, that it's all right.

Lacroix pulls him forward again and chokes him. God, it's so good. Avery gets a hand on himself. He keeps his eyes locked on Lacroix, who is leaning against the glass with half-closed eyes, face flushed and breathing hard. Avery fights as long as he can, but Lacroix holds it longer this time, and the panic takes over completely. He's going to lose consciousness. It's like the darkness from the window behind Lacroix is seeping into Avery's vision and slowly taking over.

Avery never looks away. Lacroix finally pushes him back, just a little, so Avery can fight the dizziness and get enough air in his lungs not to pass out. Then he comes in Avery's mouth with a low groan. His fingers tighten one last time on the back of his neck. Avery's hand is still moving over himself, and he's not sure he's going to get off or not. He's not quite there yet, and he's not sure he'll get the time to finish. But then he feels Lacroix relax his fingers and brush his thumb lightly against the side of his neck—right against his racing pulse—and he comes. He still can't breathe, and every frantic gulp of air sends another shock of pleasure through him. It's too much—overwhelming and almost painful.

It's fucking great.

At least, until about two minutes after he comes down from the high of it. His throat and neck hurt—and he's a mess, sitting on the floor of Lacroix's office and still trying to get his breath. He presses a shaking hand to his mouth and looks everywhere but up at Lacroix because he just… can't.

He ends up taking off his dress shirt and using that to clean himself up. It's sweaty anyway. Lacroix isn't saying a word, but Avery can feel his eyes on him and knows he's looking. Usually Avery is very relaxed after sex, stretches out like a cat and grins a lot, but this is so far from his usual it's not even on the map. He's not getting up. He's just sitting there in his dress pants and an undershirt, looking at the floor.

"We have a meeting tomorrow at eight at the Knight Foundation offices. Be there at seven thirty. I want to prepare answers for any questions they may have for us so we're on the same page."

Avery jerks his head up and he nods, distracted and tired and completely uncertain of himself in a way he doesn't like at all. "Yeah, okay." Lacroix's watching him, and his clothes are all back in order, slightly rumpled, but nothing that couldn't be explained away by a long day at the office. His hair is sticking up, though, suggesting it was damp, and he ran his hand through it a few times.

For some reason that slight hint of dishevelment makes Avery feel better.

Lacroix's not an easy man to figure out just from his body language, and he tends to keep his features composed and remote most of the time. This is no exception. But his eyes are somehow less guarded, not quite as cold, though it may just be a trick of the light. "Get up off the floor, Avery."

He's too tired to argue, but it takes him a few minutes to get his bearings and not freak out about what he's just done.

"Seven thirty," Lacroix says when Avery is finally standing. He's looking out the window, but Avery can tell he's watching him from his reflection. It looks like Lacroix is going to melt into the glass and vanish in the dark.

Avery says, "Seven thirty. Got it." And that's the end of it. He leaves Lacroix's office, grabs his keys off his desk, and heads home. When he drives past the office building, he slows and turns to look. Sure enough there's a single, solitary light shining inside. Maybe it's the tint of the window or something in the night air turning the white light into yellow, but it looks like fire to Avery. Like something's burning.

"HEY, HARLAN. Remember that one time I called you and said I wanted to do acid, and you were all, 'No, Avery, I think you shouldn't do that.' And then I went ahead and did it anyway?"

"Are you really calling me at work and asking about your prior recreational drug use?"

"Yeah." Avery turns his car off and drums his fingers on the steering wheel.

"Yes. I remember." Harlan sounds like he's sighing. He sounds like that a lot when he talks to Avery.

"Remember how you tried to talk me out of it? How you said I'd probably be the guy who thought they had spiders crawling all over them and then try and jump off a parking garage?"

"Yes." Harlan snorts a laugh. "And that is exactly what happened."

"Well, kinda. I mean, they were ladybugs, and it was a bunk bed."

"Avery, you're not… doing that again, are you?"

"What?" Avery scowls, offended. How could Harlan think that of him? "No. I haven't done drugs in forever. The kids in the scene would laugh at me. Is there a scene? Are there kids in it? See? I don't even know that."

"You just wanted to call me at work and reminisce?"

"No." Oh right. Now he had to actually get to the reason he'd called in the first place. "I just wanted you to remember how I called saying I wanted to do something, and then you told me not to, and I did it anyway."

"Thank you very much for reminding me, because I might not believe you were capable of such a thing." Harlan's voice is dry. "What did you do this time?"

Stung, Avery tries to come up with some kind of snarky comeback, but Harlan knows him way too well. "Um. Remember how you were like, 'Hey, Avery, don't sleep with your boss'?"

There's a very significant pause. "Oh, Avery."

Funny, that's exactly what Harlan said when Avery told him about the acid.

"I know. I *know*. Sometimes, Harlan? Sometimes I think I do things just because people tell me not to."

"Really." Harlan's voice is so dry it could suck all the water out of the Atlantic.

"So you think that's true."

"You're really asking me this?"

Avery leans his head back against the seat. The sun is coming through the window, too bright, burning his eyes. "Do you think that's why I wanted to do it in the first place, though?"

"With the acid or your poor choice in men?"

"Shhh," Avery says hastily, even though he's alone in his car and also not the one speaking. "But yes. The, ah... last one. Did I want that just because I knew I shouldn't?"

"No. I don't think so. Also with Lacroix. He's—you have trouble resisting that kind of thing."

"Older men with no personality who tell me no a lot?"

"The 'tell me no' part." Harlan is so very patient Avery wonders if he's a robot. Or an angel sent down from heaven, like in *It's a Wonderful Life*, except one who likes to fuck their friends sometimes. "Did you... ah. Did it go well?"

Avery closes his eyes against the sunlight and immediately sees himself on the floor. He remembers what it felt like to choke with Lacroix's cock in his mouth. His body heats up immediately. A hunger that is dangerously insistent, unlike any other he's ever felt, stirs and makes him want things he can't quite name. He's been thinking about it every day since it happened, though obviously neither he nor Lacroix have said a word about it.

"No."

"Ah. Well. That's all right. We all—sometimes this happens. You're under a lot of stress, and this is a thing you've been working for your whole life." Harlan's voice is kind, and for some reason—the exhaustion, the stress, the weird sex—it makes Avery feel like someone kicked him in the stomach. He doesn't deserve unconditional kindness and understanding from Harlan. He never has. "It's understandable. I'm sorry that it wasn't very good, though."

"Oh, it was good." Avery slumps down in his seat and rubs the heel of his hands against his eyes. "I just said it didn't go well."

"I see." Harlan clears his throat. "Actually no, I don't. Can you explain?"

"It was... pretty rough." Avery needs to stop talking about it. He's not going to jerk off in the car like he did after dates in high school. No way. "I think maybe I'm into weird shit."

"I have slept with you," Harlan reminds him. "One time you told me to smack you."

"Was I drunk?" Avery tilts his head, momentarily distracted. "I don't even remember that."

"I think so. I went ahead and did it anyway because I might never get the chance again."

"Ha-ha."

Harlan makes a comforting noise, which he's impossibly good at doing. "Avery. Look. I think you were looking for some kind of outlet, and you do tend toward extremes, especially when you're under this kind of stress."

"Thank you, Mr. Meyers-Briggs." Avery chews nervously on his lip. He can hear the sound of an approaching car, tires crunching gravel. Lacroix is here, and they have to meet the contractors, which means he can't spend the entire time wanting whatever it is he wants from his boss. "I guess that's true. But I shouldn't do it again, huh."

"Oh no. I'm not falling into this trap." Harlan suddenly sounds very businesslike. "But I am very glad you called to discuss the situation, and I hope my advice was sound."

"No, asshole. You just basically said, 'I told you so' and 'don't do acid' and then refused to give me any advice." Avery knows Harlan's abrupt voice switch means someone is in his office, but it's still annoying.

"I'm happy to discuss it with you further, but I think your intuition is sound, even if you don't always think it is."

Well. Great. That's just great.

"Thanks, Harlan. I'm sure your career writing fortune cookies will be brilliant. I'll look for your work at the Peking Palace."

"Your lucky numbers are one, five, fifteen, and thirty," Harlan chirps, and then his voice sounds a bit less businesslike. "We'll talk later. Try to get some sleep, hmm?"

"I will, as soon as I drop all this acid and blow my boss again," Avery snaps, and his peevishness is rewarded with a sharp bark of laughter and abrupt silence.

Goddamn, Harlan, stop encouraging me.

Avery sees Lacroix's ridiculously expensive car pull in next to his. He sighs and rubs his eyes one last time before putting on his glasses. Then he takes a deep breath and goes to face the day.

THINGS SETTLE down eventually, or else the endless hours and meetings have become so routine Avery doesn't remember what his job was like without them.

He and Lacroix get along no better and no worse, so apparently that little incident in his office did nothing to either ease the tension in their relationship or cause more in any noticeable fashion. So. There's that.

As the weeks lead up to the initial groundbreaking, Avery spends most of his time at his desk. He reworks schematics and alters plans to fit newly created budgets—usually smaller—and allow for newly discovered problems with the site—usually larger. But most of the time, that goes all right. He gives Lacroix his designs. Lacroix nods, puts them on his desk, and then puts that glass paperweight on top of them.

They've met each other's eyes a few times. Lacroix's are as cold and unfriendly as ever. Avery mutters something under his breath and leaves, tense and worked up.

He's still attracted to Lacroix, damn it. But that's not the thing pissing him off anymore. It's remembering being on his knees and choking, remembering how it felt and touching his neck when he gets himself off, trying to hold his breath to make it feel the same. It never works.

The Spice Channel is definitely not helping. Neither is a trial pass for kink.com, but for entirely different reasons.

Finally he decides to ask for advice from the only other person he knows who has kinky gay sex.

ahextall@ratcliffandroberts.com: *hey Brandon can we go to dinner i have to ask you about total domination tuesdays.*

He taps his pen on his desk, waiting for a response to his e-mail. When one doesn't arrive immediately, he scowls and sends another one.

ahextall@ratcliffandroberts.com: *i have to know right now*

He can *hear* Brandon sighing from his desk. Avery is certain of it.

bthomas@ratcliffandroberts.com: *i am not going w/you to TDTs but i like thai food so sure.*

Avery expels a deep breath and leans back in his chair, relieved.

All he has to do now is figure out how to ask his friend what he should do about Lacroix without telling him about the whole blowjob thing. That should be easy. Avery is pretty good at talking.

"YOU BLEW him, didn't you."

"What? Shut up. You... you can't just sit down and say that. It ruins my whole...." Avery waves at the appetizer platter. "Have a chicken satay."

Brandon takes one and eats it without comment. Also without spilling peanut sauce on himself. Some men have all the fucking talent. "It ruins your whole self-denial thing. Is that it?"

"I hate you so much, Brandon. So. Much."

Brandon doesn't seem bothered. "I know. Look, Avery. I have experience dealing with someone's self-denial when it comes to both liking guys and liking kinky shit."

"Wasn't Justin at Total Domination Tuesday?" Avery says that like he's a professional wrestling announcer. Even when he just thinks it, that's how it sounds.

"I'm not going to help you if you mention that one more time, Avery." Brandon calmly eats another satay. "He was, but he thought he was there to find a girl. He played with a few. I remember watching him."

"Wait. Wait. You can go there and watch girls and guys hit each other in various combinations?" Avery leans forward, chin in his hands. "Tell me more about this magic place, Brandon."

Brandon gives him a look. "No. I told you. There are much better websites."

"I know. I have a trial membership to one." Avery beams at him. "Are you on kink.com?"

"What, as a user? You don't friend people on there, moron. It's not Facebook."

"I meant videos of you and Justin. But whatever. Are you *blushing*, Bran? That's not very dominant of you."

"I will eat every single appetizer on here and then leave you alone, without answers, Avery. I really will. Can I see a menu?"

Avery hands him one, but he can't help himself and says, "Is this the kind of shit you do at home with Justin, because that's not very hardcore of you. Does he have to safeword out of appetizers?"

Brandon throws one of the sticks from the satay at him. "You know, it makes a lot more sense to me now, why you're all hot and bothered over Lacroix."

Predictably that makes Avery scowl. "What? I am not. Why would you say that? Do you really think I am?"

"Yes," Brandon says bluntly. "You want him to make you shut up and calm down."

"How do you know that?"

"Because that's what you all want," Brandon says, looking up as the waitress approaches their table. He orders his dinner—along with some steamed dumplings and a pad thai to go. "For Justin," he explains, and Avery wonders what that must be like to have someone take care of you like that.

"All of us who?"

"Bratty bottoms," Brandon answers, which makes Avery glare at him. "Especially high-strung ones."

That's the stupidest thing he's ever heard. He's not... well, okay. He does like bottoming. And maybe he's bratty. He's most certainly high-strung. Why is Brandon right about everything? It's not fair.

"Tell me what happened. When you and he hooked up."

Avery tells him as they eat, and he's completely unaware other people may be scandalized by his story of hot guy-on-guy action. If they are, they should stop listening. Brandon listens like Avery is a client and he's taking notes for a design, with an even gaze and an occasional nod.

"You shouldn't do shit like that without some kind of safeword," Brandon tells him when he's finished talking. "What if you wanted him to stop, for real?"

"I *did*," Avery mutters. He slouches and knocks his chopsticks against his water glass. "But I kind of didn't too."

"Hmm. Look, I'm not so sure Lacroix knows what he's doing either."

"Didn't see him at the thing I can't mention, did you?" Avery continues using the professional wrestling voice for "thing I can't mention," because now it's a habit.

"Nope." Brandon snorts. "That would have been awkward as hell. Wow. Anyway it doesn't sound like either of you know what you're doing or what you want. This should be entertaining. Or would be, if I didn't like you. You're supposed to come to dinner, by the way. If Justin asks if you want to have a threesome, tell him no."

"But why?" Avery looks up at him through his lashes. "It'd be fun."

"Yes, I'm sure it would. But we work together. And if you could stop thinking about Lacroix long enough to hook up with someone else, you would have done it by now."

"I tried." Wow. That sounds pathetic. "I mean, I… tried to convince a fuck buddy of mine to take me to bed, but apparently *he* thought the same thing, and he declined. Why does everyone know shit about me before I do?" Avery grouses and stabs one of his chopsticks into a steamed dumpling.

"You know it. You just need someone to make you admit it." Brandon gives him a slow grin. "Justin said it was a good thing you had no idea about any of this, or else you might have jumped me before he did."

"Yeah. Maybe. But I'm not a long-term kind of guy. We'd've been all into the awkward silence thing long before Justin showed up." Avery lifts his water glass in a salute. "I like him. It's nice you have someone."

"Thanks. I like him too. Look. Do you really want my advice?"

"Yes and no? I mean, I hate asking for it, and it's going to make you smug. But I'm kind of desperate, so I really don't have any other option."

"Wow, Hextall. Wow."

Avery shrugs and waits for Brandon to tell him what to do. Great. Now he's a study in dramatic irony. Fuck all of this, seriously.

"Okay, you're obviously—it's not going away. And it's not like he wasn't a willing participant, right? But I don't know, it sounds like you were both fumbling through it, and believe me, I know. He won't want to look like he doesn't know what he's doing or like he's too interested, because I bet that would scare you off. And I really can't believe this is our boss we're talking about. Ew."

"He's attractive," Avery protests. "Justin would get it."

"Justin likes his tops to have a little more emotion," Brandon says dryly. "You, on the other hand, have too much already. So you want someone who's not like that."

This all sounds perfectly reasonable, so Avery naturally wants to contradict Brandon and tell him he's wrong. Except he's shit at lying, so he doesn't. "I don't think he wants it again. I really don't."

"Do you believe that, or do you want me to tell you that I think you're wrong?"

Avery throws a chopstick at him. "Both."

"I think you're wrong. But I also think he's not going to do anything until you do."

"So you're saying I was right to pounce on him in his office." Avery nods.

"Well, no. But you did, and it got you what you wanted. So...." Brandon waits and watches him expectantly.

"The best predictor of future behavior is past behavior?"

"I would have taken you for a Dr. Drew guy, not Dr. Phil. You are truly an enigma, Avery. Do you know that?"

"Nah." Avery sits up and straightens in his chair. "I'm like one of those Dum Dum suckers with the question marks on the wrapper. Sometimes you can see what flavor it is through the paper, and if not, you just have to suck on it to find out all the answers."

Brandon bursts out laughing. "That was funny."

Avery bows. "Thanks. So should I just go up to him and say, 'Hey, Lacroix, want to take me home and fuck me and slap me around a little'?"

"Did you ask him the last time? Because I think what you want is to not have to worry about asking. And honestly, Avery? You'd drive me fucking crazy—in the not-fun way—because I like Justin to follow rules. I like to explain to him what the protocol is and how to do exactly what I want."

"And you really don't have videos on the website? I'm going to check, you know."

Brandon raises his eyebrows. "Check away. You won't find any. And my point is, I don't think that's what you want, and I don't think it's what Lacroix wants either. Sometimes people like the formality of it. I think that'd drive you bananas."

He was right about that. Avery had watched some "scenes" on the website, and he was bored immediately at how staged it all looked. But he didn't want to say that if Brandon was into it. It might not be his thing, but he wouldn't mind hearing about how it was Brandon's.

"Just be careful, all right? If Lacroix doesn't know he likes guys or kinky shit, it's going to be pretty rough." Brandon sighs. "And that totally turns your crank, doesn't it?"

"Who are you, Captain America? *Turns your crank?* Yeah, I guess. What if I try it and he doesn't do anything? Or has me arrested or something?"

"Then you either try harder or have your answer. And before you ask, I don't know how you decide. Only you would know that. But all I'm saying is that I know you want him to be aggressive. And you're going to have to push him. If you want that. But maybe don't because he's our boss, and have I mentioned this is a terrible idea?"

Yes, he's mentioned it. But all Avery hears is, "You're going to have to push him." Trying to talk him out of it is a lost cause. Because if there's one thing he's good at, it's pushing.

Avery waits until Brandon heads home. Then he turns on his phone and starts searching. Malin Lacroix is not a common name, so it doesn't take Avery long to find his address. He also finds out Malin is a girl's name in Sweden, which, ha!

His body feels like it's buzzing, electric. He stands beneath the streetlights and waits for a cab, humming, hands shoved in his jacket pockets. This is the stupidest thing he's ever done. He's not even thinking about whether Lacroix has a girlfriend or boyfriend living with him—or kids, or any of it.

He's just doing what he does best—rushing into something without thinking and hoping it turns out all right in the end.

In his experience, it usually doesn't.

CHAPTER 6

WELL, IT'S worth it for the look on Lacroix's face when he opens the door, if nothing else. Also someone needs to notify the apartment management that the doorman should probably spend more time watching who's coming and going, rather than talking on his phone and smoking.

"Hextall. I'm assuming you have some reason for showing up at my home uninvited?"

"Yeah." His heart is racing. Lacroix is wearing a dress shirt, unbuttoned and untucked from his dress pants. Does the man not own anything else? And he's barefoot, which is completely out of character and yet still really hot.

"And am I permitted to know what that is?" Lacroix asks.

"Can I come in?" Avery is pretty sure he knows what the answer is going to be, and he's right.

"Absolutely not. Either tell me why you're here, or I'll see you tomorrow at the office."

"Thought I'd blow you again. I can do it in the hallway, but you might give your neighbors a hell of a show. Though you could be into that."

Lacroix's expression is as unyielding as stone. "I don't wish to discuss what happened in my office. I suggest you don't bring it up."

"Okay. We don't have to talk about it." Avery steps closer. He can taste his pulse, and he reaches out and grabs at Lacroix's shirt. Lacroix's eyes flash at him, heated silver. "We don't have to talk at all." Before he can say anything, Avery pulls him in and kisses him hotly.

For just a moment, Lacroix stuns Avery by kissing him back. And then he shoves him away and presses the back of his hand to his mouth. He turns and walks into his apartment, but he doesn't shut the door.

59

"Get in here," he says, and Avery feels a low, heated rush of triumph as he walks inside and closes the door behind him.

Guess I owe Brandon a thank-you card. Maybe I'll buy him a whip or something.

Lacroix's apartment is done in the modern style, with low furniture and abstract art. The whole thing is decorated in gray and white and yellow, with bright dashes of turquoise thrown in as an accent. Lacroix has colorful accents? Huh. He came here to blow Lacroix, and instead his mind is blown. Trippy.

"Are you renting this place?" Avery clearly has no intention of honoring that no-talking promise he made. If Lacroix wants him to shut up, he can just go ahead and make him. "It doesn't seem like you."

"No. My ex-wife had it decorated, and I haven't really gotten the urge to change it."

"But there are things in here that are turquoise, Lacroix. Turquoise. You don't strike me as the whimsical type."

"Likely why she isn't here to enjoy it." He walks toward the kitchen and gets a bottle of Scotch—of course he drinks Scotch—and pours himself one. He doesn't offer any to Avery, which is fine. Avery doesn't need to drink. Lacroix is fucking with his equilibrium enough.

Avery walks around, looking at the apartment. There are no pictures, no magazines, no books, no television Avery can see, and there's no music playing in the background. Everything is spotless—no shoes on the floor or jacket thrown casually over the sofa.

This is weird. Avery's a fairly tidy guy. He's not messy or anything, but his apartment looks like someone actually lives there. He has pictures, magazines, shoes by the door. A cat. Things.

"What do you do here?" he asks at length because his curiosity is overwhelming. "How do you entertain yourself?"

"It's quiet. I spend time thinking. Some of us do that on occasion, Hextall." Lacroix walks over to him. His nearness makes Avery skittish. He's never been this attracted and anxious around anyone. Ever. Even those hot car models at that car show in Chicago he went to when he was thirteen.

"Great view," Avery says almost enviously. The wide windows are spotless, and the city is a thousand shining lights beyond the glass.

"Mmm. Watch." Lacroix hits a switch and plunges the apartment into darkness. The windows appear to vanish completely, and without any glare, it's like they're not there at all.

"That's fucking incredible," Avery breathes, turning slowly. It almost gives him vertigo. "I take all that back. You don't need anything else to be entertaining. Wow. I bet watching it storm is amazing, huh?"

Lacroix is suddenly standing right in front of him. "Why are you here?" He reaches out and lightly traces Avery's mouth with two fingers. It makes Avery just as dizzy as the view, and it definitely makes the vertigo worse.

"I told you," Avery answers, feeling that electricity flare up hot between them. This can't be just him. It *can't.*

"You want to put your mouth on me again. Is that it?"

Avery can barely speak. He just nods, and Lacroix's fingers start to press against his lips. Avery opens his mouth immediately as Lacroix slides them inside.

"You don't need to. It will never influence a single thing I do at work, will never get you any favors, and I will never, ever bow to blackmail attempts or give in to threats."

Avery snorts and bites Lacroix's fingers. He is so not that devious, but it's kind of awesome Lacroix thinks he is. "What the hell? Why would I think any of that?" The words are muffled around his fingers but easy to understand.

"Honestly? Why wouldn't you?"

"Because you're hot, and I want you to smack me around," Avery tells him, still muffled. But the sound Lacroix makes, involuntary and sharp, is proof he understood that too.

"You don't like me, Avery. You think I exist to crush your dreams." Lacroix takes his fingers out of Avery's mouth, and then drags them, wet, down his cheek.

Avery finds it hard to breathe. He's also fairly certain Lacroix knows exactly what he's doing, because holy *fuck* this is getting him wound up tighter than a ball of twine wrapped around a spring.

"Technically you are the one who made my dream come true," Avery says, and he means it as a joke, mostly. But it doesn't sound that way because he's so fucking turned on he might die.

Lacroix makes a rough sound, grabs his shirt, and hauls Avery toward him. "If this is gratitude, I don't want it. Whore yourself out for someone else, because you won't do it for me."

"It's not," Avery assures him, eyes wide. "Besides, my design was fucking awesome. I'm not going to be grateful that you're not an idiot. You did your job. I did mine. Isn't that how you told me it worked?"

"*Oui.* I believe so."

French again. Fuck. Avery presses closer and starts unbuttoning Lacroix's shirt. Lacroix grabs his wrist and won't let him. "So you're telling me you came here without wanting anything at all from me?"

"Oh, I want stuff, Lacroix. Nothing about work, though. Other stuff. Hot stuff. Like the hair-pulling, choking-me-with-your-cock kind of stuff. Like we did before, with the smacking me in the face. Remember?"

"I'm fairly certain I would remember smacking you in the face," Lacroix tells him, and to Avery's shock, he lets go of his wrist and doesn't stop him from unbuttoning the shirt. "I'm disappointed to tell you that I didn't."

"Oh. I just wanted you to." Avery finishes unbuttoning his shirt. They stand there, both of them breathing harder, neither moving. "You remember the other stuff, though. Right?"

Lacroix gives him a sudden shove, pushing him backward with a violence that startles Avery and almost makes him trip. "Hey—"

"Shhh," Lacroix says, advancing on him. "You talk too much." He shoves him again, and Avery realizes he's not so much pushing him away as pushing him somewhere on purpose.

"Then make me be quiet," Avery tells him, shoving him back. He sees Lacroix narrow his eyes dangerously, and Lacroix shoves him harder. Avery shoves back just as hard. "You want me to go somewhere, make me."

"I am," Lacroix says, grabbing his shirt.

"No. I'll fight you. Make me go there. Don't you get it?" Avery searches Lacroix's cool, pale gaze, and he makes a frustrated noise. "I came here. I want it. I'm telling you. I'm not just going to do something because you tell me to. You want me to shut up? Make me, Lacroix."

Lacroix is silent for a moment. "Malin," he says, his voice very quiet and threatening in a way Avery's never heard before but really, really wants to hear again. "My name is Malin."

"Malin," Avery answers, his voice already gone to hell. He says it wrong on purpose and waits, breathing faster and saying *please, please, please* in his mind. Maybe out loud. Who knows?

And then Lacroix—Malin—smacks him on the mouth. Hard. "Say it again. Correctly."

Avery's answer is a low, broken moan. Malin smacks him again, harder, and grabs his hair in one hand. "Say it, or you're going home, Avery."

Avery doesn't believe that for a second, but he plays along. "Malin," he gasps, and then his gasp turns into a moan as Malin starts pulling him by the hair toward a door that he hopes to God leads to a bedroom.

It does, but Avery doesn't see much of it. Malin slams the door and pushes Avery against it, and then kisses him. Avery kisses him back like he's desperate for it, and he is. The windows are the same in the bedroom as they are in the living room—seamless, invisible—as if there's nothing between the two of them and all the light.

This time when he gets Malin's pants open, he's already hard. But it takes longer because Malin makes certain it does. He won't let Avery touch himself either. He tries to tell him to stop, but Avery almost laughs and keeps doing it anyway. Finally Malin pulls out of his mouth, smacks him again, and pulls him to his feet. Avery is shivering and confused. Malin shoves him to get him to turn around. But then Avery feels him grab his wrists and pull them roughly behind his back, and Malin's breath is hot on Avery's neck as he ties Avery's wrists with his belt. The touch of the leather on his heated skin makes Avery moan. Malin doesn't make a sound, but Avery can feel his fingers shaking slightly as he secures the belt.

When Malin's finished tying the belt, he turns Avery around again and kisses him roughly. Then he shoves Avery down to his knees again. Avery blinks up at him, tugging at the leather and enjoying how he can't pull his wrists free, even if he wanted to. Malin looks down at him, predatory eyes glittering, and gently rubs his thumb over Avery's bottom lip. He doesn't say anything, but he doesn't need to. Avery knows what he wants.

He leans forward and opens his mouth, and Malin's not hesitant this time when he pushes his cock in deep, making Avery gag. Malin makes a rough noise, but he pulls back almost immediately. The conscientiousness of the gesture would make Avery grin, if his mouth wasn't full. Instead, he hums around Malin's cock and winks up at him, trying to let him know that it's all right to just go for it, that Avery wants him to and that he can handle it. Malin brushes his fingers over Avery's cheek in an oddly tender gesture, and then his hips push forward, and this time he doesn't stop.

Avery pulls against the leather on his wrists while he chokes. Malin is breathing hard, his head thrown back against the door while Avery sucks him hard. He makes a sound when he comes. He says something Avery can't hear because his blood is roaring in his ears, and he's dangerously close to passing out. Malin pushes him away after it's over, and Avery drags air back into his starved lungs while he waits for whatever is going to happen next.

Malin gets on the floor behind him and loosens the belt around Avery's wrists. He puts it around Avery's neck, pulls him up, and kneels behind him. "Get yourself off." He starts pulling on the belt, choking him.

Avery drops his head back. He can see Malin's eyes, dark gray like storm clouds. "Make me," he gasps, because he wants Malin's hand on him, wants Malin to be the one who gets him off.

Well. He really wants Malin to fuck him, but something tells him they're not quite ready for that.

"Do it, or you don't get off," Malin growls, pulling the belt harder—hard enough Avery reaches up and grabs at it instinctively. He pulls at the leather and tries to get it away from his neck. Malin seems angry about that, or maybe it's just turning him on. It's hard to tell.

Avery's been with guys who have never touched another dick in their lives, whether they've thought about it or not. And something tells him Brandon was right. Malin Lacroix hasn't touched one either. *You'll have to make him. He won't want to look like he doesn't know what he's doing.*

Avery grabs Malin's hand and pulls it around his body. He settles back and wraps Malin's hand around his cock. He moans immediately at how good it feels. He starts moving, showing him how to do it before

Malin can protest. Avery looks back at him and says, "I can still breathe. Come on." Malin chokes him with the belt again.

Malin picks up the rhythm of it easily enough, and it's not like it's going to take very much to get Avery off. He drops Malin's hand, and Malin doesn't stop moving it. The choking gets so intense he's thrashing and he can't move. When he breathes—when he's allowed to breathe—the sudden influx of oxygen pushes him toward the edge with the intensity of a knife catching skin.

Malin holds the belt long enough to send thrills of fear down Avery's spine. When he hears Malin's voice next to his ear, soft and menacing, he expects a threat of some kind. And he wants that, or at least he thinks he does.

Instead, Malin drops the belt and wraps a hand around Avery's neck. He doesn't squeeze or choke, but just keeps it there like a reminder. And instead of the threat Avery's expecting, Malin says, "Let go. Stop fighting me."

And that's exactly what Avery does. He comes with Malin's hand on him, his head thrown back, one arm raised and hooked around the back of Malin's neck like he's drowning, and there's nothing else that can save him.

AVERY GOES into the bathroom when they're finished, intending to take a shower. But first he spends some time staring at himself in the mirror. He's all drowsy eyed and relaxed, and his neck is already purpling with bruises. He touches them gently and shivers a little.

Malin has a really great shower, which has spray coming from every single direction—the top, all three sides. It's fucking amazing. He puts his hands on the tile, bows his head, lets the water slide over his neck and back, and then tilts his head up so it runs down his throat and chest.

He feels weird—quiet and calm. Yet he knows if he keeps thinking about what just happened, he'll get all worked up again. It's late. They have an early meeting. Maybe he should just go home. But what if this is it? What if this never happens again?

Malin's soap smells like him, and when Avery rubs it over himself, he gets hard again. *Damn it.* He isn't sure Malin will just get in the shower with him. The guy seems to be weird about his personal space. And he's fairly certain he'll be leaving when he gets dressed, but the thought of getting off in Malin's shower is both a damn shame and sort of weirdly hot.

He's idly rubbing his soapy hands over his cock when Malin comes into the bathroom. He's wearing a white undershirt and his dress shirt, which is untucked and unbuttoned. His dress pants are zipped, but the button is undone. It's not *fair*. Why is that so hot?

Avery studies him with frank interest, taking in his pale eyes, his white-blond hair touched with silver at the temples. He has no idea how old Malin is, but looking as relaxed as he's ever seen him, Avery thinks he's probably younger than he first thought. His eyes definitely are his most striking feature and give him a menacing look, even though there's nothing particularly threatening about him at the moment.

Malin seems to be studying him the same way. Avery wonders what he's thinking. He cocks his head and grins, turns to face him, and leans back against the shower wall. He has never been shy about his body, and he's always figured if someone is looking at him naked, they must be at least a little into him.

"You can choke me anytime if you let me use this shower afterward. This is great. Holy shit."

"I was wondering why you were still in here." Malin's eyes lower briefly to Avery's cock, which is definitely not relaxed anymore. "Was I interrupting?"

"Nah. I told you I just really like the shower," Avery deadpans. To his shock, Malin actually smiles briefly. Then his face settles back into that inscrutable expression. Avery soaps up his hands and rubs them over himself, wondering if that will do anything to convince Malin to get in there with him.

But there is something he likes about being on display. Fuck. Avery had no idea he was so weird. But like most things, he decides to just go with it. Malin is watching him, and Avery gives up the pretense of washing and starts jacking himself, slow and easy, tilting his head back against the tile and letting the water slide over his closed eyes.

Save the sound of his breathing and the water, there's absolute silence for so long that Avery opens his eyes and half expects to be alone. But he's not. Malin is leaning against the counter, watching,

LET THE WRONG LIGHT IN

arms crossed. He looks almost bored. Avery bites his lip and stalls his hand. Why does Malin Lacroix make him feel so uncertain? It's not like this is the first time he's shown off for someone in the shower, man *or* woman.

"Is there a problem?" Malin's voice is cool and distant. Why it gets Avery going is completely weird, but it does.

"No," Avery says, shaking his head. "Just, you know."

"No, Avery. I don't know." Malin stares at him. "Are you not interested in continuing?"

Why can't he like normal people? "Are *you?*"

"Did I tell you to stop?" When Avery shakes his head, Malin shrugs. "Then why did you?"

"Because you make me nervous," Avery answers without hesitation.

Malin gives a small, pleased smile. "Do I?"

"Yeah. Look—"

Malin holds his finger up to his mouth. He doesn't even say "shh." "Tilt your head back so I can see your bruises. Then you may continue."

"Oh fuck." Avery does so. He moves his hand faster, arching his back and tilting his head like Malin told him. He's close, and Malin doesn't say anything else. Now Avery can't see him, but he can feel him watching, and he bites his lip. He smacks his other hand hard against the tile as he feels himself about to come.

"That's very good, Avery," Malin says. Avery wants to believe it's just that Malin has good timing, and not that some part of him wanted to hear those words so badly they make him come the second Malin says them.

When he finally opens his eyes, he's alone in the bathroom. He takes a moment to compose himself, then gets out of the shower and dries off with a really crappy towel. Why would you have that awesome shower and terrible towels? It's like buying a Ferrari with cloth seats instead of leather. He pulls his clothes on, runs his fingers through his hair, and pads into the main living area. It's still dark.

Malin is sitting on the couch, smoking a cigarette. He's not looking at Avery.

Suddenly Avery wants to climb on his lap. Not because he wants sex—or not only because of that—but because he wants something else. To be touched or praised or… something. But instead, he's getting a cold and silent dismissal. And it's causing a rash of confusing feelings. He should just go home and deal with them alone.

"I'm gonna head out," he says and nods toward the door.

Malin nods, and barely. He takes a drag off his cigarette.

"I'll… see you at our meeting, then." Wow, that's not incredibly awkward or anything. But what else should he say? *Thanks for choking me and getting me off and letting me use that awesome fucking shower. I'll see you at work, where we'll pretend this never happened.*

He's turning the doorknob when Malin speaks. "Avery. You are not permitted to call me by my first name at work. Do you understand?"

"Keep the hot side hot and the cool side cool?"

"If you wish to make jokes, we can simply end this right now."

Avery sort of wants to hit him. "What *is* this, Malin?"

Malin just exhales smoke again, not looking at Avery. "Do you understand the rules or not, Avery? This is not something I will *make you* do. It's simply something I expect."

Avery stares at the ceiling and wonders when he started getting turned on by autocratic behavior. "I understand. Do you? I mean, come on. You know how I am. You want to strangle me at work all the time. And now you can. So, are you sure you'll be able to help yourself?"

"Who said anything about not choking you? I'm simply saying that you won't use my first name at work."

"Right. You mean you want to keep this… whatever it is… a not-at-work thing." Avery is transfixed by Malin and how he smokes a cigarette. He's got it bad, and he doesn't even really know what *it* is yet.

"Is that what I said, Avery?"

"Yes?"

"You don't sound very certain." Malin leans forward and puts the cigarette out, directly on the glass table in front of the sofa. "What have I asked you not to do?"

"Call you Malin at work." Avery can't, for the life of him, figure this out. "But why isn't—I mean, you're saying you want to keep this a not-work thing. Right?"

"Avery, I am growing very tired of repeating myself. Perhaps if you listened to what I'm saying, instead of what you think you're hearing, that would help."

Avery walks over and stands next to the couch. Even with his height advantage, it doesn't feel like anyone but Malin is in charge. "Okay. Well, can I ask a question?"

"Yes."

"Don't you *want* rules about... what we do at work? Like, say, 'Avery, don't come in and try and suck me off in my office,' or 'Avery, get your hand off my dick. We're on a conference call.' I mean, you know me. Right? I'll try shit if you don't tell me not to."

"All you have to do, Avery, is that one thing."

"So should I try and suck you off in your office? You really have no other rules at all about this? Do you think you should think about that, maybe, and get back to me about it tomorrow?"

"I expect you're not stupid enough to jeopardize your career. And do tell me if I'm wrong for trusting that you have an investment in your future in the firm, or at the very least, in architecture."

Avery feels completely at a loss for words. "I wouldn't intentionally. But sometimes I don't think, and I do impulsive shit without thinking about consequences and things."

"I'm aware of that." Malin almost—almost—sounds amused. "And I will take care of it. All you need to do is what I've told you. I'm capable of dealing with your behavior, so it's not something you have to worry about."

That is so incredibly weird, infuriating, and also attractive that Avery has no idea what to say. "So I should just act like myself and let you deal with me?"

"You should not call me Malin at work," Malin says slowly, like he's talking to an exceptionally stupid three-year-old. "I didn't realize this would be so difficult for you to understand."

"No. I get that. I don't understand why you don't want me to behave any different. Seeing as how you get annoyed with me all the time."

Malin gracefully gets to his feet and steps closer. "Because, Avery. You told me I would have to make you. Remember? That's what I'm going to do." He leans in, voice pitched low. "You give me all the control, or you give me none. That's your only choice. And by coming here, we both know which one you chose."

Avery shivers at the way Malin's breath ghosts across his neck. "All right. Then I'm going to try to blow you at work, you know."

"If you try, and I'm not in the mood, I'll make certain you stop."

Avery can't imagine not being in the mood for a blowjob, but he lets that go. "As long as I don't moan your first name in the office."

"Yes." Malin steps away from him. "As long as you follow that one rule, I will make you follow the rest."

"What about kissing. Can I do that? As in right now?" Avery asks, because he wants to and because he's feeling totally off-balance. It's similar to what Brandon told him earlier, which is annoying, because Brandon needs to be wrong about *something*.

"Try it and see."

The uncertainty is both exciting and nerve-racking. Avery steps closer and slides a hand into Malin's hair. He holds his head still and presses against him. He kisses him slowly, heatedly, and Malin eventually responds and kisses him back.

Avery pushes him to the sofa and climbs on top of him, just like he wanted to do earlier. He settles on Malin's lap, and their kisses get heavier and more intense. Malin's hands are warm on Avery's back, lightly tracing over the contours of his muscles. Before long Avery is reaching down to get Malin's pants off.

Malin lets him, and while he's on his knees, Avery thinks about how he really should get home and the meeting they have in the morning. But if Malin wants him to leave, then he'll tell him to do so. There's something nice about not having to worry about it.

So when he opens his mouth, it's not because he wants to say something. Malin is still rough, but he doesn't choke him this time. When it's over, Avery puts his head in Malin's lap and catches his breath. He feels Malin gently stroke his fingers once through his hair.

And then he starts to pull.

THE SKY is light when Avery drives home to change. He's tired and sex-dazed and he just wants to go to sleep. His bruises hurt. And ow. Fuck. Malin really, *really* likes pulling Avery's hair. But he's also grinning and so goddamn pleased with himself, he can't stand it.

He takes another way less exciting shower, dresses, and shaves, and then sends Brandon a text message while he brews himself a hell of a pot of coffee.

Me: *thnx for the advice man just got home.*

Malin didn't say anything about telling his friends. Right? And he can make him not send text messages if he wants. He just isn't here. Which isn't Avery's fault.

It's going to be a long day. But man, was it totally worth it.

THREE WEEKS later, Avery still has no idea what's going on.

The project is running smoothly, and the groundbreaking will take place in a little more than two months. The frantic pace of meetings and redesigns has come to an end, and Avery goes back to a somewhat normal schedule. Work, gym, dinner, and stay up stupidly late being smacked around by his boss. The usual eight-to-five grind.

He doesn't always see Malin outside work, but when he does, it's always at Malin's apartment. So far the only kinky thing Malin's done at work is pull his car off the side of the road on the way to a site visit and make Avery suck him off. That was really hot because Malin was right back to normal when they met with the guys from the Knight Foundation.

But sometimes Avery just goes home, torments his cat with a laser pointer, and watches terrible action movies.

He hangs out at Justin and Brandon's place. They get drunk, have dinner, and play *Call of Duty* on Brandon's PS4. It's pretty badass, and Brandon has a surround-sound entertainment system, so it's just like being at war. Only without the likelihood of physical danger or bothersome ethical considerations.

It's so much fun that Avery buys himself a PS4, the game, and the little headset that goes with it so he can play from his place. Brandon usually wins, Avery accidentally kills their entire unit by being overly generous with explosives, and Justin's strategy usually revolves around talking shit to the other online players and making them angry enough to stop playing—until Brandon tells him to quit it.

Avery watches their dynamic, and he knows it's not a full-time thing, the kink stuff. He knows because he asked Justin, who is fast becoming a good friend and who'll tell Avery just about anything he wants to know. But he will not show Avery any of their toys or his collar.

Justin is a lot more easygoing than Brandon. He reminds Avery of himself. But Brandon doesn't remind Avery of Malin at all. Brandon smiles and makes jokes and touches Justin all the time when they're at home.

Malin doesn't make jokes. His touches lead to bruises, and his smiles all end in teeth marks. But Malin does smile, though not often. Still, it's not something Avery thought he'd ever see.

One night over takeout—because neither Justin nor Brandon can boil water to save their lives—Brandon catches sight of one of Avery's bites peeking out from beneath the collar of his worn T-shirt.

"You do have a safeword. Right?"

Avery changes the subject. Brandon tries to give him a lecture about consent, and Avery pretends he has an early meeting so he can leave without hearing it. He doesn't like talking about it to Brandon because he's pretty sure what he and Lacroix are doing is not the same thing Brandon and Justin do. Living in that apartment with Malin would be almost laughable.

He can't even play *Call of Duty* because there's no television. Though maybe Malin would be good at it. Who knows? The man was as easy to figure out as stereo instructions.

Earlier that day Malin stopped Avery in the hallway to tell him he had to attend an event that evening. Avery nodded and told him to have fun. Because that was clearly Malinspeak for "Don't come over. I won't be home tonight." Right. Check.

Except it wasn't because Malin's response was "It should be over by ten thirty. I expect you to be there when I get home. I'll leave a key with the doorman."

Avery thinks about not doing it. But his libido is louder than his pride, so he shows up at ten thirty. He takes a nice long shower because that's the only entertaining thing in the apartment.

And the windows. Avery has discovered if you stand too close to them with the lights off, and you fall forward, there's a moment when you think they're not there and you're going to fall through the glass and tumble into the city below.

That's only fun for about ten minutes, though. After that and the shower, Avery looks through Malin's dresser and his closet. He marvels at how neat and utterly boring everything is. No wonder the man likes kinky shit. He doesn't even have any wacky ties or neon socks. And if there's porn in this place, it's well hidden, and Avery doesn't want Malin to come home and find him snooping through things.

Apparently Avery is the only one into sexy-architect espionage. What a shame.

Because there's nothing else to do in the apartment, Avery decides to take a nap. He should probably get sleep when he can. His schedule is ridiculous. And he's not as fond of *thinking* as Malin. Lately his thoughts have been insistently telling him something he doesn't want to hear.

He's woken violently by Malin pulling his hair. *Hard.*

"Get up," he snarls, and he seems angry, which is rare.

"What? I took off my shoes," Avery protests sleepily, grabbing at Malin's wrist. "Ow." He swings his legs over the side. "Wouldn't fall asleep if you had anything to do here besides take a shower and fall on your windows."

Malin blinks. He seems confused, but the expression only lasts a moment before his eyes turn icy with rage. He backhands Avery, which he's never done before and which makes Avery's head snap to the side. That certainly wakes him up, and he gingerly touches his split lip. It's bleeding.

All of Avery's warning signals go off at once—a cacophony of bells ringing, sirens blaring, and that voice saying, "Danger, Avery Hextall, danger." Over and over. Because something is wrong, and Avery notices. He's actually worried about Malin. So he decides to put the pain-slut thing on hold and says, carefully, "Is everything all right?"

Malin goes to backhand him again, but Avery catches his wrist. "I don't think so. Fuck you." He grabs him, shoves him on the bed, and climbs on top of him. Malin is hard, which is thrilling and kind of worrisome. Avery pins his arms to keep him still. This feels all wrong, sort of, but it's also fucking hot.

"Get off of me," Malin hisses. But he's not fighting. He's so fucking weird. Avery rolls his hips down and tries to kiss him.

Bad idea. Malin bites him right on the split lip, and when Avery rears back in pain, Malin shoves him away.

"You are in a fucking mood tonight. Jesus. What the hell? I thought you went to a fucking party."

Malin laughs, but it's not any laugh Avery's ever heard before. It's too loud, for one, and he's still lying on the bed in his really hot suit. And oh fuck. There's a smear of blood on his jaw from Avery's mouth.

"I hate parties. *Hate* them."

That's the most personal information Malin's ever shared. And his voice is accented more than usual, which means he's definitely mad about something.

"See? This is why you shouldn't repress your emotions," Avery tells him. "You have a simple dislike of parties, and it makes you a raving lunatic who smacks guys around."

"If you don't want me to smack you, Avery, you're free to leave." Malin is staring at him, his face flushed and his pale eyes gleaming. Avery sucks on his bleeding lip and looks at Malin.

For the first time, Avery thinks about what Malin gets out of this. He seems much the same before they start as he does after they're finished. Sometimes he smokes afterward, but that's about it.

Really? Is it?

Avery is aware he's at an important juncture. If he leaves, this will be the end of it, no questions asked.

He won't like it if he doesn't know how to do something.

Oh, Brandon Thomas. You are the wisest man I know. Avery takes a deep breath and moves toward the bed. Malin wants something, and he's trying to ask for it. He just doesn't know how. And he hates asking for anything. That's obvious.

Malin is leaning up on his elbows, breathing heavily. Avery can see he's still hard. He starts to take off his own shirt. "Think I'll stay. That's what you want, isn't it?" He gives Malin a crooked smile. "Don't worry. I'm going to be quiet."

"How did I luck into this miracle, exactly?"

Avery shrugs. "You look like you've had a bad day, that's all."

There's a flash of something hot in Malin's eyes. He stands up and crosses to Avery, grabs him by the back of the neck, and forces their gazes to meet. "Don't make this something it isn't, Avery. I didn't come home to you so you could fix me a drink and ask me how my day was."

"I know." *You came home to me so you could hurt me and get off on it, and watch me get off on it too.* He reaches out and starts taking off Malin's belt. His fingers are shaking. He can't believe what he's going to ask Malin to do to him. Avery leans up and kisses him impulsively, presses the belt into Malin's hands, and goes to lie on his stomach on the bed.

Silence.

Avery waits, arms stretched out above his head, grabbing at the headboard.

Silence.

Finally he looks over his shoulder to ask Malin if he's an idiot, and does he need to explain what you do with a half-naked man on your bed and a belt in your hand? His words die on his lips because.... Oh fuck. Malin looks so goddamn hot, and he's looking at the belt like he's starving.

"I could hurt you very badly," Malin says, and his voice makes Avery hard immediately. It's probably supposed to be a threat, but Avery's body takes it as a promise. Fuck. Maybe he's the stupid one here.

"Yeah," he says, dropping his head again. "That's the idea."

"Avery."

"Yeah?"

"I won't stop until I want to."

Avery bucks his hips restlessly against the bed, seeking friction because—holy fuck—that was hot. "I know." He's shaking a little from nerves, and it's cold in the apartment, especially without a shirt. The anticipation is making him light-headed. He can hear Malin shift behind him, and he tenses his back and waits.

It turns out that Malin might not know about jerking guys off or blowjobs or whatever, but he's pretty good with a fucking belt. He lays into Avery's back without hesitation, and he's making sounds and saying things in French Avery can't pay attention to because it hurts so fucking much. But he takes it, even when the belt wraps around the tip of his shoulder and brings tears of sudden pain to his eyes.

"Tell me to stop," Malin says, and Avery makes a noise like "no" and shakes his head, feeling a little sick to his stomach. But his cock is still hard. He still wants something to push against.

"Tell me to stop," Malin hisses, and he's hitting Avery with the belt doubled up now. It hurts even more that way, especially when he strikes places that are already red and purpling into bruises.

He grits his teeth, and when that doesn't work, he bites the pillow beneath him and shakes his head again. He's going to pass out. He's an idiot. This is the dumbest thing he's ever done.

"Avery. Goddammit. Tell me to fucking stop!"

Holy shit. Malin is shouting at him. Avery finally realizes what he wants, and at the next blow, he says, "Stop."

Malin doesn't. He just keeps hitting him and saying, "Oui, oui. Dites-moi d'arrêter," over and over. Avery takes that to mean he should keep saying it, and he does. At some point, it turns into the truth. Malin seems to know. He stops abruptly and drops the belt to the floor.

Avery is shaking on the bed, and his back is on fire. He's not hard anymore, but he can't remember if he came or not because he can't think. His head feels fuzzy, and he's shivering. Then he feels Malin climb on the bed. Malin straddles him, and at the thought *He's going to fuck me now*, his erection comes back with a vengeance.

But Malin doesn't fuck him. Avery has no idea what the noises are all about until he turns his head to see. And there's Malin with his pants undone and his cock in his hand, staring at the ceiling and gasping while he jacks himself off. He sees Avery watching and he shoves Avery's head down onto the pillow. He doesn't see when Malin comes, but he feels it, warm on his back.

Then Malin gets off the bed and leaves the room. Avery doesn't know what to do. He's in pain, and the idea of moving is too much. But he never spends the night. He always goes home, at some point. Even if it's late. Even if the sun is up.

When Malin comes back, Avery's jeans are half-buttoned, and he's sitting on the edge of the bed, taking deep breaths.

"What are you doing?" Malin asks and sits next to him.

"Should go," Avery mutters, his fingers clumsy as he tries to pull on his shirt. "Shouldn't I?"

"Did I tell you that?"

Avery shakes his head.

"Then you aren't leaving," he says simply. He presses something into Avery's hand. A glass of water. Avery drinks it thirstily. Some of it spills down his chest.

Malin takes the shirt out of Avery's hands. And then to Avery's shock, he leans in and gently kisses the back of Avery's neck. His hands are warm on Avery's shoulders. "You need a shower. I'll put something on your back."

Avery lets himself be maneuvered into the bathroom. Malin helps him get his jeans off and helps him into the shower. Avery leans against the wall, watching in quiet surprise as Malin strips his own clothes off and joins him.

He's never seen Malin naked—ever. And he grins even though the water hurts like a bitch. Malin has a *tattoo*—a skull and crossbones on one shoulder. "You're kidding me," he says, reaching out to lightly trace it with his fingers.

"I was young," Malin says. His hair is slicked back off his forehead, and it makes his cheekbones sharper and draws attention to his hawklike eyes. "You have a dragon tattoo on your chest, Avery."

"But dragons are awesome," Avery mumbles and lets his head fall down. "Like this shower."

"I'm going to clean your back. It might hurt."

Avery grins over his shoulder. "Oh no. We wouldn't want that. Hey, you look like you feel better."

Malin looks at him for a long time, then turns his attention to Avery's back. "Yes."

Avery nods, pleased. "So I did all right, then. You're really good with a belt. I didn't think you would be. Well, not that you couldn't figure it out. But that was pro-level skill right there. If they have competitions, you should totally—"

Malin starts kissing him, his hands on either side of Avery's head. Avery kisses him back. He places his hands on Malin's slick, heated skin. This is the most he's ever been permitted to touch, and he likes it a lot. So does his cock, which is reminding Avery he didn't get off yet.

When Malin pulls away, they stare at each other for a few long moments. Avery slowly and deliberately lowers his gaze. There's no sound but the rush of the water and the two of them breathing. It sounds almost obscene in the close confines of the shower. Malin gently turns him so he's facing the shower wall. He takes Avery's wrists, lifts his arms, and places Avery's palms on the wall.

"Keep them here." He bites at Avery's neck, and Avery moans, shivering with pleasure. "Good. Make noise. I want you to."

"You are being really hot right now," Avery tells him and swallows hard.

"I want you to make noise, Avery. Not speak." He starts to clean Avery's back with soap, and that gets a slight gasp of pain from him. His body twists in instinctive protest. But he doesn't drop his hands or stifle the sound.

"Good," Malin says. Occasionally he presses his fingers against a welt and gets a surprised, pained noise from Avery.

By the time he's finished, Avery is a wreck. His skin is oversensitized to the point where the water is almost a torment, and he's having a hard time standing still and keeping his hands on the wall. Malin presses against him, takes his hands again, and turns him this time so Avery's back is against the wall. It hurts a little, but it isn't nearly as distracting as how hard he is.

But nothing is as surprising as watching Malin Lacroix get on his knees for him, because... holy fuck. "What—" Avery doesn't even know what to say. He had absolutely no expectations Malin would ever do this for him. Ever.

Malin tilts his head up. He still looks like he's in charge, even though he's kneeling. "Hands against the wall, Avery."

Avery smacks them there, too eager. "You're really—" He can't seem to finish a sentence.

"Yes," Malin says, sliding his hands briefly up his thighs. He leans in, but he doesn't take Avery's cock in his mouth. Not at first. He bites Avery on the inner thighs—both of them—and it hurts so badly that Avery's knees buckle, and he desperately grabs at Malin's hair.

Malin immediately stops and grabs Avery's wrist. "Hands against the wall. I won't tell you again."

That doesn't seem very fair, but Avery does it while Malin bites him again, then brushes his fingers over the teeth marks on Avery's skin. "Hey, this is not what I—Oh, holy *fuck*."

Malin takes Avery's cock in his mouth while he presses lightly on the teeth marks, and that makes it feel completely different. The pleasure chases the pain, and it's nearly too much for him all at once. He's going to embarrass himself by coming really quickly if Malin doesn't stop.

Not being able to move his hands is killing him. He wants to grab Malin's hair. He wants something to hold on to. But he doesn't have that. He's unbalanced, and it feels like it did with the windows. But this time there will be nothing there to catch him, nothing to keep him from falling.

AFTER THEIR shower, Malin bandages his back, smokes a cigarette, and then makes Avery an omelet.

Avery lies on the couch, on his stomach, his head on his arms. It's got to be close to two in the morning, and he's tired enough that he thinks he might be dreaming. "Do you ever sleep?"

"Infrequently." Malin is smoking while he cooks. It's hilarious to think this man in a simple white T-shirt, wrinkled dress pants—he really needs some pajamas—and smoking a cigarette is the same man Avery hates with a fiery passion.

And beat the shit out of his back with a belt. And just sucked him off in the shower. *Okay. Fine.* He doesn't hate Lacroix at all. *Get a clue, Avery.* He groans and repeatedly bangs his head on his arms. *Shit. Shit.*

"I didn't realize my sleeping habits were such a problem for you."

Avery's head snaps up. Suspicious, he narrows his eyes at Malin. "Was that a joke? It was, wasn't it? Quit it. You've knocked me around enough for one night."

He's pretty sure Malin rolls his eyes.

Malin brings him the omelet. He puts his cigarette out on the glass table and sees Avery watching him. "My ex-wife hated when I smoked in here," he says. There's the slightest hint of a smirk. "Also, I hate this table."

"Stop acting human. You're freaking me out," Avery says, pushes himself into a seated position, and winces a little. It feels like he pulled a few muscles, but nothing too bad. "You didn't even get any ashes in this omelet. I would have. Did you have to practice that? This is really good."

"You talk when you're nervous, you talk in bed, and you talk when you're relaxed. Are you ever *quiet*, Avery?"

Avery takes another forkful of the omelet, chews it with relish, and smiles at Malin. "Nope. Not unless I've got something in my mouth."

Malin lights another cigarette. He's not eating. "As if I needed more incentive."

Avery winks at him and goes back to his omelet. At one point, the hilarity of the situation hits him, and he starts to *giggle*.

Malin raises his eyebrows at him. "Quoi?"

Avery laughs harder. "I'm sorry," he gasps, his eyes tearing. His fucking back hurts, but he can't help himself. "It's just... can you take a look at what's happening right now?"

"You're having some sort of breakdown on my sofa?"

Avery is shaking with laughter, hunched over while he tries to catch his breath. "It's two in the morning, my back hurts because you hit me with a belt, we've had sex, and now I'm eating an omelet on your couch. While you do nothing but watch me, chain smoke, and put cigarettes out on your table. This doesn't seem the slightest bit funny to you?"

Malin shrugs in that effortless way of his and inhales sharply from his cigarette. "And that's why we settled on the turquoise accents. My version of whimsy apparently offended my ex-wife's sensibilities."

Avery is so shocked he just stares at him. "That was funny," he says slowly and reaches out to poke Malin in the shoulder. "I mean actually funny. Not, like, funny because you're weird. I think you hit me too hard this time. I really do."

Malin exhales like a movie villain. "I doubt that, Avery."

You're being clever and witty, and I'm starting to think you're nothing like the man I thought you were, and that is bad news with a capital B.

"I don't know anything about you," Avery says slowly. "Except that you hate glass tables, parties, and noise."

Malin doesn't crack a smile. "Avery, we're not having a conversation about this right now."

"Are we going to? Ever?"

Malin puts his cigarette out, brushes the others onto Avery's discarded plate, and goes to the kitchen without answering.

"It drives me nuts when you do that," Avery says. He is peevish, as if this is an actual relationship and not just... whatever it is. He gets up and gingerly stretches. Fuck. His back feels like it's on fire. He hopes he has aspirin at home. Does that even work? Maybe he'll check WebMD.com.

Avery goes to the bedroom to find his shoes. Malin is getting ready for bed. When Avery picks them up off the floor, Malin asks him what he thinks he's doing.

"Getting my shoes?"

"Why?"

"Because I need them to drive? Because it's cold outside? Because this is New York City, and I don't want to get a tetanus shot because I walked home barefoot? Take your pick."

"You're not going home tonight, Avery."

"What? I'm not?"

"No." Malin disappears into the bathroom, and Avery hears the water running in the sink.

"But you're going to bed," he points out, and then he stands and holds his shoes like an idiot—until the water switches off and Malin walks back into the bedroom.

"And so are you," he says, as if this is normal, as if they've ever done this before. "But not in jeans. And you should sleep on your stomach. Here." He holds something out to Avery.

Avery opens his hand out of instinct and pure, unadulterated confusion. Malin drops an Advil in his hand.

"For your back," Malin says slowly. Like he's not sure if Avery speaks English. His gaze suddenly sharpens. "I shouldn't have done that."

Avery takes the Advil with the glass of water on the nightstand. He isn't sure what to say. "I asked you to, remember?"

Malin sits on the other side of the bed, staring down at his hands for a moment. Then he looks back up at Avery. "It doesn't matter," he says. "I was angry, and I...I won't do that again."

Avery climbs into bed, completely and utterly confused, unsure if he's glad about hearing that or not. But it hurts when he tries to lie on his back, so maybe Malin has a point. "Yeah, okay. Maybe it was too much," he says, shifting on his side.

"It was," Malin says, in the "you're not going to argue with me" voice. Avery does it anyway, on occasion, but this time he keeps his mouth shut. He leans closer and kisses Malin instead, like he's trying to argue with him that way instead of with words.

But Malin just kisses him, holding him closer with his hand on the back of Avery's neck while he does so. The gesture is possessive instead of rough, but that gets Avery's blood going all the same. Apparently everything Malin Lacroix does turns him on.

Malin presses some button that makes the curtains sweep closed and block out the light, pitching the room into darkness. "Avery?"

It's so rare Malin asks him anything that Avery takes a moment to respond. "Yeah?"

There's a very brief moment of silence, and then Malin says, "Thank you."

Avery is so shocked he doesn't know what to say. So he settles down with a yawn and mumbles, "You're welcome. Next time maybe don't go places that piss you off that much."

"That means I'd never leave the house," Malin says, and Avery doesn't think he's ever heard Malin speak English with an accent because he's relaxed

Avery's glad he was able to help with that, even if Malin was probably right about them taking things too far. And he knows there are things he should be worried about—like how he doesn't know anything about Malin, not really, and how this is supposed to just be about sex, but now he's staying over. Instead, Avery just closes his eyes and listens to Malin's breathing, deep and even, until he falls asleep.

CHAPTER 7

THE BAR where Avery meets Justin after work is crowded with hipsters. Everyone is wearing black-rimmed glasses. Avery is too, but he needs his, and... he had his first. Whatever. They're also all on iPhones. The Instagram servers are probably jammed to capacity from this IP address alone.

Justin has a table in the corner and is drinking a beer. There's a pitcher and a nice empty glass waiting for Avery. "Beautiful," he says and falls dramatically into the chair. He is so tired he's going to die. He pours himself a beer and drinks it like it's water.

"Slow down, Ted Kennedy," Justin jokes and makes a motion for the waitress. "Can we have another pitcher, please? And can my friend get a water?"

"Sure thing," the waitress says. She's got brown hair pulled into a sloppy ponytail, a great smile, and a killer pair of legs Avery and Justin both take a moment to appreciate as she walks toward the bar.

"Sometimes I feel bad for Brandon," Justin says and sighs. "How can you not want to sleep with girls? Look at them. They're all so pretty."

"Right?" Avery watches all the girls at the bar as they interact. They lean in close with each other, giggle, and sometimes pet each other's hair. "If this were the Spice Channel, they'd be making out by now."

"Where do they film those shows? Just showing up and having a drink as an extra doesn't count as cheating, does it?" Justin clears his throat. "Don't tell Brandon I said that."

"Oh, come on. Brandon would totally let you fuck a girl, I bet." Avery likes to make statements he cannot back up in the slightest with actual facts. "If he does, can I come over?"

"My sex life is not a Spice Channel movie, Avery," Justin laughs.

At least yours isn't a Call of Duty level like mine is.

83

When the waitress comes back with his water and another pitcher, Avery realizes they're at a table for two. "Hey. This is romantic and all, but isn't Brandon coming? Are you going to sit on his lap? Because that might be too much for me to handle. You two are disgustingly happy." He doesn't mean that—well, he does, kind of—but all of a sudden, Justin's smile falters, and he looks away.

"Whoa, whoa. That is international bar language for something is wrong." Avery leans closer. "What is it? You two aren't fighting, are you?"

"Oh no. It's not that," Justin reassures him. "Just… Brandon's not coming tonight. That's all."

"Why?" Avery looks at him with suspicion.

"He's training for another ridiculously long running thing, you know. He has to sleep eight hours a night and drink water and eat carrots. Beer is too tempting." Justin is looking everywhere but at Avery, who snorts and takes another drink of his beer.

"Out with it, Justin. You're as bad at lying as I am."

Justin sighs. "Fine. We're…. Brandon's worried about you."

"Huh?" Avery takes a minute to parse that one. "Your boyfriend is worried about me, so he's not here?"

"No, he… uh… sent me to talk to you."

"What is he, the king of goddamn France?"

"What? That doesn't make any sense." Justin leans in, like anyone could hear them talking if they wanted to. "No. He just wanted me to, y'know. Check on you."

"First of all, why the fuck doesn't he check with me himself? Second, why are you doing it for him?"

"That's the same question, Avery."

"Goddamn it." Avery's temper is frayed around the edges, and he knows he has to fix his sleeping schedule—pronto. "Fine. I still want to know."

"Look. I like you. I think you're hilarious. I would totally be up for a drunken threesome if Brandon would just…. This is beside the point," Justin says hastily. "And Brandon really is worried about you, and he thinks you might want to talk to someone who is into stuff like you're into."

Avery laughs. He can't help it. There's a wild edge to it, and he's grateful Justin is there, because he does need to talk someone. But he's pretty sure Justin isn't into anything Avery is doing with Malin. "That's great, and I appreciate it, but tell him it's cool. I'm fine." He studies the coaster with rapt attention. It's very colorful.

"Now who's lying?"

Avery slumps in his chair. "I really don't think we're into the same kind of stuff, Justin."

"That's why Brandon's worried about you," Justin says, refilling Avery's glass.

"But you just said—"

"Okay, into stuff that you want to be into, but are instead with a fucking moron who doesn't know what he's doing and who is going to hurt you."

Avery is horrified to feel himself blushing. He hides it by glaring at Justin. "That's the point, isn't it?"

"No, Avery. It isn't." Justin looks sad.

Avery stares at him, and his mouth closes on whatever he was going to say. That's going to take him a second to get over.

"Look, man. Not to be all… that guy who overshares, but I'm going to be that guy who overshares," Justin says bluntly. "I thought I could do this shit without emotional involvement too. I went looking for someone to hit me, not to fall in love with. Or even have sex with afterward. Especially not a guy."

"Brandon says you were looking for a girl," Avery peevishly points out, uncertain why he's being such an ass. Probably because he's not getting any sleep.

"Yeah. Well, Brandon has his own issues," mutters Justin. "I love the guy, but he's kind of…. When he thinks he knows something, it's hard to convince him otherwise. But my point is, if he's just hurting you, that's fucked-up."

"He's—what, so it's okay if he's sucking my dick after he does it?" Avery kicks his heel against the floor of the bar. He can't look at Justin. He knows what his friend is trying to say, and he doesn't want to hear it. Malin hasn't hurt him nearly as bad as the night with his belt, but Avery hasn't stayed over again either. He just keeps having rough not quite sex until all hours of the morning, eating an omelet, and driving home when the sun comes up. That's all perfectly normal, right?

Yeah, right. Maybe if Avery were nineteen.

"No, it's not. Look. You're giving him something, and he's not giving you anything back. It doesn't seem like it, anyway."

"What's he supposed to give me? Diamonds?" Avery skates his fingers along the edge of the table and over his glass. "He gets off. I get off. That's what we're doing."

"Does he ever say anything nice to you?"

Avery snaps his head up. He laughs. "Have you ever met Malin Lacroix? I don't think he's in this to be nice to me."

"That's—don't you see why that's a problem? Look. I know maybe we're not exactly into the same things because Brandon tried using a belt on me once, and he kept apologizing. I don't really get off on pain or anything, and Brandon's not much of a sadist."

"And why are we into the same thing, again?"

"If you would let me finish."

"Starting to see why Lacroix wants to hit me with things, are you?"

"Ha-ha. Look. I let Brandon tell me what to do and wear a collar because I like not being in charge of things. And that's pretty much Brandon's favorite thing—ever. I swear to God, he gets off being the banker while playing *Monopoly*."

Avery snorts. "I can totally see that."

"Right? Anyway. He's happy. I'm happy. And he's not acting like I fucking owe him or like he deserves it without having to do anything in return. It's a relationship, you know. Outside of all the other stuff."

"Right. Well, we're not in a relationship. We're just fucking around."

"It doesn't matter. He should still…. Look, he's supposed to do things. Take care of you."

"Oh my God, what?" Avery groans. "I'm not his mistress. Jesus Christ, Justin."

"After the kinky shit, moron. And you don't have a safeword? What if you want him to stop?"

"I don't."

"Yeah. And that's the fucking problem," Justin mutters, raking a hand through his short hair. "You don't want him to stop, so you never tell him to stop."

"Uh...." Avery finishes his beer. Fuck. He's so tired he can't think straight. "Right. I don't tell him to stop because I don't want him to."

"You don't tell him to stop while he's hitting you so that he doesn't end it. That's why, isn't it?"

Avery looks up at him silently. *Fuck.*

Justin nods, taking that for the answer it is. "You know, when I first met you, you were a lot different."

"That was like three months ago, dude."

"I know. And you were exhausted all the time then too. But you looked... fuck it. You looked happy. And now you look goddamn miserable, and Brandon is two seconds away from storming into Lacroix's office and giving him a piece of his mind about how he's abusing you." Justin's face is dead serious.

"He didn't send you, did he?" Avery rubs his hand over his face. "You just don't want him to lose his job."

"Are you kidding? He could come work with me, and it would save so much fucking time in the morning. And we could fuck in my office. It'd be hot. But he doesn't want to, and I am worried about you, dude. That's what I mean. You automatically think it's not you I'm worried about, because no one is taking any fucking care of you." Justin sounds angry.

Avery doesn't know what to say. "Do I look that bad?" he quips. But it falls flat, and he knows why. Justin's right. He does look terrible. He's seen the dark circles under his eyes, and he's constantly in a state of near exhaustion. He can't remember the last time he got a full night's sleep. And omelets at two in the morning are not enough to sustain him through ten-hour workdays.

"Yeah. You do. And you don't look happy at all." Justin is staring at his own beer glass. He looks embarrassed. "I know we just met and all, but I like you. And so does Brandon. And this isn't the only way you can get what you want. You don't have to take it from him."

Yes. I do. Because he makes me, and I like it. Avery pushes his glass away and fumbles for his wallet. "I have to go."

"Aves," Justin says, worried. "Don't—Look. I'm sorry. I know that came out of nowhere."

"No. It's all right." Avery's hands are shaking. "I can't... I just can't right now." His eyes search Justin's, hoping to God he sees what Avery's not saying.

Justin nods slowly. "C'mon, let's get out of here. We can share a cab."

"No, I'm going to walk. I think."

"You're not. Or if you are, you better promise me you're going home." Justin adds some cash to Avery's and looks at him obstinately.

He isn't thinking about going to Malin's, but maybe he is. Avery feels hysterically near tears, which is all sorts of fucking crazy. "I'm going home, Justin. I promise. I just need to get out of here."

Justin nods, and the two of them make their way to the front of the bar. The crowd is picking up, and the noise is deafening—too loud. The energy isn't washing over Avery, it's drowning him.

And that's when he knows Justin's right, and something's got to give.

AVERY TURNS his cell phone off, calls in sick to work for the first time in his life, and sleeps for three days straight. He wakes up only to eat regular meals, take a shower, and go back to bed.

On the third day, he takes a look at himself in the mirror. He's covered in faded bruises from the last time he was with Malin. When he touches them he gets the same heated rush he always does. But he looks better. His brain doesn't feel like mush.

He sends Justin a text message.

Me: *thnx man and tell bran not 2 yell at boss.*

When he goes back to work, he spends the entire day checking e-mails and fixing issues with the Knight Foundation Center design.

When he sees Malin, it feels like electricity sparks up his body. The want is there immediately, sharp and hot, and he can barely breathe when he goes in to hand Malin some schematics he asked him for.

Malin doesn't mention he was out sick or ask if he's feeling better. Avery doesn't bring it up either. He doesn't go to Malin's that night or the next.

A few nights later, he picks up a girl at a bar. Her name is Allison, and she's in New York with her sister, who's at some work conference for the week. She's cute and friendly, smokes cigarettes, and drinks whiskey.

He takes her back to his place, and she giggles and tells him over and over, "I never do this." She sits in his lap, takes her clothes off, and touches him almost shyly. Avery loses himself in how she's soft and warm underneath him, and he comes when she scratches her nails down his back against bruises that are still fading. She apologizes and says she doesn't mean to hurt him, and he buries his face in her shoulder and doesn't say anything.

Avery takes her out for pancakes the next morning, then back to his place and right back to bed. He pulls her legs over his shoulders and kisses up her thighs. There aren't any bites or bruises, just soft, sweet skin. She curls her fingers in his hair, but when she pulls it doesn't hurt. She twists when she comes against his mouth, gasping and arching on the bed.

When she goes down on him, he grabs the sheets, and he's careful—so careful not to choke her. Her mouth is deliciously soft and wet. He washes her in the shower, and she giggles at how much attention he pays to her breasts. She's got great tits. He's missed those.

She leaves Sunday morning, smiling and her hair all sex tousled. Avery is pretty sure her name isn't Allison, and he doesn't think she even has a sister. But he understands she needed the same thing he did. He kisses her good-bye and tells her thank you. He's grateful for the reminder that it doesn't always have to hurt to feel good.

His sheets smell like her. It makes him smile.

Two nights later Avery lies in bed and pulls his own hair while he gets himself off. Frantic, he kicks his heels against the mattress in frustration. Nothing works, not the memory of that gorgeous girl and her long legs wrapped around his hips or the way she rode him and moaned with her nails in his chest.

Nothing but the thought of Malin staring at him with his glacial eyes, his belt around Avery's neck. Avery shoves his wrist into his mouth and bites it hard enough to break skin. Only then does he finally, finally come.

It's so good it's almost unreal. He lies in his darkened bedroom and stares at the clock, watching the numbers change. He doesn't understand what's wrong with him. He doesn't know what he wants.

Chapter 8

About the same time as Avery started at Ratcliff and Roberts, Harlan opened his contracting company, Blackwood Inc. He told Avery it was in reference to a Shirley Jackson story he loved as a kid. Avery told Harlan he had no idea who that was.

"She wrote *The Lottery*," Harlan said, and Avery nodded sagely, pretending to know what he was talking about. "Anyway, the name's from a book called *We Have Always Lived in the Castle*."

Harlan is like that. He reads smart books and knows how to do construction and owns his own company. He owns a walk-up, and it even has a guest room. He's four years older than Avery, and he's always been completely on top of things. Including, on many memorable occasions, Avery. He's also very good at giving advice and being patient. Sometimes Avery thinks it's like that movie, *A Beautiful Mind*, and he's totally made Harlan up.

Harlan's office is in a converted deli. Every time Avery visits, it makes him want a sandwich. Today is no exception, but there are no sandwiches. Just his friend, boots stacked up on his desk—actual leather cowboy boots, because Harlan is ridiculous. He is on the phone as always. His dark-blonde hair is streaked with gold and is slightly too long, so strands are constantly getting in his face.

The hair thing drives Avery crazy, to be honest. He leans over and brushes it out of Harlan's face. Harlan swats at him and keeps talking.

"Well, sure. Now, I'm absolutely positive that's what the guy said, but you don't have to worry, we'll get it straightened out."

Avery falls back in a chair and glares. Harlan is in jeans, a buttoned-up shirt without a tie, and boots. Avery is wearing a three-piece suit and uncomfortable shoes. His hair is a little too short. His weekend playdate, Allison, asked if he was a marine. Avery responded, "Only if you count *Call of Duty*." It was better than explaining he went for a cheap haircut. And he hasn't cleaned the lenses on his glasses in so long he's gotten used to seeing blurry spots everywhere.

In short, he feels like the boring accountant friend of the dashing cowboy romance-novel hero. Not that he reads those or anything.

Avery knows he's a good-looking enough guy, but what generally gets him laid is his charming personality and sparkling joie de vivre, otherwise known as impulsive decision making. But right now he doesn't feel charming, and if there's any joie in his life, it's all from getting a normal amount of sleep.

Harlan's still trying to sweet-talk whomever he's on the phone with. He's got a bright smile, and his eyes have the right kind of lines on the sides—from smiling, instead of staying up worrying too much about a sadistic kind-of boyfriend. His laugh is infectious and even makes Avery smile. Fucking hell.

"Why can't we just fall in love?" Avery asks. He is dramatic and immediately slouches in the chair. That's the only thing he can do that makes him not feel like he's here to do Harlan's taxes.

"Hey. I'll have to call you back," Harlan says and hangs up the phone. "What?"

"I said why can't *we* just fall in love? It'd be so much easier. I could design you a better office, and you could teach me to wear shirts like that with jeans and not look like a frat boy. We could have crazy fucking sex every night, and you would get us so many chicks the threesomes would be epic. The threesomes, man. Think of the threesomes."

Harlan stands up and walks over to the small minifridge, takes out two beers, and hands him one. "First of all, I like my office. Second, you were in the engineering fraternity in college. That doesn't make you a frat boy. Third, we tried living together once, and we almost killed each other." Harlan sits down, props his boots on his desk, and tips his beer back to take a drink. "We did have some epic threesomes, though. I can't argue with that."

Avery opens his beer and takes a drink. It's a Budweiser, because it's the middle of the day. Harlan has weird, arbitrary rules about drinking that he says are "Southern" and Avery thinks are "made up." But he has one anyway, as it's Harlan's way of saying "Yes. I will listen to you angst at me," and joins in the moment of silence for threesomes past.

"We lived together as roommates, though," Avery points out, smiling slightly. "That was a terrible idea." It was. Harlan wasn't quite as neat as Avery, and he was also constantly trying to open all the windows and let some light in. In the middle of New York City. In February.

"Just don't tense your muscles and stop shiverin', and you'll be fine," he'd tell Avery.

Avery, who was a miserable, sleep-deprived grad student, huddled in a blanket and trying to keep blueprint paper from blowing away. When Avery's cousin, Heather, decided to fuck having a grown-up job and take off for the Peace Corps two years ago, Avery jumped at the chance to sublet her place. The apartment technically belonged to Heather's father, Avery's uncle Clarence, but Clarence spent most of his time with his third wife down in that creepy Disney town in Orlando where everyone drove golf carts. The apartment was a one-bedroom and even had its own parking space, meaning he could finally bring his Prius up from his parents' house in Akron. Avery had to watch Heather's cat, Sheba, as part of the rental agreement—but the cat was a way better roommate than Harlan ever was. At least she couldn't open a window and wasn't responsible for any of the bills.

"Besides, my parents would go tits up in a cornfield if I took you home," Harlan continues cheerfully. That expression literally makes no sense, given his parents are from Louisiana, but Avery doesn't mention it. "They already think I followed you up here to the godless North. If they knew we fucked, you would never make the family Christmas exchange ever again."

Avery grins around his beer bottle. "They do like me, huh."

"Besides being a godless Northerner, yeah."

"I'm from Akron," Avery points out, rolling his eyes. He loves Harlan's parents, though. Even if they sort of terrify him. "Ohio's not the godless anything. It's not that interesting. And it's the Midwest. Your parents need a map."

"Son, anything above Kentucky is the godless North." Harlan laughs, settling back.

"My parents, on the other hand, would be fucking thrilled if you and I got gay married. That's what my mom calls it. 'Honey, you know your father and I will be happy when you get married or gay married, whatever you want.' Ugh. I can't even disappoint my parents correctly. I suck."

"What on earth is this?" Harlan narrows his eyes at him. "Are you still sleeping with your boss?"

"Umm," Avery says, looking around. "Is that painting new? I've never seen it before."

Harlan cranes his neck. "That's a picture of a ham sandwich I haven't gotten around to removing, Avery."

"Well, I like it. It's very ironic."

"Avery."

"What?"

"You know what."

"That's not the correct definition of irony?" Avery smiles at him. "Thank you, Alanis."

"You're in love with him?"

That stops Avery and his attempts to steer the conversation away from the thing he came there to talk about. "What? What in the fuck made you say that?"

"You came in here being mopey and looking like one of those guys from The Killers and asking why you and I aren't in love."

Avery drinks his beer in silence. "I think you meant The Hives."

"Do what?"

Only Harlan can say that and not sound like a hard-of-hearing octogenarian. "That crack about The Killers. Did you mean that because I'm in a suit? They don't wear suits."

"I meant because you looked like you were having feelings, but sure. That'll work."

"Some of us have to wear suits to work, cowboy," Avery snaps, but he's smiling.

"You ain't at work," Harlan drawls and winks at him.

Avery studies him for a moment—the way he's leaned back in the chair—with an architect's eye for design. Harlan is a good-looking man, and Avery has always thought it would be impossible for any guy to think they were straight if they could go to bed with him. He's kind and generous, hot as fuck, gives amazing head, and reads literature. He can build things.

Avery makes a frustrated noise. "I don't understand why I'm not in love with you."

Harlan lowers his feet to the floor, his face serious. "Because you're not. Why would you be?"

"Why wouldn't I? Who wouldn't? Harlan. You have no faults and are technically and physically perfect."

"Do you need to borrow money?"

"No, I mean—I think there's something wrong with me."

"Thanks," Harlan says dryly.

Avery waves his hand. "I'm just wondering what I'm holding out for, you know?" He's pretty sure this is either going to end up with Harlan laughing at him or punching him in the face. He's not going to think about which would be better.

"Well, Hextall," Harlan says, and the way he drawls the last syllable of Avery's surname is exactly what got Avery in bed with him in the first place. That, a six pack of Corona, and some cheap whiskey because Avery is a lightweight. "There could be the whole thing where I find you cute as a button, but you ain't really my type either."

"So now I have unrequited theoretical love for you? Ugh." Avery starts pulling at his beer label and grins at Harlan from beneath his lashes. "Could I have a blowjob so I can feel better?"

"No," Harlan says and stands up. "You can have another beer, though. And tell me what the hell brought this little visit on. Aren't you supposed to be working?"

"Probably. I have a site visit soon." Avery sits up and puts his half-finished beer on Harlan's desk. Suddenly he doesn't want to talk about why he's there because he's not sure why he is. "I'm kind of sleeping with him and kind of not," he says slowly, answering Harlan's question.

Harlan starts another beer. "Out with it," he says, and Avery takes a deep breath and spills his guts. He hasn't talked to Harlan in a while. It makes him realize that Justin was right about how fucked-up he's been over Malin.

"So," Harlan says when he's finished. He has that same vaguely angry look on his face Justin had, back at the bar. "You're saying this asshole beats you up and doesn't even take you out for dinner?"

"I don't need to go out to dinner," Avery protests.

"Avery, I smacked you once, and it was pretty fun. But you know why?"

"'Cause I have a big mouth and never stop talking?" Avery answers immediately. Self-deprecating is a talent of his, along with drawing and naming songs from eighties action movies.

"Because it drove you fucking crazy, that's why. Like, you got so hot for it, for me, that I wanted to do it again, even if it was weird, and I had to stop myself from asking if you were all right or if it was too hard."

Brandon tried hitting me with a belt once and kept apologizing. What the fuck was wrong with him? "Yeah?"

"Yeah. You have no idea how much girls like that story too," Harlan says with a smirk, but he still looks concerned. "You know, this is something about you that I don't get."

"What? Wait. There's more than one thing? Harlan, how can you not get something about me? You've known me for years. Fuck. You knew I liked guys before I did. You and my parents."

Harlan flashes a grin at him. "I don't know about that."

"I'm like the easiest person in the world to know," Avery protests and stands up. Harlan's office sucks for pacing. It's not big enough. And he really does want a sandwich. "I'm not complicated in the slightest. I'm an open book. I'm—what? Why are you looking at me like that?"

"Because you're not, Avery. You're one of the most complicated people I've ever met."

Avery gapes like a proverbial fish. "What?"

Harlan looks like he's thinking how to say something. Or at least, Avery thinks that's how that would look, as he's never done it. "Okay. First things first. While all that nonsense about me being perfect was sure nice for my ego, you're crazy if you think it's true. I'm not perfect. No one is. But how about this. I agree that life would be a lot easier if I could be in love with you. How's that?"

"You're joking. I'm impossible."

"Yes," Harlan sighs and rubs his nose. "You are. But you're brilliant, you're funny, and you're fun, Avery. You've got a fascinating career, you're tenacious, you're hot, you have great taste in friends...."

Avery smiles, but he's already trying to find something to hide behind. This is silly. And making him feel funny.

"And you're the least pretentious person I've ever met. Do you know, when you showed up at that construction site, every single person, to a man, thought you'd be gone in a week?"

"What? My scrawny, pale northern Ohio ass didn't inspire confidence? Of course I knew that. Everyone hated me."

"They didn't hate you, idiot."

"Well, they thought I was an after-school special waiting to happen. Don't go hanging around construction sites. That kind of a thing."

Harlan looks like he's praying to someone for patience. "They thought you were a college kid trying to get your kicks by slumming it with the good ol' boys, Avery. And not just any college kid—a rich one, seeing as you went to Rice."

Avery is well aware those guys were skeptical of him at first, but they seemed to come around by the time the summer was over. Or maybe he was too busy fucking Harlan to notice. Either way. "Rich kids do cocaine in South Padre for kicks, Harlan. They do not take construction jobs in Houston. In the *summer*."

"I know. And I fucked around with you because I thought for sure you'd hightail it out of there the second I came on to you, and you'd be gone in a week."

Avery's known that one for a while, so it's not new information. But it still makes him laugh. "Ha! That totally backfired. You haven't gotten rid of me yet."

"I know. You're a loyal friend. Jesus, Avery, do you know why I'm even here?"

"Because you said the previous owner was up to his pastrami in debt to the mob and highly motivated to sell?"

"In New York," Harlan responds and throws a pencil at him. "Not this office. I mean New York. Look. Do you remember when I came to your house and met your parents?"

"Yup. My mom called you pretty and said I had good taste. I think she was disappointed when I said we were just friends."

"She also showed me all your architectural drawings. From when you were five."

"I know. She does that." Avery picks things up, looks at them, and puts them back down. "That one with the two-way waterslide was awesome. Don't deny it. I'll build that someday. You watch."

"I believe you," Harlan says, and something in his voice makes Avery stare very hard at the counter and not want to look his friend in the eyes. "Very few people grew up to do what they wanted to do at the age of five, Avery. And you did. Me, I just needed a job, and the classified ad for 'bartender' had a phone number that was busy when I called it. So I just went down to the next one on the alphabetical list. Bingo. Construction."

"You would've been a sexy bartender, though," Avery tells him, trying for a smile.

Harlan doesn't smile back. "The reason I came to New York is because I thought I could open my own business. And I thought I could do that because I had this friend who believed in me despite my having nowhere near a tenth of the education he does. I don't have a college degree, Avery. You have six of them."

"Three," Avery mutters. "And stop it. Are you kidding? You're the one—"

"We're not talking about me," Harlan yells—*yells*—at him and glares hotly.

"We're not talking. We're yelling," Avery shouts and throws his hands in the air. "And I don't know why. I'm really glad to hear that, Harlan, even if this is making me uncomfortable, and there aren't enough Budweisers in that minifridge to make this conversation acceptable for the time of day it is."

"I've got some whiskey under the counter there. If you need it."

"No. Don't you remember that trip to Destin? I do not need whiskey," Avery says firmly. "I forgot why you were yelling at me. It was about Lacroix, though. Which, go ahead. I'm a moron for even thinking about it. Everyone told me it was a bad idea, and yet I went ahead and did it anyway."

"Avery, why do you think this is your fault?"

Avery stands for a good fifteen seconds, staring at Harlan like he's never seen him before. "Why do I think what is my fault?" He can't even come up with a quip or a clever joke.

"Malin Lacroix."

Avery sits down in his chair. He stares at his hands. "I don't," he says softly. But maybe it's not true. Maybe he does. "I changed my mind about that whiskey, Harlan."

"Avery, you didn't do anything wrong," Harlan says very quietly.

"Then why is everyone mad at me?" Avery snaps and leans his head back on the chair. "Sorry. It's just you, Justin—"

"Justin?"

"Oh. Brandon's boyfriend? I introduced you guys last month at poker, remember? The two guys who were obviously together but weren't sure if anyone knew, so they were just awkward about it until everyone got drunk."

"Ah. Right. See, that's another thing, Avery. You make friends everywhere, and you want your friends to be friends, for God's sake. Why you're wasting your time on this fucking asshole Lacroix is beyond me. You don't invite him to poker."

"Because he'd win all our money," Avery says under his breath. The idea of Malin at his poker night is almost hysterically funny. If people find terror hilarious, which apparently Avery does. He studies the sandwich poster again. "Were there other sandwich posters, and if so, why did you just keep this one up?"

"Avery."

"What? I'm curious. I thought maybe, if there was a corned beef one, I'd put it in my office. Or in Brandon's. He has no sense of humor."

Avery briefly envisions the ham poster in Malin's apartment, hanging right above his bed. Except now he's thinking about Malin's bed. Great.

"Would you stop trying to switch the subject? You're the one who came here, you know. And it was not to discuss sandwich posters." Harlan's voice goes flat. "Make a joke about my meat, and I'm kicking you out."

Avery scowls at him. "But it was going to be funny."

"Stop trying to be funny. Did you come here for advice? I told you before it was a bad idea, and that's when I didn't know what was going on. Now I'm going to tell you again. This is not something you should be doing. Avery, you have worked too hard to fuck it up over this asshole."

"I know." Avery's going to go back to him. He knows he is. "It's hard to explain, Harlan."

"No, it isn't." Harlan sounds angry again, and Avery decides it's time to go before he causes his friend to lose any more respect for him. "And my advice is to stay away from the guy. If he wants to hook up, let him come to you. And then tell him to take you out for a goddamn date or something, Avery."

"He won't, but thanks for the advice." Avery stands up, takes his beer bottle, and looks around reprovingly. "Where's your recycling container?"

"Avery."

Avery puts the bottle next to a stack of others—fuck, is Harlan an alcoholic, or is this just how construction guys do business? It's a lot better than suits and pointed looks and angry phone calls. Maybe he's in the wrong business. "I'm sorry."

"For what?"

"For whatever it is that's making you mad at me. I guess this is what I do now. Make people mad. You, Justin, Brandon...."

Harlan is suddenly right in front of him. "Avery, goddammit. Don't you understand why we're angry?"

"Yeah. Because I don't listen, I do stupid shit, and then I come and whine about it." Avery gives Harlan a crooked grin. "I'll be fine. Don't worry. Malin won't break me. He can't. Also I'm not a horse, and this isn't one of those movies Brandon let me borrow about lusty male slaves."

"What in the actual hell are you talking about?"

"Lusty male slaves.... Never mind. I'm fine." Avery claps his friend on the shoulder.

Harlan is having none of it. He puts his hand on Avery's shoulder and squeezes firmly. It doesn't hurt, but Avery wishes it did. Oh, how he wishes it did. All of his problems would be solved.

You'd just get a whole new set of problems and you know it.

"Avery, me, Justin, Brandon. We're not mad at you, moron. We're mad *for* you. You don't get that at all, do you? Because you don't think you're worth being treated better than this fucker is treating you, and we all know you are. And we wish you knew it too. That's why we're mad, Avery. Because you're not mad enough."

"Sorry to disappoint you," Avery mutters and turns to go. Harlan holds him firm to stop him.

"You deserve better, Avery. You deserve a guy who does things because you like them, not just because he's got some fucking rage issues and likes getting his dick sucked."

Avery pulls away, wincing. "Fuck off. I get it. I should have more pride in myself or love myself more or whatever the fuck."

"No, he's not good enough for you," Harlan snaps, his voice raised again. "You deserve someone who doesn't just want you around between the hours of six p.m. and eight in the morning. You deserve someone you can take to poker night, who you can invite to your fucking birthday party. And, Aves?"

Harlan's voice is all choked, and it makes Avery suspicious. He looks at his friend and wishes he hadn't, because Harlan's bright summer-blue eyes look like they got hit with an afternoon rain, and that's doing awful things to Avery's equilibrium.

"Yeah?"

"You know why you're not in love with me? Because you also deserve someone who isn't afraid to take you home and tell their parents about you. That's why."

Avery stares hard at the door. There's a knot in his throat, and his eyes are suddenly burning too. Harlan, in perfect understanding of the guy code when it comes to tears, pretends not to notice.

The answer seems to be pretty clear, all around. Avery should forget about Malin Lacroix and go back to his normal existence of happy hookups, poker nights, and girls like Allison who like dumb horror movies and playing with his cat. It's not like it's really even a problem. In the last two weeks, Malin hasn't said a single word to him about anything that isn't related to work. So in all probability, that isn't even an option anymore.

So what if he still can't sleep without biting his wrist until it bleeds, and if he sometimes gets himself off with a belt around his neck? That has to be better than disappointing everyone he knows. Right?

Right.

CHAPTER 9

TWO DAYS after his conversation with Harlan, Avery stands in line for a coffee at Starbucks. In front of him are two men he recognizes as "I've seen you somewhere recently but nowhere fun," which means he's intently studying his phone while playing *Candy Crush Saga* and pretending not to notice them.

"*I don't know, but Benedict told me Lacroix's on the warpath—again.*"

"*Oh, not again. The commission thing? Can't he just stick to terrorizing architects?*"

Avery's ears perk up. He slides one of the candy pieces down the screen and watches as things react excitedly to his obvious genius. He moves closer to the two men as casually as he can.

"*No. That one's fine, but apparently there's going to be some overhaul of the irrigation procedures again, because Lacroix found some theoretical reason why there should be.*"

"*Does he fucking dream up this shit, or what?*"

Avery remembers who they are now. They're on some architectural-design committee for the city, and he met with them briefly when they were finalizing contract issues for the Knight Performing Arts Center. They had some boring job that made Avery think about insurance and other things that incited immediate drowsiness, so he didn't pay much attention to them.

But he has a good memory, especially for faces. And he remembers Justin that night he met him and Brandon at the bar, and what he said about Lacroix's reputation and how he pissed off so many people by being hard to work with.

"*He'd cooled it for, like, a month or two. Someone told me he was actually acting like a human being for a little while, but that must have stopped.*"

"*Oh yeah?*"

"Yeah. Jason Robbs from Slaterly and Brown? He told me he saw Lacroix at some fancy event, and he didn't even snap his head off like every other time Robbs tried to say hi to the guy. I mean, if I had to go to my ex-wife's parties, I'd be pissed too. But geez."

"Yeah, no kidding. Family holidays at that house must suck, huh?"

"Seriously. But Robbs said he about died of shock that Lacroix even remembered his name, and then he said something halfway complimentary about the Denmark Building. And that's a contract Lacroix wanted and didn't get."

"And he's back to being an ass?"

"Yup. Lacroix is on that planning and zoning committee. He called Robbs by the wrong name three times and then told him it didn't matter what his name was, he wouldn't be there that long anyway."

Avery tries not to grin at that. Malin is an ass, but whatever else he is, he's still Avery's boss.

"Robbs said he thought maybe the guy was getting laid, but guess that was short-lived."

Avery pokes at his phone some more and watches the candies dance in happy joy as they fall and disappear from the screen.

"Sir? Sir? Can I take your order? Sir?" There's a giggle. "Are you playing *Candy Crush Saga?*"

Avery looks up and blushes hotly to see that he's next in line, and the cute young barista is grinning at him. He proceeds to order the most ridiculous sugary confection they have on the menu.

"Do you want whipped cream on that?"

Avery likes flirting. He forgot about that. He also likes whipped cream. "Of course. Extra sprinkles, and you'll make my whole day."

"Consider your day made, then." The girl takes his credit card. "It's the little things, isn't it?"

"It is," Avery agrees. His brain is whirling. "Hey. Actually can you make me two of those? Might as well make someone else's day, if I can."

"You betcha. Same with the sprinkles?"

"Can you put even *more* on the second one?"

"Sure can." She rings in the purchase, runs his card, and then hands him the receipt with a wink. "Hope whoever's day you're making appreciates it."

Avery signs his name to the receipt with a flourish. "You and me both." He pockets his wallet and steps aside to wait for his drinks. He watches the two men leave with their coffees—why would you come to Starbucks and not get anything with whipped cream?—and thinks about what he just heard.

At work, he heads straight to Brandon's office. The groundbreaking on the Byrne Building is coming up, and Brandon is also busy with work on another design. Avery's barely seen his friend, and he also didn't know what to say about the whole "Brandon wants to knock Lacroix out" thing Justin told him about. So it's a good idea to clear the air.

"Here. I brought you coffee. Or whipped cream and sprinkles with a little bit of coffee on top," he says as he walks into Brandon's office.

"Why?"

"Thank you, Avery. That's so nice of you," Avery sings and puts the beverage down.

"Thank you, Avery. That's so nice of you," Brandon parrots flatly. But he gives the coffee drink the eye. "Is that caramel? It is, isn't it?"

"You like caramel," Avery tempts and sprawls in the chair in front of Brandon's desk. "Look how sad everyone else is in their little aquarium boxes. No one brought *them* coffee, with or *without* whipped cream."

The junior associates all work in a centralized area, with individual desks and offices encased in glass. It's like being in an exhibit at a zoo. *Junior Architects at work, please do not feed or tap on the glass.*

"I do like caramel," Brandon concedes. His eyes close briefly in enjoyment as he takes a drink. "Fuck you. This is delicious."

Avery toasts him with his own, which is half-gone. "Hey. So thanks for offering to beat up our boss for me."

Two minutes later Avery is still laughing, and Brandon is still coughing and cleaning coffee off his shirt. "I can't believe you said that."

"I can't believe you would *do* that," Avery responds, still amused. "Look. Don't ever put yourself in danger of losing your job over *me* and my stupid decisions, Brandon. You'll end up homeless. Or designing strip malls."

"Same thing," Brandon says and shudders. He gets a Tide To Go pen out of his desk drawer and starts working on the coffee stain. He sees Avery watching him and shrugs. "If you had any doubt I was gay. Right?"

"Sometimes you make gay-stereotype jokes because you're worried someone else will make them first." Avery nods and Brandon's ears turn red. "I am sometimes astute when it comes to other people."

"Just not when it comes to you," Brandon retorts, capping the pen. "You're my friend, idiot."

"Thank you, dumbass. You're my friend too."

"I meant that's why I was mad at La—ahem." Brandon drops his voice to a theatrical whisper. "Lacroix."

"Brandon," Avery whispers back, leaning closer. "We're surrounded by glass. And he works here. You can say his name."

"Yes. Well, I'm just trying to keep your sordid work-affair secrets for you."

"I appreciate that."

"You're welcome. What is it you wanted in exchange for fucking up my blood sugar levels at eight in the morning?"

"I'm going to ask you an embarrassing question, that's what." Avery drinks more of his sugary beverage. The girl was really generous with the sprinkles. He leers at Brandon. "I'll let you swallow this time."

Brandon winks at him. "Big of you."

"Damn it." Avery stares at the ceiling. "That's what he said?"

"Lame."

"I tried."

"What is it? As much as I'm glad you're not half-asleep, I'm not sure I want hyped-up-on-sugar Avery in my office either." Brandon's enjoyment of the coffee beverage is almost obscene. "God, this is so good."

"Enjoying a latte, are you?"

"Yes. But if my choices are between horrible puns and embarrassing questions... can you just leave?" Brandon smiles to show he's joking, then picks up a mechanical pencil and clicks it a few times. "Okay. What is it?"

"Why did you go to find someone to, um... totally dominate?"

"Why did I know you were going to ask me about that?"

"Because I'm predictable?"

Brandon sighs. "I guess I should be glad you didn't use the Sunday Night Football-announcer voice."

"It was a professional wrestling announcer. Come on. I'm not as classy as football. The question, if you would, Mr. Thomas."

"I wanted to. I mean, I don't know what else to tell you, Aves. It's just a thing I guess I needed, and I wasn't getting it. I wasn't getting any, actually," Brandon says, laughing. "So there was that too."

"But can you get some without... without it?"

"Without what?"

"Doing whatever you do? I don't know, just keep talking."

"If this is getting you off, I'm charging you by the minute."

"I brought you a delicious coffee treat!"

"And I appreciate it." Brandon beams at him. "A latte. I'm just not sure what you're asking. And Avery, this is not the place for me to give you a step-by-step accounting of my sex life."

"Where is that place, and can we go there?"

Brandon's response is an eye roll. Avery takes that as a no. "You have four minutes before I'm done with this conversation. Because I have a meeting, and I need to get ready for it. I swear that should have been in the grad-school curriculum."

"That and how to run a PowerPoint presentation if you're giving a webinar." Avery wonders if he too is supposed to be in this meeting. He'll have to check when he gets to his office. "It ruins all the mystery if you prepare for meetings. That's what I say, anyway. And I'm just trying to figure out what you get out of it."

"Meetings?"

"Brandon. What made you finally go and find someone? Do you get all tense and whatever passes for high-strung if you're you?"

"Sure. I mean, Avery, you know what it's like to be stressed out. Right? It's like that, and I'm just sort of restless, I guess. And I want to get laid. Justin says...." He chews on the pencil.

"Yeah?"

"Sorry. This is really not the place to discuss this." Brandon waves his mechanical pencil in frustration. "Justin says I get twitchy. And concerned about being constantly in charge of things. And putting things back where they belong. I'm apparently the only person who thinks that's a good idea."

Avery watches as Brandon messes with the pencils on his desk, moves the calendar minutely to the right, and starts dusting off his keyboard.

"So acting like you are right *now*, then?"

Brandon glares at him. That's a pretty good signal he's right. Brandon's version of "twitchy" is as understated as British comedy. "You and Justin didn't have a fight, did you?" What if they did, and it's all Avery's fault?

"Yes. It's all your fault." Brandon stares levelly at him and then smirks. "Kidding. He's at a conference in Seattle and then visiting family in Oregon for a few days."

"So you can't even go, what? A week without totally dominating someone?"

"Avery, get out of my office." Brandon picks up his latte and practically inhales the rest of it through the straw.

"One more question. Whatever. Stop glaring. You can't look threatening with a thick straw in your mouth. Do you ever have sex without it?"

Brandon starts giggling. "No. I've been pretty fond of *thick straws* since I tried kissing that girl at the school dance."

"Tried? What happened?"

"Her older brother. Anyway, listen. Obviously I can have sex without putting Justin in a collar and making him kneel first. Sometimes you just don't feel like going through all the… elaborate setup procedures."

Avery stares at him, fascinated. "Hot. Wow. Are you *sure* you won't put those videos on kink.com? My trial membership is up, but I'll totally get a real one for that."

"I'm sure. And look, there's always some element of it in there, I guess. Because that's just how I am. Now I'm thinking about things I shouldn't, and I have to go to a meeting, so would you please get out of here? Next time you need to put Kahlúa in my fancy coffee if you want me to talk about sex before ten thirty in the morning at work."

"*Kahlúa*? Oh, Brandon."

"Is that one of those gay stereotypes I should make fun of myself for?" Brandon asks. He stands up and assembles his various gadgets for his meeting. Architects like gadgets. Avery uses his iPad mainly to play

Candy Crush Saga in staff meetings, but he has some smart-sounding apps on there too. He's never opened them, but they're on there.

"You should definitely be making fun of yourself, but not because it's a gay stereotype. Because it's Kahlúa." Avery has a sudden memory of kissing Malin, tasting cigarette smoke and Scotch. "Thanks, though. I mean it. For everything. You and Justin are good friends."

"You are too," Brandon says, knocking him with his shoulder. "Be careful, Avery."

"I probably won't be, but thanks." Avery follows him out of his office and walks to his own. Happily he is not expected in any meetings, at least according to his calendar, and he spends a few minutes checking e-mail and thinking about what Brandon said to him. About what he heard that morning in the coffee shop.

Then he does some work—because he's been shit at that lately—and for the next few hours, all he thinks about are lines and angles, things that make sense.

AVERY SPENDS the next two days working on a design for an office complex in Chicago. He's trying to figure out how to make sense of the specs and how exactly one is supposed to design an open floor plan around the need for sixteen individual offices when his phone rings.

His office phone. Avery stares at it in confusion, like he's not sure why it's making such a weird noise. The only time he's ever used that phone was to set up the voice mail, which he also doesn't use. "Is this a going to be a call for a fax machine? Because that's not nice. I'll unplug you."

The phone rings again. It sounds offended. Avery picks it up gingerly. "Hello?"

Instead of a fax beep, it's another sound that sets his teeth on edge for entirely different reasons.

"Hextall, you're needed at the Knight Center location in an hour. I need you to bring the specs from the last meeting, and O'Keefe will give you a copy of the contracts. Bring your blueprints and don't be late."

Avery makes a face at the phone. Why do people say that, as if anyone *plans* on being late? "Why?"

There's silence on the other end of the phone. Avery stays on the call, curious to see which of them will hang up first. Like they're teenage girls in a Disney Channel movie. "An hour, Hextall," Malin says and then hangs up.

Avery listens to the phone click over to a dial tone and then hangs up. If this is a Disney Channel movie, maybe he could be Miley Cyrus. She's old enough to find attractive. Avery knows this because he checked on imdb.com.

Avery scarfs down some leftover veggie pizza from the fridge in the break room before he heads for the site. He's not entirely sure if it's actually his or if those were actually vegetables. It's one of those perfect autumn days that make people speak fondly about sweaters and gloves as if they've forgotten how horrible winter is. Avery sings along with the radio—loudly and only sort of off-key—and he doesn't even care about the weird looks he gets at the stoplight when he's belting out "Party in the USA."

Totally a coincidence.

Avery hasn't seen much of Malin in the last few weeks. They didn't discuss Avery's no longer showing up at Malin's apartment, and Malin hadn't asked him to come over either.

He only ever did that once, the night of the party, when he used the belt on Avery's back.

And was nice to someone named Robbs, apparently. Or fine, maybe not nice, but at least less of an asshole.

That's the thing Avery wants to know more about. Not Robbs specifically. Avery has a vague recollection that the guy is stuck back in the un-ironic seventies mustache era, which is all he needs to know. He wants to know how Malin knew Avery would be there when he got home that night, and why he was less of an asshole at the party. Evidence suggested hurting Avery did something good for Malin, but either he didn't realize it or didn't want to admit it.

The little voice in his head keeps whispering, *But what does it do for you?* The possibility that his masochistic sex urges are actually destructive has never occurred to him, but that seems to be what everyone is telling him.

Avery wants answers but doesn't know what questions to ask. He doesn't have time to think about it either, because Malin's sleek black

Jaguar pulls in next to his Prius. He can't sit in his car, listening to pop songs and angsting over his sex life.

I'm not Miley Cyrus. Fuck it. I'm Justin Bieber. Miley would kick his ass. She could kick mine too. That's a nice thought. Maybe I'll sit here and—

There's a sudden loud rap on his window, knocking him out of a very inappropriate reverie, and Malin is standing next to his car. Avery feels his heart slam into his chest and his mouth go dry at the sight of Malin in his severe black suit and dark glasses.

Avery opens the door and climbs out into the fresh October air. "Hi," he says and closes his door.

Malin stares. Avery stares back. This is like the phone conversation but infinitely worse. He can feel himself getting hard, and he can't even see Malin's *eyes*. What the actual hell is wrong with him? Why does this man do this to him?

"The schematics? The contract? Please don't tell me you left them in the office when I specifically told you to bring them."

Oh. Right. Avery turns, opens the door, and grabs his messenger bag to get the requested documents. "People don't decide to forget things, Malin," he says quietly and hands them over. "It just happens."

Avery knows Malin is furious with him. It's in the way he jerks the folder away, in the way he tightens his jaw and flattens his mouth into a straight line. *"Don't ever call me by my first name at work."* Avery could plead ignorance and pretend site visits didn't count, but he knows very well they do.

And now there are no more rules for Avery to break.

Malin turns on his heel and walks toward the delegation from the Knight Foundation. Avery doesn't expect anything different.

Right before they go in for the obligatory handshakes and "how are yous," Malin surprises him by saying, "People decide to forget things all the time, Avery. It just doesn't work. No matter how much you want it to."

Avery is so shocked he nearly trips on a rock as he goes to shake hands with the VP of something or other. He apologizes profusely for nearly knocking her over.

"I almost did the exact same thing," she says, shaking his hand firmly. "Please, don't worry."

"Ah, but you're wearing heels," he jokes, smiling easily at her. She's an older woman. Her dark hair is streaked with silver and wound into a knot on the top of her head. Avery has no idea how women do that—make their hair disappear so prettily—but it's awesome. "My only excuse is that I never look where I'm going."

"Well, maybe tripping over a few rocks will teach you to start," she says pertly, which makes him laugh.

"You'd think that, wouldn't you?" Avery looks at Malin and grins. "It hasn't happened yet."

CHAPTER 10

MALIN DOESN'T look surprised in the least when Avery shows up at his apartment that night with a bag of takeout Chinese and a cold six-pack of beer from a local brewery.

"I was under the impression our association was at an end, Mr. Hextall."

Avery shifts the paper bag in his arms and stares at him, momentarily dumbfounded by his ridiculous, villainesque formality. "Are you going to put me in a death trap that doesn't work now?" He clears his throat at Malin's unfriendly stare. "I forgot you don't think I'm funny."

"Not even a little. What exactly do you want, Avery?"

"To die, Mr. Bond. I want you to die!" Avery sighs. "Nothing? All right. I brought dinner. You know. It's a meal people eat. Someone needs to tell the good folks at Peking Palace that, since they apparently think Kung Pao beef and a burning box of coals are the same. Maybe that's what Kung Pao means. I dunno."

Avery is watching Malin very carefully during his little spiel. His expression never changes, and he doesn't get out of the way either. But Avery knows he's going to. Eventually Malin steps back to let him in.

The apartment is as depressingly empty of entertaining things as the last time he was here, but the late-evening sun throws a beautiful golden light into the room. "I like what you've done with the place since I've been here last. Is that a new speck of dust I see?"

He doesn't expect an answer, and he doesn't get one. Avery walks to the kitchen, unpacks the boxes, and starts going through Malin's cabinets. Most of them are empty.

There are three simple, serviceable plates that look like the ones you buy at the dollar store. A few bowls and some plain glassware occupy one cabinet. He finds a similarly sad amount of silverware in the drawer. "I'm not sure what you like, because we've actually never

111

eaten a meal together, unless you count the omelets you make me at oh-God o'clock in the morning. So I just got you something spicy too, because I'm not sleeping with someone who eats sweet-and-sour chicken." He busies himself putting food on two plates and not looking at Malin, as if this is perfectly normal.

He also puts the six-pack of beer in the fridge, takes two of them out, and opens them with the bottle opener on his keychain. Whoever invented those is a genius, because searching for a bottle opener isn't sexy at all. "I also have steamed dumplings and crab rangoon, but there isn't crab in it, I don't think. I doubt there's even crab-with-a-K in it, but you can't call them cream cheese rangoon. That's just giving up."

He takes the two chopstick packages out of the bag, opens them, and puts one on each plate. He does the same thing with the fortune cookies and then carries it all over to the glass table. Avery goes back for the beers, takes a mental breath, steels himself for the possibility of being brained upside the back of his head, and hands one to Malin.

"It's a local beer. My friend Harlan was the contractor when they built their second location last year."

Malin takes the beer, because Avery practically shoves it at him. His cool eyes are unreadable. "What are you doing?"

"I brought you dinner. You never eat anything. It's the Midwesterner in me. We like to feed people. You're lucky I didn't bring a casserole." Avery clinks his beer bottle against Malin's. "We should probably eat it before the food gets as cold as the welcome you're giving me right now."

Malin takes a drink of his beer. "They're crepes," he says, apropos of nothing. "Not omelets."

"That's why the filling wasn't actually... inside. I just thought you were bad at flipping them. Why didn't you tell me that before?"

"When has that ever done any good?"

"Well, you've got me there. Come on. Come over here. This is really good, I promise." Avery sits down on the floor and picks up his chopsticks. "You didn't already eat, did you?"

Malin doesn't smile, but his voice is benign when he answers. "Maybe you should have asked me that before you showed up."

"You know what wouldn't kill you?"

"What's that?"

"Well, I was going to say using a contraction, but then you used one. So thanks for ruining my small talk. And dinner. Hello?" Avery gestures with his chopsticks. "Kick me out when we're done. But seriously I'm starting to think maybe you're a vampire."

Malin does sit down, places his beer on the table, and picks up his plate. He and Avery eat for a few moments in a silence that is not companionable, but isn't combustive. So that's something.

"What do you like?" Avery asks. And it isn't because the silence makes him uncomfortable. It would be easier to fall back in that trap rather than ask questions. But he's not doing that anymore—sleeping with someone he doesn't know and letting them beat the shit out of him without learning their preferred takeout order.

The problem is that Malin isn't very chatty, and Avery feels like he's at a corporate retreat, doing icebreakers with a bunch of introverts. "For dinner. Chinese food? What do you like," he repeats very slowly.

"Szechuan pork."

"Excellent. Hates parties, glass tables. Likes Szechuan pork." Avery takes another drink of his beer. "Those are the three things I know about you that aren't related to work. Oh. And you have a tattoo. I bet no one at work knows about that."

Malin puts his chopsticks down. "What is it you think we're doing, here, Avery? Dating?"

"Yup," Avery answers, nimbly sawing a dumpling in half with his chopsticks. He's eaten a lot of takeout. At some point, it might be a good idea to learn how to cook.

"You're fucking kidding me."

Avery's head snaps up at that because Malin rarely swears. It gets his blood rushing, though, because it means he's getting worked up, and Avery definitely wants that to happen. "Okay. Why don't you tell me what we're doing here?"

"Besides having an extremely uncomfortable meal together?" Malin takes a drink of his beer, but Avery catches an expression that might have been a smile.

"Besides that, yeah," he agrees. "And don't give me some bullshit answer either."

"Such as?"

"Well, I'm not going to tell you, because then you'll use it."
Avery feels his tension easing slightly as he watches Malin push his
chopsticks around on his plate. It's one of the few times Avery's seen
him look uncertain about anything.

"I don't know," he answers, at length. "I didn't invite you here. I
never asked you to bring me dinner, and I didn't ask you to get on your
knees in my office either."

"And I didn't tell you to wash my back, make me an ome—crepe,
or get on your knees in your shower. Not that I minded."

"It's obvious you have a point. So make it." Malin takes his crab
rangoon off his plate and gives it to Avery. "I don't like these."

"What?" Momentarily distracted by both the uncharacteristic
gesture and the blasphemy inherent in that statement, Avery peers at
him with interest. "You don't?"

"No."

"Why?"

"Avery," Malin says. He sounds tired. He looks it too, with the
heavy dark circles under his pale eyes. "What is it you want?"

"You," Avery says before he can think better of it.

"Why?"

Avery gets up on his knees and faces Malin across the table. He
keeps his face straight, his voice even. "There's really only one obvious
answer to that, you know."

Malin watches him, looking wary, and takes another drink of his
beer. "Is there?"

"Your shower," Avery answers, deadpan.

Malin smiles. And then he laughs. It's a short and tired laugh, but
it's genuine. And the smile reaches all the way to his eyes. For the
briefest of moments, he looks ten years younger and almost like a
different person. "Oui, bien sur."

To say Avery is charmed is a bit much, but he's a sucker for
accents. "I don't want to say I don't know, but…."

"You don't know?" Malin takes another bite of his dinner.

"Look. We're obviously attracted to each other. I think we
figured that one out easily enough."

"We did?"

114

"I'll throw this crab rangoon at you, Lacroix." Avery feels a lot better about this, all of a sudden. "And come on, can we just agree on that, at least?"

"That you'll throw something? Probably. You're very dramatic, and I've seen you do it before."

Malin's expression hasn't changed, but Avery would bet that was supposed to be funny. It's also true, but that's not the point. "Funny. If we weren't attracted to each other, would I even be here? Come on. You know you think I'm annoying as hell—"

"Avery," Malin interrupts. "Stop telling me what I think. It's irrelevant, because you're usually wrong."

Avery stares up at the vaulted ceilings and sighs. "This is one of those times I don't know why I like you at all. Besides the part where you're hot, have a nice shower, and those are pretty good crepes."

"You seem to like me to tell you what to do and hurt you."

"See, that's the thing," Avery responds, ignoring the sudden flare of heat. "If I'm the only one who likes that, why am I here?"

"That," Malin says with a tired sigh, "is what I'm trying to find out."

"Are you attracted to me? Because I think I know the answer to this, but maybe I don't."

There's a long moment of silence. Avery suddenly can't swallow past the lump in his throat, and he can feel himself flush with embarrassment. This is going to be a short date if he says no.

"I think so."

"You think so?" Avery stands up, hands on his hips. "You *think* so. Really?"

"Yes, really." Malin looks up at him. "I've never been with a man before, Avery."

Even though he suspected that, it's still weird. And flattering. Also hot. "Well, considering we've gone to bed together, shouldn't that be easier to answer? Or do you want to sleep with me again to find out if you think I'm attractive, because I'm perfectly okay with that."

"I do think you're attractive. That's not what you asked. You asked if I was attracted to you."

"How did you get through the ARE exam, anyway? Did you just write questions in response to all the questions? God. You're Socrates. They poisoned him, you know."

"Yes. Because he liked to derail conversations and talked too much." Malin's look is pointed.

"I don't think they had that word, back then. Derailed. That word was made up by people on the Internet," is Avery's brilliant response. He's slightly mollified at being told Malin thinks he's attractive. That's apparently how easy he is. Good to know.

"I'm not like you, Avery. You don't just wear your heart on your jacket, you wear it on everything you own."

"On your sleeve," Avery corrects him. "The expression. It's on your sleeve, not jacket."

Malin waves a hand. He's clearly annoyed by Avery correcting him. "Regardless. That's not where I wear mine."

"Yours is at home in the closet," Avery says without thinking. He winces. "Sorry. Poor choice of words."

"No. Actually that's rather apt." He stands up, picking up the plates, and carries them to the kitchen. Avery keeps waiting for him to say something else, but he doesn't.

"So you... may or may not be attracted to me, think I'm attractive, and okay, say what you want, but I was there all those times you got off. So you at least liked it when we were in the middle of things."

Malin does that thing where he pinches his nose between his fingers. "I don't understand you, Avery. You stopped coming here, so I assumed that you weren't interested."

Avery picks up the rest of the detritus from their meal and the two bottles, and joins him in the kitchen. "That's not it. I just don't think we were being smart about it."

"I can't argue with that," Malin mutters, raking a hand through his hair.

"I can't function without sleep, and I don't know how you do it. Is this a thing that comes with age? How old are you, anyway?" Avery tried to find this information on Facebook, but to no surprise, Malin did not appear to have an account.

"Forty-six. And I've had a lot of practice. So that's what this is about? You want regularly scheduled hours?"

Avery maneuvers carefully around to Malin's other side. He starts drying the dishes. Apparently Malin was telling the truth about why he

116

doesn't have a dishwasher. He just left out the part where he only had four plates. "No. Well, part of it is that. Look. I really don't have any idea what's going on either," he admits. "You acted like you couldn't care less if I stopped coming around, like maybe you were just doing me a favor. But you weren't, were you?"

Malin is scrubbing at the plate as if he's trying to get the finish off. "No."

"That's what I mean. I have no idea if you want this. Not really," Avery says bluntly. "Give me that plate. There's nothing else you can clean off of it, and you're wasting water."

Malin lets him have the plate, but he starts doing the same thing to the next one.

"I'm glad you were nicer to me than your dishes when you washed my back in the shower after that thing with the belt. Ouch."

"What do you want me to say?" Malin says, and Avery can feel how tense he is, even from a distance. "You're here, aren't you?"

"Yes, but you didn't exactly invite me," Avery points out. "Would you have if I hadn't shown up here?"

"No. I'm not chasing you. That's ridiculous."

"But you want it again, and you weren't going to say anything. Is that right?"

"Yes, Avery. That's right," Malin snaps, clearly losing the thread of his temper. It's surprising it took this long. "I wasn't. But you're in my apartment. Again. And I don't see what else there is to talk about."

Avery's never said that in his entire life. Ever. "I'm not staying up all hours of the night. I'm not going to let you hurt me without knowing if you like it. And I'm not giving you all the control, because that's stupid, and it'll just make me mad."

Malin turns to him, his gaze cold. "Is that all?"

"One more thing. If I want you to stop, and I mean really stop, I'll say, uh...." Avery casts around for a word he won't forget and that will immediately make him want to stop having sex. Something that isn't his parents' names, because ew. He decides the best option is the name of his hockey team's archrivals. "I'll say 'Flyers.' Because fuck those guys, seriously." Avery meets his gaze evenly. "And if that's not going to work for you, find someone else to hit. And you're welcome for dinner. Your turn."

"For what exactly?" Malin sounds tired again. Avery wonders if he's put it together—how that happens when you stay up all night.

"Rules. There have to be some. I thought we didn't need them, but what I'm getting is that maybe we do."

"You broke the only one that I had," Malin reminds him.

"Because that's a stupid rule," he says bluntly. "I wasn't going to call you by your first name at work. I only did it because you told me not to."

"Then why is it we need rules, again? So you can break them?"

Now Avery is starting to feel tired. Is this how people feel about him? Maybe he has more sympathy for his friends, if so. "The rules are for here. I figured out that you don't want to have rules, because then you have to admit you like this and think about what you're doing. I just let you do whatever you wanted, because I thought I was giving up control or whatever the fuck. But really I was doing the same thing."

To his surprise, Malin actually seems to be considering that.

"So if you want to come up with rules and share them, cool. If not you're not touching me again. Because fuck you. I'm not a goddamn punching bag."

Malin is still quiet, but he looks away. Avery notices he has very long eyelashes. Pale but thick. Like girls' eyelashes. "And now you see why I didn't say anything when you stopped showing up here."

"Why? Because you can't do this if you have to admit you like getting your dick sucked by a guy? Or sucking cock? You liked that, I remember. Believe me. I think about it all the goddamned time."

"No. Because of what you just said. You're not a punching bag. Avery, I've never done anything like this before."

"Me neither. That's what I keep telling you." Avery moves closer hesitantly. Malin tenses, but he doesn't turn away.

"*Now* you keep telling me."

Oh. He maybe has a point. Avery shrugs and tries to ignore the flush of embarrassment. "I guess maybe I acted like I knew what I was doing." Which, of course, made Malin do the same thing. Brandon was right about that. Avery was just wrong about how to deal with it.

The light is starting to fade in the room as the sun sinks below the skyline. The apartment is so quiet it's making Avery twitchy. He considers just going ahead and getting on his knees right there, but Malin surprises him by speaking.

"When we were finished, I could sleep. It was quiet." Malin looks at him. There's more there—in his body language and the sharpness of his gaze—but Avery understands what he's not saying.

"Usually when I make people quiet, it's because they can't get a word in edgewise." Avery smiles at him encouragingly. "See? That was good to hear. I'm sort of a whore for praise, you know."

"I've noticed." Malin is studying him, his head tilted.

"You look like that velociraptor in *Jurassic Park* when it figured out how to open the door."

"Because I have figured something out." He looks pleased with himself, which gives Avery a delicious thrill of anticipation.

"What's that?"

"It would be easier just to show you," he says. "Come here."

Avery isn't sure he just heard that correctly. "Um." He doesn't know why, but having Malin actually want him to be closer is making him nervous. Which is dumb. Isn't that what he wanted?

He moves closer, and his equilibrium is thrown, so he hooks his fingers in Malin's belt loops and tugs playfully. "So I guess that means you want to do it again."

Malin smiles. It calls up that same mix of uneasiness and excitement. Malin reaches down and takes Avery's wrist in his fingers. "You want rules, Avery?"

"Yes," Avery says immediately, breath caught in his throat. "If that means I get laid, definitely yes."

"All right. Don't touch me without asking me first. And if I tell you to be quiet, and you're not, I'm going to smack you in the mouth."

These are not rules Avery expects to hear. He was thinking of ones that would lead to more touching. But whatever. The smacking is nice. "Sure. You look really proud of yourself. Seriously. You look like how I feel finishing a sudoku puzzle." He opts for that over *Candy Crush Saga*. Math sounds sexier than candy.

"Oui, I am. Would you like to know the third rule?"

"Sure. Is it a sexy one? Can you say it really slowly?" Avery smiles. It's hard to keep himself from moving closer until he remembers he could do that—technically. He just couldn't touch him.

"Shh," Malin says, touching his fingers briefly to Avery's mouth. And it works, because Avery's brain turns immediately to mush at how hot that is. "The third rule is—no more manipulating me into doing what you think you want, Avery."

"I don't know what you're talking about. I never do that." Avery nips at his fingers. "Does the touching thing include biting?"

"Yes."

"Oh." Avery lets it go. He's still interested in this strange new version of Malin, who no longer looks quite so tired. "Things I think I want? What does that even mean?"

"That we are going to do this my way, which is what you wanted all along, isn't it?"

It's suddenly really hard to think. Avery has trouble making sense of that, so he finally just says, "It is?"—like an idiot.

"Yes. It is." Malin presses his fingers into Avery's mouth. "Suck," he says quietly.

Avery does, and he also nearly falls over. Fucking hell.

"You don't tell me you want me to hurt you and then hand me a belt." Malin is sliding his fingers in and out of Avery's mouth—less of a seductive gesture and more like he's trying to tell him something. "You tell me you want me to hurt you, and if I want to use a belt, I will." He pulls his fingers out and draws them wetly across Avery's cheek.

He's done that before, Avery remembers. That night when Avery got on his knees in his office. It's doing the same thing that it did then, making him glassy eyed. He can hear himself breathing, trying to clear the haze of sudden lust from his brain so he can keep up.

"And what if I *ask* you to use a belt?" Avery asks. And is that his voice? Because it sure doesn't sound like him talking.

"I suppose it will depend on if I think you deserve it or not." Malin strokes gently down Avery's throat, making him shiver. "But not if I'm angry. I'm never doing that again."

This isn't really what Avery had in mind, but there's no denying that it's turning him on just as much as it did when Malin backhanded him. "Deserve it how?"

"It doesn't matter right now." Malin puts his fingers on Avery's mouth again, to quiet him probably.

Avery opens his mouth, and Malin laughs and takes his hand away. He seems pleased about something. He also looks just as turned on as Avery, which is excellent.

And a little nerve-racking, but it's been a few weeks.

"You do understand, don't you, Avery? We play this time with my rules, not yours."

"That is maybe the hottest thing anyone's ever said to me," Avery informs him, because it is. "I wanted rules the last time, remember? You were the one who was all 'oh just let me take care of it.'"

"You're right. I did say that. And now I'm going to do it. I want to make sure you understand."

"Then ask me again, after you take me to bed, because I can't remember my own name." And it's true. He's also having a hard time standing upright and not grabbing Malin and kissing him.

"No. I'm asking you now." He slides his fingers back into Avery's mouth and hooks his thumb under his jaw. It's a strange gesture that isn't about sex as much as obedience. But it's clearly working to make him think about sex too. He nods, and Malin takes his hand away. "Good."

And then Malin takes *him* by the belt loop on his jeans and pulls him in. He lowers his head so his mouth is right by Avery's ear. "Ask me to hurt you."

"You're getting off on this, aren't you?" Avery's stalling, but he's not sure why. There's something he doesn't like about asking for it. And besides, isn't he making it pretty clear that's what he wants? He all but says as much, to which Malin responds by biting him on the ear.

"I—hurt me," Avery tries, thinking that has to be good enough.

"Try again."

Apparently not.

Avery isn't sure he likes how much Malin is enjoying this. Malin's hands are on Avery's hips, holding him still, and he nips sharply on the skin right beneath Avery's racing pulse. "Try using my name."

"Because someone else might think I'm talking to them? Come on. I brought you dinner." Avery tries to kiss him, but Malin won't let him.

"You think you're going to make me do it without hearing what I want to hear, and you're wrong. I have a lot more patience than you." Malin's fingers are bruisingly tight on his hips. He bites gently at the shell of Avery's ear again. "Ask me for what you want, Avery. That's the only way you're going to get it."

That makes him moan, and he's not sure why. "I... would you... hurt me, Malin?" There's nothing about his intonation that sounds like a question until the very end, when he says Malin's name.

"Mmm. Better." Avery has never heard Malin's voice like this, low and amused, heated. And he would really like to hear it again, only without the infuriating insistence on correct grammar and sentence structure. "Try saying *please*."

"Seriously?" Avery's voice is wrecked to hell and back. He's almost panting, he's so hot for it. And it doesn't make sense. They're not even doing anything—not really.

Malin responds by shifting just slightly. He presses his cock against Avery's, and he's hard. Oh fuck. That's about the end of Avery's resistance. "Would you please hurt me, Malin? Pretty please? I'll put a fucking cherry on top, or lime, or whatever you want."

Malin stops his frantic monologue by biting him on the neck. "That's good enough for now. In the future, if I say I want you to ask me for something, Avery, that's what I want to hear. That's all I want to hear. You may spare me the commentary. Do you understand?"

"Yes," Avery answers, staring at Malin's shoulder. He feels like a chastised schoolboy. Except for the part where he wants Malin to fuck him on the floor—right now.

"Look at me and tell me."

That's really hard to do, for some reason. Avery looks at him and nods once. "I understand."

"Good. Now go wait for me in the bedroom."

"How long exactly—"

Malin taps him on the side of the face with his hand—not quite a slap but almost. "I'll tell you if I want you to speak. If I don't, then be quiet. Nod so I know you understand, Avery." When Avery nods, Malin leans in and kisses him. "Good. Go."

And Avery goes.

He doesn't do anything in the bedroom, because he's not sure if he's supposed to. And this is stupid. Why aren't they even in the same room right now? Avery feels like he's lost all sense of control, and it's infuriating. *I guess that's what Justin means about how it doesn't have to hurt all the time.*

He sits on the bed, waiting.

Malin comes in a few minutes later, and he leans against the dresser and casually starts taking off his tie. "I like hurting you, Avery. I like it very much. This morning I got myself off in the shower thinking about your back, how it looked marked up from my belt. Take your shirt off."

Holy fuck. That image is going to be in his head for forever. Avery takes his shirt off and tosses it on the floor. His skin feels too hot, and the cool air makes him shiver when it hits his naked chest.

"Do you remember when you came storming into my office, calling me names and shouting at me, when all you wanted was to know why I didn't choose your design?" Malin takes off his cufflinks—which, who even has those?—and starts rolling his sleeves up. Avery's mouth goes dry.

Which he tells himself is the only reason why he nods instead of speaks his answer, and not because Malin didn't tell him to talk. He's going along with this to get laid. That's all. Right.

"Are you aware that nearly every other junior designer under my supervision schedules a meeting with me so that I can do that exact thing?" Malin unbuttons the collar of his shirt. He's holding his tie loosely in one hand. "Well? Yes or no. That's all I want to hear."

The switch in subject is so sudden his head feels like it's spinning. Like Malin backhanded him again, maybe. "No." That's embarrassing. He should have known that.

"I didn't think so." He comes closer and nudges at Avery's ankle so he'll widen his knees and Malin can stand between them. "I kept expecting you to ask me for feedback like the other junior associates, but you never did. At first, I thought maybe you saw yourself as above the need to learn anything new. And I don't like that attitude at all, Avery."

Avery is almost horrified to hear that, because he wasn't trying to suggest that, and he had no idea it would have come across that way. "I wasn't, I—"

Malin smacks him—hard—across the mouth. It doesn't split his lip or knock his head back. It just makes him be quiet. Malin rubs his fingers lightly over his cheek, and the sensation of the caress on his reddened skin makes Avery bite back a moan.

Malin's pale eyes are burning. He smiles slightly. "That's all right. You can make noise. I like that. I've told you that before. Just no talking. As I was saying, if you thought that I disliked you, that would be why. And you might be wondering why I didn't say anything about meeting with me, but every other designer made the appointment of their own initiative. I'm a busy man, and I will make time if it is requested of me, but—as I said earlier—I'm not going to chase you down."

Avery looks down at the floor. He's still flushed and restless. He's turned on, but he's also weirdly upset to hear this and not be able to defend himself. And apparently Malin isn't done yet.

"Did you also know that, as a senior project manager, I'm allowed to choose my own design team?"

He shakes his head slowly. He didn't know that either.

"I chose you as a designer because your work was bold—innovative—and I liked your approach, your lines. Unapologetic use of contrasting symmetry, I believe, is one of the notes I made on your portfolio. Some of your designs are a bit too flashy for my tastes, but those are aesthetic differences, and we do have a variety of clients."

Flashy? Says the man with the vanishing windows and turquoise accents in his apartment. Avery wouldn't have said that out loud even if he hadn't been told not to talk. He still wants this to end with him getting off, not hailing a cab.

"I expected you would, at the very least, challenge me on occasion. But you didn't. And I was frustrated because your designs were often the second or third on my list. And I knew they'd be higher if you would just take a few minutes to *listen* to me. But you didn't. And if you're not willing to take the initiative, I am certainly not going to take it for you. I wanted to have you moved to another project manager. I thought if you couldn't learn from me, you should learn from someone. I never hated you, Avery. I expected better. I was disappointed in you."

Avery doesn't move or say anything or even look up from the floor. He just sits, breathing unsteadily, with something tight and painful coiling in his chest. He wants to apologize, but he doesn't want to say anything because he's not supposed to. He's surprised to feel

Malin rubbing a hand over his back, up and down—not sexual, just soothing. A verbal belt lashing and a back pat. This is definitely not like anything he saw on kink.com, that's for sure. Avery leans slightly into the caress, focusing on Malin's gentle touch.

"But I realized something when you came storming into my office that day, all angry and threatening to throw my paperweight at me—which was a graduation gift, so please leave it alone. Do you want to know what it was?"

Avery does, but he doesn't want to hear it right now. "Does it matter?" He braces himself for the smack that Malin delivers to his mouth. It stings, but he can't deny that he's still turned on. He doesn't let himself moan, though. He has some fucking pride left.

"You didn't think you were too good to ask me for feedback. You were afraid you weren't good *enough*. And you were determined to prove yourself, every time, so that's why you never asked. You don't like to ask for things, do you, Avery? I think you actually hate it. So you push and push, until you get what you want without having to ask at all."

Oh, fuck this. Avery is angry. He's not here for a pop psychology lesson. This isn't getting laid and having rough sex, so why the hell isn't he just *leaving*? This is not what he signed up for. It so isn't.

Malin crouches so he's at the same height, takes Avery's chin in his fingers, and forces him to look up and meet his eyes. "This isn't what you had in mind when you asked me to hurt you, was it?"

Avery shakes his head, horrified to feel his throat tighten and something hot gathering behind his eyes. He's supposed to be getting laid, not demoralized.

"But it hurts, doesn't it? You may answer me."

Avery has to swallow three times before he can answer. "Yeah." It feels like he took sixteen lashes with a belt and had lemon juice and salt rubbed into the wounds for good measure. In fact, he would have preferred that to... this.

Malin leans in and presses his mouth to Avery's. "There are a lot of ways to hurt someone, Avery. I know a lot more than you seem to think I do. This is what I mean when I say we're going to do this my way instead of yours. Understand?"

Avery tries to jerk his head away, but Malin's holding him by the chin and won't let him. His mouth is still against Avery's. Avery nods in the most recalcitrant way possible, which isn't very much at all. His eyes are turned toward the wall, and there's nothing holding him here. He's not restrained in any way, but he still can't leave.

"And to answer an earlier question, I am very, very attracted to you right now." Malin says, and then kisses him. It's forceful, and Avery tries not to kiss him back. That doesn't work out so well, and he does so—almost desperately.

Malin pushes him on his back on the bed and climbs on top of him. He takes Avery's wrists in his hands and pins them above his head. Avery stares up at him, breathing hard, pushing his hips up because he can't help it. Malin feels so good on top of him, and it's better than thinking about what he just heard.

Malin kisses him on the neck. "Is that enough, or do you want more?"

Avery shakes his head. "No. I mean, yes. It's enough. And no, I don't want any more."

He can feel Malin smile against his skin. "And that didn't even take three hours. Do you see? Would you like me to make you feel good now?"

He does, but it's hard to ask for it. He doesn't want to. He doesn't. But the look he's giving Malin right now is just as loud as the words he won't say, and it's clearly what he wants.

"I was wrong about you, and do you know how I realized it? I saw you when I was explaining why I passed on your proposal. You were listening, just like you are now. And I knew, Avery. I knew that when you turned in a design to me again, I would put my name on it and submit it. And I was right."

Avery's still staring at him, silent. Malin kisses him again—gently, almost sweet. And then he lets Avery's hands free and kisses up his neck and back to his ear. "And I was very proud of you and happy to see I wasn't wrong about you, after all. You can touch me now, if you want."

Avery grabs at his shirt, pulls him down, and buries his face in Malin's neck. He doesn't do anything else, doesn't say anything, just breathes quietly—in and out—until his head clears.

"Why did you do that?" Avery pulls back and asks. He thought he'd be embarrassed, but it turns out, he's not. The tight thing in his chest has loosened and uncoiled, and he's forgotten for a moment what else he's there for.

"To show you what it's like."

"What *what* is like?" he asks, starting to unbutton Malin's shirt. His fingers aren't quite steady, and for some reason, it doesn't bother him that Malin will notice.

"Being quiet." Malin kisses him. He works at Avery's jeans, and his hand isn't steady either. And that reminds Avery about the whole getting laid thing—and vehemently so.

"Why did you like that?" Avery asks him. They're both breathing hard now, kissing with increasing intensity. It's usually so much rougher between them, but this is maybe the best it's been since the first time.

"Because I like how you look when I'm finished hurting you." Malin bites him on the chest. "And I like how much you want to take it for me."

"So this means you're going to just go through my inadequacies all the time? And I really can't make any requests for just choking me with your cock or something...?" Avery hears Malin's sharp intake of breath and tilts his hips up so Malin can get his pants off.

"I didn't say that. Stop it, Avery."

Avery, who was in the middle of rubbing his hand over Malin's cock through his pants, furrows his brow and scowls up at him. "Doing what? This?"

"No. Stop trying to figure me out. I'll give you what I think you need, which, I'm starting to learn, is seldom what you think you do."

Avery goes completely still beneath him. That sounds serious, the kind of serious Avery has avoided like the plague, because it only ends one way—and that's *badly*. "I didn't think that's what this was about," he says very carefully.

"It wasn't. Now it is." Malin's gaze is steady. "If it isn't, then you wouldn't have come back."

Avery tries to argue with that, but he can't, at the moment. There's always later. "I didn't think you'd want that, though," he offers, gasping as Malin moves his hand over his cock.

"If I didn't, I wouldn't have let you inside." Malin lowers his head to kiss him again. "Tell me what you want."

"Again?" Avery puts his hands on Malin's chest and stops him. "Stop smiling at me. It's weird. This is not what I expected."

"Avery. You have one last chance to tell me what you want, or I'm going to gag you with my tie. That way I won't hear you say anything about whatever it is I decide to do."

"That sounds nice," Avery murmurs. He puts his hands back to other pursuits—namely getting Malin's pants off.

Malin keeps biting him. Apparently he's really into that—ow—and Avery twitches beneath him, hissing in pain.

"There's something you want."

"Well, your hand is on my cock so... ow. Why are you like this, with the biting? Fuck." Avery lifts his head. "Can I bite *you?*"

"Not at the moment. But yes, later." Malin looks up at him. "Why is it so hard to shut you up and then impossible to make you talk?"

"That's just how I am. Sorry. But you're signing up for it apparently." That still terrifies him, as undefined as it is. "And I want to get off. Do you really need me to ask?"

"If I want you to. You want something, Avery. I can tell. What is it?"

"Stop trying to figure me out, Malin," Avery mimics, and Malin actually laughs—and then bites him on the inner thigh and slowly increases the pressure until Avery is thrashing and clawing his back. "Fuck. I want—"

"Finish your sentences." Malin bites his other inner thigh. He likes symmetry, just like Avery. Fucking architects. He should date an abstract impressionist or something.

Date? Did I just think that? He did, though. So if he can't ask for what he wants, they're going to have a problem. He grabs Malin's hair, trying to make him stop biting, even though it's getting him hot for what he's about to ask for. "Fine. I hate you. Fuck me. That's what I want."

Malin stills, and Avery gives him a challenging look—like it's a dare. Which it is, isn't it? "Malin, I like blowjobs, but I'm not going to be with a guy without getting fucked into the mattress sometimes. So if you think that's too gay or something—*ow*—would you stop?"

"I will if you stop telling me what I think." Malin's breath ghosts over the bites on his thigh, which actually feels good and makes Avery tighten his grip on Malin's hair. "Ask me again."

Avery groans. "Why are you so into this?"

"I'm surprised you don't have an answer for that." Malin bites his lower stomach, not hard, just in warning. "I like how it sounds when you say it, Avery. That's why."

"Oh. Well." That's different. Avery grabs his shoulders, and he moans when Malin settles on top of him and grinds his hips against Avery's. He could get off just like this, even though the friction is a little too much to be entirely without pain. Or maybe that's why he could get off. He doesn't even know anymore.

"Fuck me, Malin. Please, fuck me, Malin. Malin, comma, please, fuck me, exclamation mark. How's that? Hey, what are you—mmph." Avery glares at Malin, who has slapped his hand over Avery's mouth.

Malin doesn't even say anything. He just looks at him until Avery rolls his eyes as theatrically as possible and nods.

"I've never done this before. I need to concentrate."

If he'd just said that at first, Avery would have been quiet. Because that's hot.

"Point taken," Avery says solemnly. Malin moves toward him, and Avery feels a little nervous. Which is silly. He's done this before. A lot. He's even let a girl fuck him once too. But even though he's the one with the experience, it doesn't feel like that at all.

He's mostly quiet, though he does say things like "yeah," "fuck," "that's good," and "do that again." Or single-word exclamations like "God" and "yeah" and "ow" because sometimes that happens, even when it isn't the first time. And they're going really fast. Avery can tell, because he's the one telling Malin, "It's fine," "another one," "hurry."

Eventually Malin stops and murmurs something in French, then presses a kiss to Avery's neck and slows down. It's annoying but also hot, which is apparently their thing.

When Malin presses inside of him, it hurts a little more than it usually does, because it's been a while. And Avery is nervous—tense in a way he never is. But he hardly notices the pain, because the sound Malin makes is so hot it's all he can concentrate on.

Avery looks over his shoulder and sees Malin on his knees behind him, all fierce eyes and panting breaths. He's flushed and so determined, like he's at work. Oh wow. If Malin fucked him over his desk while on a conference call, Avery would be reduced to ash.

Avery wants Malin to like this, and also to make that noise again. "Harder. Come on," he moans, and pushes back to meet him. That's maybe goading him into doing something. But hey, he asked, and it doesn't sound like Malin minds that at all.

When Malin grabs the back of Avery's neck, Avery pushes his head back into Malin's grip and struggles to stay upright while getting a hand on himself. That ends with Malin smacking him on the thigh and saying, "Arrête ça," which Avery is pretty sure means "stop doing that" but pretends not to know.

And then suddenly Avery's not on his hands and knees anymore. He's on his back, and Malin is kissing him and pushing back inside of him—almost like he's trying to go slow, but he can't. He's saying something in not-English, and that's excellent. Avery likes that a lot. It's nice to see him lose his cool, and it feels fucking amazing. He puts his hands on the wall behind him and pushes himself forward, grinning at the noise *that* gets. And there's a little voice that says, *Isn't this better than pissing him off until he hurts you?*

The constant commentary even annoys him on occasion. Luckily it's quieted the second Malin grabs one of Avery's hands from the wall and says, "Oui, maintenant," which makes no sense, whatsoever, until Malin puts Avery's hand on his own cock. That's his new favorite French phrase, whatever it means.

Avery jacks himself with sure, firm strokes while he watches Malin—and the way his eyes drift closed, the tension in his arms. His thrusts get more sporadic, and his breathing is fast and harsh. Avery can tell he's close. And then his eyes open, startlingly bright, and he looks around almost wildly, like he's not sure where the hell he is or what's going on.

He meets Avery's eyes, and Avery tilts his head up and shows his throat—because he did watch those lusty slave boys videos Brandon sent him, thank you very much. He's not above research to improve his technique. And he can't prove that gets Malin off, but he likes to think that's why he suddenly tenses, moans, and shudders hard.

Avery doesn't last very much longer, but it's long enough to feel a little smug about it.

"You're in really good shape," Avery says the minute he can breathe again. Fuck. That was amazing. "What the fuck do you do at the gym for your thighs, because that's a goddamn workout."

Malin is lying beside him, and he turns his head and looks at Avery. He doesn't smile often, and he doesn't do it now. He studies him quietly for a moment. "I go running," he says, completely serious.

Avery stares at him, too fucked out to know if he's being serious or making a joke. "Oh, okay. Thanks for clearing that up."

Malin nods. Avery's starting to get used to his expressions and how his eyes make him look fierce or predatory or angry when he's really just... quiet. Introverts are so weird. "I liked that better, though," he says, and Avery hears a smile in there somewhere. That's good enough for now.

CHAPTER 11

AVERY WAKES up on Sunday morning, covered in bites and feeling really goddamn smug. He also wants to go tell his friends how he's figured something out, and things are much better. But he's enjoying his weekend too much to do so. Also his phone is dead.

He can hear something in the living room. A man's voice speaking French. Malin on the phone. He's taken a few calls that weekend, because apparently you never get a free weekend when you're the project manager. The bedroom door is closed, so either Malin is working on secret architect espionage, or he didn't want to wake Avery.

Which is nice, but Avery's a morning person, and he would have been up first, if someone could sleep before 3:00 a.m.

He grabs his jeans and tugs them on. Even though it's daylight, and no one could possibly see him in the windows, he's still too polite to walk around naked. Without a sex-related reason, that is, because those will usually trump manners.

He leaves the top two buttons undone, because it's effort and he wants coffee, and walks into the living room, yawning. "I wouldn't say no to a crepe when you're off the phone," he says, and then stops dead in his tracks. Oh. Malin's not on the phone. The reason the door was closed has nothing to do with espionage or being considerate to the guy you kept up all night. It's because there's someone else there.

Good thing I put on some pants.

The woman is beautiful, with dark hair loose around her face eyes that are the same color as the delicious coffee he's in search of— and as cold as the coffee would be if he found a cup of it three weeks later. She says something and looks at Malin.

That seems like a good plan. Avery does the same thing. He has a feeling he knows who she is.

"C'est Avery Hextall," Malin says. Avery has trouble reading into his tone when he's speaking English, much less French, so he has no idea if Malin is pissed. "Avery, this is Marie Lacroix."

He doesn't offer any more information, but he doesn't have to. Avery smiles brightly and pretends this is totally normal and there's no reason why he shouldn't hold his hand out and say, "Hi. So, you're the one who likes turquoise."

And then he shakes Malin's ex-wife's hand, goes to get some coffee—he just went through all of that, he's earned it—and walks back into the bedroom and closes the door behind him.

At least he's got the shower to keep himself entertained.

When he's finished showering, shaving with Malin's razor, pressing on his bites, and getting all turned on, he goes to get dressed. He liberally borrows what he needs from Malin. If you can fuck a guy, you can let him borrow your toothbrush and a T-shirt.

When he's finished he sits on the bed and listens carefully for yelling. He doesn't hear any, so he listens even more carefully for talking. He doesn't hear any of that either.

What if Malin and his ex-wife are in the middle of a hot, hate-sex thing? Is he just supposed to stay in here and miss how hot that would be? No. That's cruel. Except, wait. He doesn't like that idea, and that makes Avery consider his life and his choices. He has never had an unkind thought about a threesome. Ever.

What's happening to him?

He opens the door a little forcefully, but Malin's standing by himself, looking out the large windows at the expanse of the city. It's a gorgeous view, and he doesn't look like he's enjoying it at all. He has a look that means *don't bother me*, but Avery thinks he just looks lonely.

I like things to be quiet.

I'll give you what I think you need, which, I'm starting to learn, is seldom what you think it is.

That shit goes both ways. There's a dynamic between Malin and him, and it's something Avery wants. But it doesn't mean he's not going to do anything.

"So that was your ex-wife," Avery says cheerfully, walking toward him. He has no idea how it's going to be received, but he puts his arms around Malin from behind and kisses his neck.

Malin tenses immediately, but Avery can tell he's trying not to pull away. He endures the embrace for longer than Avery thought he would, and then disentangles himself and reforms his personal space bubble.

"Yes. That was my ex-wife." Malin's got the unfriendly-hawk eyes going while he waits for Avery to say something.

Which, if there's one thing Avery can do…. "Well, you obviously have a thing for brunettes," he says and shrugs. Maybe it's getting fucked all weekend, but he decides to leave this one alone for the moment. "Want me to make us breakfast?"

"Absolutely not," says Malin, but he looks like he relaxes a fraction of an inch. It's a start, but Avery can do better. Not with cooking, though, so he needs to offer something he's actually good at.

"Want to fuck me over that stupid table you hate?"

"Oui," Malin says immediately. "Very much."

That doesn't work very well, because the fucking table keeps jabbing Avery in the side, and the hardwood floors are a little too much on their knees. But it's enough to make Malin satisfied they at least tried. He ends up fucking Avery over the couch, which is rough, but deliciously so.

When they're finished Malin smokes a cigarette, and Avery examines the damage to his side from the glass table, lying on the sofa with his head in Malin's lap. "Oh, I see she went with the *seppuku* model. Last-season Ikea. Right?"

Malin laughs—and then keeps laughing—hard enough that he starts to cough. If that isn't shocking enough, he gives Avery an honest-to-God grin and says, "All right, *cher*. Maybe you're a little funny."

And that's when Avery realizes he's in love.

Well, hell.

LET THE WRONG LIGHT IN

CHAPTER 12

THE PROBLEM with being in love and being Avery Hextall is that Avery likes to share things that make him happy. Like caramel lattes, his favorite IPA, and most of all, his friends. He's always been a social person, and he likes when his friends are friends with each other.

Except that doesn't work with a secret boyfriend. Also his friends think Malin is evil, so they probably don't want to be his friend anyway.

Avery is getting plenty of sleep. But that's irrelevant, because he's in love, damn it. Malin has no idea Avery is in love with him, and that's fine. Avery is just glad to experience it. If he keeps telling himself that, he's got to believe it at some point.

He tries to tell Harlan that no, really, things with the secret work boyfriend are great. Avery stood up for himself, and isn't Harlan proud of him?

"Has he taken you to dinner yet?" Harlan asks, doing his best impression of a grandmother from the 1950s. Apparently crepes don't count.

"You never took me to dinner," Avery points out.

"I brought you takeout at the computer lab."

Harlan has an interesting selective memory. "Only because you didn't pay the bill, and the power went out while I was working on my final capstone design, and you felt bad."

"Oh. Well, it probably did you some good to get out of the house. Try telling your *boyfriend* that too."

"That he should stop paying his power bill?"

"Good-bye, Avery."

"I'm not in fake love with you anymore," Avery informs him, but Harlan's already hung up. Jerk.

He sends Blake a text.

Me: *hey i have a secret boyfriend just like in college!*
Everett: *didnt u have 3 or 4? is this the republican?*

Apparently everyone thinks Avery has horrible taste. Except he doesn't know how Malin votes. Malin's rich and drives a Jaguar—and he's also sexually repressed and secretly sleeping with a man. These are not good signs.

Well, I got him to switch sides once. I can do it again.

Whatever. It doesn't matter, because Avery's happy. He goes to poker night and signs up to run a 5K with Brandon, plays *Call of Duty* with him and Brandon when he's home, and unsuccessfully tries to convince Malin to get something that makes noise for his apartment.

"I did," Malin tells him, giving him a pointed look.

He tries in all seriousness to talk to Brandon about Malin. But Brandon tells him flatly that he doesn't want to know. "You seem happy, and that's weird but great. I'm happy for you even if I don't get it. But please don't tell me about it. Tell Justin."

"Doesn't he just tell you anyway? And don't tell me you two don't discuss my sex life, because he asked me some questions about *Sex Slaves of the Sultan* that seemed very in-depth."

"Yes. But hearing it from him, I can imagine it's not my boss." Brandon has been stressed about something lately, and he won't tell Avery what it is. He's not running an absurdly long distance race, and he and Justin seem fine, so Avery doesn't push.

When they meet for a beer, he grills Justin about it, instead. "Is something wrong with Brandon?"

Justin's eyes widen, and he slowly shakes his head back and forth. "No. Why do you ask?"

"Justin, what the fuck? That's so obvious, even *I* know you're lying. I'm not that dim." Oh. Wait. Apparently he is. "Ah… you wanted me to know you were lying. What is it?"

"I don't know," Justin says, sinking in his seat. He looks defeated. "I was hoping you did."

He corners Brandon and tells him that Justin's worried. But Brandon tells him it's nothing and then engages one of the newest junior associates in a discussion and escapes while the guy is telling Avery all about his architectural influences.

This is what junior architects do, so Avery gives in and listens, takes the kid to lunch, and tells him if he gets a design rejected, to schedule some time with the project manager to find out why.

He finally asks Malin about his ex-wife's visit. It's a carefully plotted conversation. Avery begins with a series of conversational twists and turns, so it seems very spur-of-the-moment. He starts by telling Malin something about a site visit and his car and a French language CD, and ends with Malin giving him the penetrating stare and saying, "Is there something you want to ask me, or are you talking to hear yourself talk?"

"Both. And I wouldn't have to do that last thing if you would just get some music in this place," Avery complains. Then Malin suggests he do something else with his mouth, so Avery does that, instead.

Later he asks what Malin told his ex-wife when she saw Avery.

"I didn't tell her anything. She doesn't need to know anything about my personal life."

"She was at your house, though."

"Yes."

Avery waits, but that's all he gets. And this is after-sex Malin, who sometimes smiles and tells him things—but not this time. Avery lets it go. He tells himself it's fine, it doesn't matter. It's not like he's introduced Malin to anyone, including people he likes. That they already know him and don't like him is beside the point.

His parents call and tell him they're going to be gone for the holidays. His mom is worried about where Avery will spend Thanksgiving, even though he's a professional who hasn't lived at home since he left for college at eighteen.

"We don't have to go on that cruise," his mom says, and she sounds guilty. Avery wonders if he should mention he hasn't even thought about the holidays this year, or booking a plane ticket home— what with the whole sleeping with the boss thing.

"It's fine, Mom. Really," Avery assures her. "I know how much you and Dad are looking forward to it."

"But you'll be lonely. It's Thanksgiving." Now she sounds like Avery is the one who's going sailing to Majorca or whatever it is they're doing. "You could come with us."

Avery loves his parents, he really does. But the thought of being stuck on a boat with them for an extended period of time is a little too much. "That's all right. I get seasick, remember?"

"Avery, you were twelve, and those were bumper boats," his mom reminds him. "Promise me you won't eat takeout on Thanksgiving."

"I won't eat takeout on Thanksgiving." He doesn't promise, because he's totally going to.

"You could make a turkey breast in the Crock-Pot," she says hopefully. Avery's mother is a Midwesterner, so she thinks you can make anything in a Crock-Pot. She's also delusional if she thinks Avery has one.

"Where do you even get a turkey?" Avery has no idea. In his mind, you get deli-meat turkey for sandwiches at the grocery—which is a mystical place he rarely visits—because they don't assemble your sandwich for you. Maybe he should get a Crock-Pot. Do they make sandwiches?

"Son, if you say that, I will cancel my cruise and move in with you."

"Kidding. Anyway, it's fine. You guys go and have a good time."

"But your father has that conference in Rome, so we're going to be gone during Christmas." His mother sighs. "I'm a terrible mother."

"You're not," he assures her. "Mom, you know me. If it bothered me, don't you think you could tell?"

"That's true," she says slowly. "Maybe your father and I will come visit in the spring, when it's warmer. We can go see your building."

"Ah, it won't be finished for a few years," he reminds her. "It's not made out of Legos."

"Well, we can see whatever they've done," she says breezily. "I can't wait to see what it looks like, even if it's just some bricks and mortar."

"I sent you the schematics and the blueprints. Remember?"

"Avery," his mother says sternly. "You know I can't make heads or tails of those things. They make no sense to me." His mother teaches existential philosophy to eighteen-year-olds. That doesn't make sense to Avery, which he tells her all the time.

"Well, I Kant understand your job either," he tells her, and she giggles. Avery's mother always laughs at his puns. That makes up for all the cruises and missed holidays. He tells her that, but she shushes him, even though he can tell it makes her feel better. They're a lot alike.

"Maybe you can go home with Harlan," she tells him, because his mother is as good at subtle as he is.

"Never going to happen, but thanks for being supportive." He wonders what she'd say about Malin. Why is he thinking about that? Secret boyfriend means "don't tell your mother." He promises her he won't be a lonely and bitter man and complain in therapy about her ruining his life.

Three days later he gets a package in the mail from Amazon. It's a Crock-Pot.

THE FIRM gives them the weeks of Thanksgiving and Christmas off, and Avery is looking forward to having nothing to do but have a lot of sex and—fine—maybe use his stupid Crock-Pot. He refuses to leave it plugged in during the day because he's afraid of something catching fire. It doesn't matter if that's the point of the damn thing. It's hard being high-strung. It really is.

On the Friday afternoon before their week off, even stressy architects fuck around at work after about three in the afternoon. Avery finds himself in Brandon's office. O'Keefe is still at his desk, and Avery can't just walk into Malin's office if he's there. Apparently "So I can blow him" is not an appropriate reason to request a meeting.

Brandon is obsessively straightening his office, moving all the stuff on his desk around to various locations, and filing.

"Do you think they'd give me another filing cabinet if I asked for one? I just like having legal-size folders. Why would they give us these normal paper-size folders when all the contracts are legal size, Avery?"

"Wait. Back up. Why do you have a filing cabinet in the first place?"

Brandon stops moving the pencil cup and looks at him with an expression of disdain. "To file things. Don't you do that?"

"Yes. But I use something called electronic files, which you find on a computer. Jesus, Brandon. I'm surprised you don't have an abacus."

"Those are cool," Brandon mutters, not looking at him. "Well, I like to file my contracts that have been signed, all right?"

"But you have one," Avery points out, because sometimes annoying Brandon is both more entertaining and also easier than *Candy Crush Saga.*

"Fine. I'm anal retentive and obsessively neat. What's your point?" Brandon snaps, then sits back in his chair and sighs softly. "Sorry, Aves. Sorry, I'm just… ready to go for the holiday, I guess."

"I'd say you're ready to go for something else," Avery leers, but Brandon just starts messing with the pencil cup again. Avery leans forward and takes it away from him. "Stop acting like me. What's the matter? I thought we were friends, and there's something bothering you. I will not give this back unless you tell me what it is."

"Mind your own business," Brandon says, grabbing for the pencil cup.

"No. Tell me." Avery shakes it at him. "Come on. You run marathons. This isn't going to work for me for very long. And look. I don't know how else to express concern, other than by annoying you."

Brandon smiles briefly at that. "I'm going to Justin's for the holidays."

"You live together, Brandon."

"No. I'm going to his family's Thanksgiving thing. In Oregon. He told them about me when he was out there a few months ago. Remember?"

Avery nods. "Okay. That makes sense. You're nervous about meeting his family."

Brandon drums his fingers on the desk. "Not really."

"Brandon." Avery levels him with a stare, then hands him one single mechanical pencil. Architects might use tablets and software, but their mechanical pencils will need to be pried out of their cold, dead, carpal tunnel-warped hands.

Brandon grabs it like it's some kind of magic, life-saving device. "Justin was really nervous about telling them. And they didn't seem all that pleased about it. Or at least, his stepmother and his dad, who he lived with growing up. His mom, though. She was cool. Then again she runs Hula-Hoop camps for hippies, so it's not like she's the type to care about that stuff."

"Well, at least you're not going there for Thanksgiving," Avery points out. "They have camps for Hula-Hooping? Are you sure? Is it that hard to learn?"

Brandon waves his hands. "I don't know. But we might go visit. It's not that far from Portland."

"Is it hard to get there, or do you have to—"

"Don't make any jump through hoops jokes, Avery."

"Fine," Avery huffs. Now he's messing with Brandon's pencil cup, but he does that shit all the time. "You hate fun, Brandon."

"I know. I hear that a lot. Anyway, yeah. So we're going there."

"But you're not nervous about meeting them?"

"No. I mean, it was his dad's idea. Which is really great. So they're trying."

"And you're an impressive young man, Brandon Thomas." Avery almost hands over the pencil cup, then thinks better of it. "Then why are you so nervous?"

"Avery, can you keep a secret?"

"No," Avery says immediately, and smiles. "Yes, of course. I mean, if you tell me it's a secret and specifically who I'm not supposed to tell."

"You're not supposed to tell anyone. That's the point."

"No one really means that, though. Right? It's like saying you need alone time." Avery has never understood the idea of wanting to be by yourself if you could hang out with people you like. If they're not available, then you take a nap.

"You and I have literally nothing in common," Brandon says and shakes his head.

"Well. We have one thing. Half a thing, maybe. The whole thing about liking cock," he says dryly at Brandon's slightly quizzical look.

"That's not—that's like saying we have eyes, so we have something in common. I mean, it isn't the sort of thing friendships are based on."

Avery lifts his eyebrows. "It isn't? Really?"

"No. I mean, yes, it helps. But you can't just say, 'we like cock, so let's get married.'"

"Married? Brandon, I'm flattered, but you know I just like you as a—" Avery drops off, his eyes widening. "Wait. You're nervous and twitchy even though you're getting laid, you keep looking at the clock—yes, I noticed—and you're going to visit Justin's family. Oh my God. Are you guys getting married?"

Brandon looks slightly queasy and also hopeful, which is how engaged people probably feel, so it seems like Avery's right. He's halfway across the desk to hug him, in fact, when Brandon steps back so fast he almost trips over his chair. "Whoa, Avery, stop. Hang on. That's not... just wait a minute," he says desperately. "Sit back down, okay? I haven't...I haven't actually asked him yet."

"Oh." Avery hugs him anyway. "But whatever. That's still great. You're going to, and it's not like he's going to say no. I mean, you don't think he is. Do you?"

Brandon shakes his head.

"Then why are you so nervous?"

"I'm not nervous about Justin. I think he will say yes obviously, or I wouldn't ask him. It's... me."

"Brandon, it's kind of like saying yes already, if you ask him."

"No. I mean... all the other stuff."

"Your wedding night?" Avery leans in closer. "Sometimes when two men love each other very much—"

"Avery," Brandon says. The quiet worry in his voice makes Avery stop talking, because he does look upset. And not in the "jokes will make you happier" way either. "I haven't told my parents."

"That you're asking him?"

"That I'm gay."

"Oh. You haven't? Really?" Avery considers that. "Do you think they'll be mad?"

Brandon laughs a little wildly. "Yeah. Maybe? I don't know."

"They'll come around. Don't you think? If they are. And Brandon, you know, everyone loves weddings," Avery points out, trying to be helpful. He only likes weddings that involve open bars and hot single people, but whatever.

"Avery. It's not just my parents. It's everyone. I haven't really told anyone." Avery realizes Brandon looks ashamed. "Justin and I have been together for two years. He didn't even know he liked guys, and he told his family."

Avery thinks back to that lunch they had months ago, when Brandon told him he was gay. "Yeah. But you took me out to lunch, and you were going to tell me."

"No. I thought you knew already."

"And you were going to yell at me for caring about it, right?"

142

Brandon leans back in his chair. "I wanted you to stop hating me. And wow, thinking about that is funny now, because you don't hate anyone, Avery. It's like you don't know how."

"What? I do so." Avery goes through his mental list of enemies. Many of them are fictional characters or movie directors. "And your parents will come around. They'll meet Justin, and it's impossible not to like him. Right?"

"Well, I think so. But I'm biased, since I love him."

Avery smiles encouragingly. "I like him. And I'm not in love with him. So there you go."

"Avery, you like everyone. And the thing is they've met Justin. They came up to go to a Broadway show last year, and we were living together. They thought he was my roommate, and they liked him a lot."

"That's a good start. Isn't it?"

"Maybe." Brandon is quiet for a moment, while Avery runs through lists of things to say to make him feel better. Some of them are off-color jokes, some are bad puns, but most of them aren't helpful. "It's okay, Avery. There's nothing you—or anyone—can do. Just me." At Avery's look, he laughs. "I could tell you were trying to think of something to say. Even if I've never seen you actually do that before."

"I don't really say everything I think, you know. Most things, sure. But not all things." Avery is well aware that he will never be mysterious, but sometimes he likes to pretend.

"How do you have room for all those words?" Brandon asks, looking momentarily envious. "I wish I were like you, Avery. You just are who you are, and you don't care what people think. I really admire that. I can't see you ever living with a guy for two years and letting everyone think he was your roommate."

It's flattering Brandon thinks that, but he's giving Avery way too much credit. "No. But Brandon, that's because I'd forget and use the wrong word or something. But what I could do, you see, is lie to myself. And then it'd be really easy to tell everyone I had a roommate. That's the part of being me that sucks."

Something is nagging at the back of Avery's mind. When he says that, he realizes there are a few things he's lying about right now. But it's not fair to burden Brandon with his own problems, not when Brandon has finally confessed what's been bothering him.

"But you want to marry him, right? I mean, don't just do this so you have to tell everyone."

"Who would do that?"

Me. "Umm. I think I saw that in a movie…. Anyway. Never mind. I'm just checking."

"I want to marry him. And that's the thing, Avery. I love him. It's not fair to pretend he's just my roommate."

"Good roommates are very important, though." This is so not what Avery needs to hear. He says that kind of desperately, but Brandon just thinks he's kidding and keeps talking.

"And what am I supposed to say in ten years, if we're still living together?"

Avery snorts a laugh despite the sudden inner turmoil he's pretending not to notice. "I don't really think you'll need to say anything, at that point."

"That's what I mean," Brandon says quietly. "I want to say something. I'm proud of him. I love him, and we're happy. We're fighting for equal rights, and what does it say if, when we get them, we don't take advantage of them because we're ashamed?"

"You're not ashamed of him, though. That's not why. You're just worried about losing friends and family. And it's not like it hasn't happened to people. Which, I'm not saying it will, just that I really don't think it's shame that's kept you quiet."

"Fine. Then what is it? Fear? Isn't that all the same thing?" Brandon throws his pencil down, but Avery sees him eyeing it to make sure it isn't broken. "Besides it's not me who's got a problem with it—or Justin. That would be one thing. But it's other people, so what's my excuse? I'm not going to do something I want very much because of them?"

It's not me who's got a problem with it. It's other people.

"Maybe you're just trying to keep your personal life to yourself," Avery says with as much nonchalance as possible. And Brandon's caught up in his own situation—rightly so. He totally doesn't notice Avery's sudden inability to look at him.

"I did say that. All the time. When it didn't matter and it was just sex? Sure. But it's not my personal life when I'm sharing it with someone else."

She doesn't need to know anything about my personal life.

Avery exhales slowly. Fuck. *Think about Brandon. You've got time to freak out about your own shit later.* "What if Justin hadn't said anything to anyone? Would you still be asking him to marry you?"

"Of course I would."

"And would you want him to tell his family, even if he didn't want to?"

Brandon meets his eyes squarely. "Yes, absolutely," he says without hesitation. "I tried to tell myself it wouldn't bother me, but I guess I can lie to other people, but not myself. And once I realized that, what other choice do I have? And you know what, Avery. Maybe... maybe you're not so wrong when you said, 'Are you doing this so you have to tell people?' Maybe that is part of it. And fuck. Is that even fair?"

Brandon looks miserable, and Avery feels a sudden, frustrated anger at the world for being full of judgmental pricks who care who other people fall in love with. "You know what you're doing, Brandon? You're showing Justin that love is stronger than fear and that he means more to you than what other people think. And that's... really goddamn brave and fucking amazing of you. And if everyone did that, people wouldn't be afraid of being in love in the first place, and this world wouldn't have its priorities all fucked-up."

There's a moment of silence after Avery's little speech. "You're so dramatic, Avery," Brandon says, but he looks a lot more cheerful. He stops messing with the pen and doesn't seem to mind that it's lying at an odd angle on his desk. "Thanks. I should have talked to you earlier. I know. I just don't like it when I can't take care of things myself. Can I have my pencils back?"

Avery is now jostling the cup of pencils. Damn it. "Oh. Right. Yeah. Here you go. So how are you going to propose? Don't tell me you're going to do it at the Hula-Hoop camp."

"Nah, but I thought about it. I figure I'll know when the time is right. I've got to trust my instincts, at some point, I guess. They've done pretty well for me so far."

"And then you can have a wedding. Am I invited?"

"No. Of course not." Brandon adds his mechanical pencil to the cup and idly sorts them by cap color, even though Avery can tell he's trying to be all casual about it. "Why wouldn't you be invited, idiot? Actually...." Brandon coughs, and his ears turn red. "This is kind of getting ahead of myself, but I thought, you know, if we do get married and you don't mind, that you'd maybe be... in it. You know."

Avery grins, delighted. "Of course. I was in my college girlfriend's wedding. It was fun. I was a groomsmaid. Or something. That'd be great, but can I make a suggestion?"

"Like you wouldn't even if I said no?"

That's very true. Avery keeps talking. "Don't tell Justin you asked me to be in the wedding before you asked *him* to be in the wedding."

That makes Brandon laugh, which makes Avery happy—or would, if he weren't quietly freaking out. "I should go. We both have to pack, and the flight's in the morning."

Suddenly Avery doesn't want him to leave. Because then he has to face the latest lie he's been telling himself, and worse, he has to do something about it. "Wait. Did you get him a ring?"

Brandon's eyes brighten. "Yes. This is really cool." He types something on his keyboard and swings his monitor over so Avery can see. "Look. It's made out of dinosaur bone and a meteorite. Cool, huh?"

Avery might be mired in his own drama, but he does like shiny things. And also dinosaurs.

"That's badass. I didn't know he liked geeky shit."

"Oh yeah. When we went to DC to visit his best friend from college, we spent half the day in the Smithsonian natural history museum. I always get him those boring documentaries for presents and then take naps when he watches them."

"Those are his?"

"Right?" Brandon grins and switches off his monitor. "Everyone assumes they're mine. I don't know what makes people think I'm the one into dinosaurs." Brandon is watching him expectantly. "Avery?"

"Hmm? Oh, am I supposed to answer that?" Avery is busy thinking that he has no idea if Malin likes anything other than sex, cigarettes, crepes, and quiet. The only present Avery could get him would be cufflinks, but he also has no idea when Malin's birthday is.

"I was just expecting some kind of joke about a giant bone, but don't feel obligated on my account." Brandon stretches, looking much more cheerful. Avery, on the other hand, feels like shit. "Okay. I just saw O'Keefe walk out with his seventies-style briefcase. I swear my dad had one just like that. But if he's gone, then I'm out of here, because he never leaves if the boss is in his office. Especially if you're still here."

"Maybe he didn't see me, since I'm not in my office. He probably thinks I left at noon."

"I don't know. He's pretty paranoid about you. I'm surprised you haven't won him over yet." Brandon turns off his computer, grabs his suit jacket and his messenger bag with his various gadgets, and then gestures for Avery to go out ahead of him. "Are you headed out?"

"Oh yeah. I have to finish an e-mail, though. It's the one thing I had to do all day, and I still managed to put it off." Avery is trying to ignore the unhappy coil of nerves in his stomach.

"Want me to wait around?"

He does, and he almost says that, but Brandon gets a text message. The way he smiles at the screen means it has to be Justin. "Nah. Go on. You've got to pack. Hey, man, congrats. Really. I'm happy for you two. I even have the perfect wedding gift for you." Avery goes to hug Brandon. "You don't have a Crock-Pot, do you?"

"Of course I have a Crock-Pot. Who doesn't?" Brandon returns his hug. "Thanks, Avery. Have a good holiday. Are you heading home to Ohio?"

"Nope." Avery tries to sound cheerful. *I was hoping to spend it with my secret work boyfriend, who apparently left the office without asking me if I'd be in town or telling me that he would. So maybe I'll throw some deli meat in my* Crock-Pot *and call it good. Oh God.* "Good luck. But I know he's going to say yes. Are you going to get down on one knee?"

Brandon's eyes gleam. "No. But he's going to get down on two," he says. The naughty effect is ruined by the blush, but it's still a racy sex reference, so Avery reacts appreciatively. Those aren't easy for Brandon.

When Brandon is gone, Avery goes into his office. He thinks about what Brandon said, and not just the things about shame and fear either. Brandon knows Justin's family history despite never having met them. And his mother's occupation, even though—wow, is that ever weird.

And he thinks about the things he doesn't know about Malin, which is all of that stuff plus things like holiday plans. He hasn't been to Avery's apartment. He's never asked Avery about his family or if they know about his proclivities—or fuck—where they live.

If Avery were going to buy a ring for Malin, what would it be made of? Avery has no idea, but he thinks it would be glass—like the windows in Malin's apartment that vanish in the dark like they're not even there.

CHAPTER 13

AVERY GOES to Malin's apartment after he leaves work, because the thought of going home and thinking about how fucked he is isn't as appealing as going and getting fucked. For the holiday, he's thankful for self-denial.

Malin has told him before, "If I want you to leave, Avery, I'll tell you so." Avery takes him at his word and lies on the couch in Malin's apartment, reading a book. It's *We Have Always Lived in the Castle*, which isn't that long, and it probably makes him look like a moron who can't read, because he's not paying attention to it at all. And yet he reads it most of the afternoon.

Malin's doing work, or at least that's what Avery assumes. His attempts at conversation involve him asking Malin what he's working on and Malin refusing to answer. It looks like he's drawing something, and Avery thought most of what Malin does involves spreadsheets.

"Hey, you want to go see a movie?" he asks later, when he wakes up from a nap. He's not used to sitting still so much. Or being without stimulation of some kind—other than sex.

Malin declines. Later Avery asks him if he wants to go out for dinner, but Malin doesn't want to do that either. He tells Avery to order whatever he wants.

Then Malin says he's going into the office during the week, because he'll be able to do some work in peace and quiet.

"What about Thanksgiving?" Avery asks, to which Malin responds, "I'm not an American. It's not my holiday."

"Aren't you thankful for anything?" Avery asks, and Malin says maybe Avery should go for a run before dinner, because he seems restless.

So he does.

It helps. But after he's finished and has had a shower, Malin asks him—in the way that is really telling more than asking—to order dinner. Avery starts to have that feeling again—a curious mixture of dread and boredom and the need to stop being quiet and do something.

Finally he can't stand it anymore. "I'm kind of not used to all this quiet," he says, keeping his voice light. "Let's go out. I know a great Thai place."

"I thought I told you I didn't want to do that when you brought it up earlier."

"Maybe you changed your mind." Avery takes a deep breath. "I would rather go out, if that matters."

"I'm not stopping you," Malin says, and Avery's too mad to catch that he sounds bewildered more than cruel.

"The point was you could come with me," he tries to explain, although he doesn't know why.

"I'm not certain I follow. Either you want to go out to dinner or have dinner with me. Which is it?"

Avery gives in and orders dinner. He doesn't eat much, and he tries to tell himself it doesn't mean anything. It's not some statement about their relationship. Malin doesn't like crowds, and it's a Saturday night, so places will be crowded.

But it's also New York City. Why does he even live here if that's a problem?

"Hey. Why did your ex-wife come by here? You never told me."

"Why would I tell you that?"

"Because I'm asking," Avery tells him flatly. "Do you go to her parties?"

"What?" Malin's eyes snap to his. "Who told you that?"

Avery puts his chopsticks down. "I heard someone mention it. That you have to go to your ex-wife's parties. Why?"

"I wouldn't call them parties," Malin mutters. "Obligations. I hear people have fun at parties."

"If you left your apartment, you might find out why," Avery snaps. That's not the right thing to say at all—but fuck it.

Malin narrows his eyes. "You're clearly upset about something and rather than trying to figure it out, I would prefer if you would just talk to me like an adult."

Oh wow. That is so not the thing to say. "Actually you know what? Let me do this the way I've been told to. Malin, please tell me

150

things about you that I don't know, such as when your birthday is, who your parents are, if you have any siblings, where you grew up, and why you don't want to be seen in public with me."

Malin's eyes go cold. "I have no idea what this is about, Avery, but I'm not indulging your theatrics."

"Indulging my—Oh, you have no idea. This isn't fucking theatrical, but I can show you theatrical, if you want." Avery stands up, so angry he's shaking.

"I'd really rather you not."

"Okay then. Do what I asked you to do. Tell me about your life— fuck—about you. About what the hell you want me here for, if I annoy you so goddamn much and you're so ashamed of me."

"I've told you before not to tell me what I think about things," Malin says coldly.

"Oh, fuck you. This isn't about you. It's about me. And if you want me to sit quietly all the time like I'm a fucking toy you can turn on and off, why do you even want me here? Because that's not me, and it isn't ever going to be either."

Malin looks at him, unreadable as ever, and even his voice is emotionless. "You didn't ask me to go to dinner. You asked me if I wanted to. I didn't."

"Would you have, if I'd told you I wanted to go? Which I did, by the way."

"I must have misunderstood you."

Avery waits, but that's all he gets. He laughs, harsh and angry. "You must have. Yeah. And that's not an answer, but why did I think I'd get one? You know how you hate when I tell you what you think about things?"

"Yes," Malin says, so tightly it seems like his jaw might crack.

"I probably wouldn't do that, you know, if you would actually tell me what you think about things."

Avery is slightly gratified to see a flash of temper in Malin's light eyes. "We're not all as gifted with words as you, Avery."

"What? What does that even mean?" Avery is about to stomp his foot, he's so mad. The only thing keeping him from doing it is that he's not wearing shoes.

Malin pushes away from the table. He's clearly trying to control his temper—which is not what Avery wants at all. "Exactly what it sounds like."

Fuck it. Avery stomps his foot anyway. "Fine. But you know, being quiet and still and isolated isn't easy for me either."

"I know it isn't." Malin's voice is very quiet, and he's not looking at Avery.

"You're not going to make me someone I'm not. And I can't—I can't stay here and let you try. Because it won't work, and you know how much I hate being a disappointment." Avery moves a little closer to him, still angry. It's unusual that Malin's not looking at him.

"I'm not going to make you stay here. I've always made that perfectly clear, haven't I? That you could leave?"

Avery closes his eyes. "Yeah. You've made that perfectly clear. What I'm not getting is that you want me to stay." He opens his eyes and finds Malin is at the windows, looking down at the city. "And don't tell me that if you didn't, I wouldn't be here."

"Then what should I tell you, Avery?" Malin's temper seems to be locked up tight again, like it was never there. "What do you want from me? Because I'm not certain why you're still here if you want me to be someone I'm not."

"I'm here because I love you, you idiot." Avery doesn't mean to say that, but he's glad when he does. That's one thing he doesn't have to keep all bottled up inside. "I've never been in love before, with anyone. And believe me, I'm as surprised as anyone, considering—like I said—I barely know you."

"You keep saying that," Malin says, turning to face him. Avery isn't prepared for the look on Malin's face—angry and resigned—like he knows how this is going to end. "What would you say if I told you this *is* me, Avery? That there really isn't anything else to know?"

"I'd say bullshit, and then I'd ask why you try so fucking hard to make me believe that's true. You're not ashamed of me. You're afraid."

"I'm not afraid of you." Malin turns his attention back to the windows. Avery wants to stab him in the neck with his chopsticks.

"You're afraid of something, and I don't know what it is. And honestly I don't know why you would be. I'm not making demands on you, am I? Is 'let's go out to dinner' and 'hey, tell me about yourself' too demanding? Because Malin, I'm serious. If they are, I'm done."

Malin laughs, and it sounds incredibly bitter. "Tell me what you think I'm afraid of, Avery. I want to know."

"No. It's time for you to do the talking. And until you do, I'm not asking for another goddamn thing. And I'm not giving you anything either." He grabs his phone, his car keys, and his shoes. "If you want to talk to me, Malin, figure out where I live. Come and see me. Do something that might actually make you uncomfortable."

Malin makes that sound again—a bitter, choked noise that can't, in any fashion, be considered a laugh. "I don't like ultimatums."

"This isn't one. I'm supposed to ask you for what I need. Well, this is it. And if you don't know me well enough to know that I'm telling you the truth, then I don't know what to tell you. And if you know I'm right and don't do it, then you don't fucking deserve to know me at all."

Malin doesn't say a word while Avery shoves his feet into his boots and leaves the apartment with a slam of the door that's far more satisfying than his earlier barefoot stomp. As he drives away, he imagines Malin up there, in the quiet of his apartment—alone. *That's exactly what you wanted, so enjoy it.*

Then he goes and gets drunk. Being in love sucks.

AVERY WAKES the next morning with a pounding headache, his cat asleep on his head—not helping—and the vague feeling he might have thrown up on someone.

No one else is in bed with him, and his pride is slightly mollified by the fact he didn't really try. Unless telling a girl you don't know that your boyfriend is an emotionally repressed jerk is a pickup strategy. In which case, he's a complete failure.

He has a vague recollection of the girl helping him to a cab. And that's good. He's glad he didn't throw up on her. But it's not like he relishes the thought of throwing up on a cab driver either. This is New York. Word gets around.

Luckily for the cabbie and Avery's future transportation needs, he didn't throw up in the cab. Unfortunately for Avery's current state of ill health, he finds where he *did* throw up. It wasn't on a person. It was all over the toilet. He curses Johnny, Jack, and Jim until the end of time and gets to work cleaning it up.

Then he takes a long shower and two aspirin, eats a piece of toast, drinks three bottles of water, and goes back to bed. He wakes up two hours later and drags his Crock-Pot out. He looks at it, discovers he has absolutely nothing to put in it—save the cat—and eats another few pieces of toast.

He feels better until he remembers why he got drunk in the first place. That's not much better than being physically ill. He retrieves his car, which wasn't towed. Even if he does have three parking tickets. Then he stops at the grocery store to buy some food. When he gets home, his head is pounding again. He's starving and miserable, and if this is the experience of being in love, Avery would like to give it back.

He puts some chicken breasts and a can of cream of mushroom soup in the Crock-Pot he's dragged out of the box. He's from Ohio, and the only thing he knows how to make involves some kind of soup. Then he lies on the couch, watching television and wondering why the delicious smell of cooking chicken is not wafting through his apartment. He eats a sandwich and ignores the Crock-Pot. Maybe it's like a watched pot. Who knows.

His hunger momentarily—if not satisfactorily—sated, Avery falls asleep with the Spice Channel on. It's comforting, instead of hot, which is so fucked-up he can't even deal with it.

Two hours later he's woken up by a pounding he's momentarily convinced is his head—again. There's someone at his door, and his apartment still does not smell like chicken. He also really needs to change the litter box.

All of this flies out of his mind when he sees who's at his door. Avery didn't expect Malin to actually come and find him. Of course, Malin could be here to fire him. Who the fuck knows.

"May I come in?"

He realizes he's standing at the door and probably looks like death warmed over—hair sticking up and still in a T-shirt and a pair of running pants. He nods and steps back, though. It would be shitty of him to tell Malin to come over and then not let him in.

"You're not going to Ohio for the week, are you?"

Blinking, Avery rakes a hand through his hair and tries to think if he can brush his teeth without causing much notice. Malin looks as attractive as ever, and he looks like a frat boy on Sunday morning. Awesome. "No. I'm staying in town."

"Do you have any obligations that would keep you from leaving town that can't be rescheduled?"

Avery would say something snarky, but he doesn't know what's going on. "No. I don't. I just need someone to feed the cat, but Harlan can do it. He's not going anywhere for the holiday, and he's got a key to my place." Sheba, his cat, is peering out of the bedroom at the strange new person. She inches closer to Malin with cautious little steps. "She's curious about people, so if you're allergic, let me know, and I'll move her. Otherwise she'll end up trying to climb you."

"Sounds familiar."

"Was that a joke? I'm hungover. Don't make jokes if I can't appreciate them. I think that was insulting, though. So never mind. But hey, what's this about?"

Malin has that "I am completely unmoved by everything" look, but Avery thinks Malin is as nervous as he is. "I'm going to give you what you asked for, Avery. Pack warmly. It's snowing."

What the actual hell? "Where are we going?"

"Mordor," Malin says, straight-faced.

Avery smiles. So he did understand that reference after all.

"The Berkshires," Malin clarifies.

"What... the Berkshires? Are you bribing me with a nice vacation, because that won't work. I'll say it will so that we can go, but it won't."

"Thank you for the warning. Now we should go. It's a bit of a drive."

"But—"

"Avery," Malin says, stepping closer, and Avery stops talking because Malin's not hiding anything suddenly. He sounds tired. There are circles under his eyes. Then he says, "Please."

Avery gets angry fast and gets over it fast. He's tempted to say it's fine. He doesn't want Malin to have to do something he hates. That's not what love is about. But he's still sort of mad. So maybe it can be a little about that, for the sake of vengeance.

155

Besides, it's not fine. And it won't be, unless this gets settled. He nods. "Okay. Give me ten minutes." He smiles, a tentative attempt at peace, considering they have a car trip ahead of them and Avery is completely unable to be quiet on car trips. More so than normal. "You can watch television, if you want. It's the glowing box with the people on it in the living room."

Malin makes some kind of face where his mouth upturns for the briefest of seconds, which Avery decides to count as a smile.

He's completely distracted while he packs, but he does throw in some lube—he's being an optimist, what?—his snow boots, and a few books. Just in case wherever they're going is as quiet as Malin's apartment. He makes a quick call to Harlan about the cat, and then brushes his teeth, changes into jeans and a sweater, and grabs his cell phone charger.

He finds Malin in his living room, sitting on his couch a little awkwardly, with Sheba next to him. He's petting the cat awkwardly too. Why didn't he realize most of Malin's weird behavior is simply that he's awkward?

Then he sees what's on TV, which is exactly what he fell asleep watching. Only this time it's a lot of coeds at a pool party, with no clothes and a lot of loud moans. Oops.

"Sometimes I miss tits," Avery says, shrugging.

Malin turns his head toward him. It seems to take him a second. "Me too," he says, and then he really does smile. Avery grins back. *Maybe this will be all right. Maybe love isn't so bad after all.*

Two hours later Avery, who is half-asleep in the car, remembers the Crock-Pot and the chicken and has a quiet freak-out about his apartment burning down and how the cat will think he did it on purpose. He can't get service where they are to call the management office, so he leaves Harlan a frantic message and hopes he doesn't sound too much like a moron.

"Avery," Malin says, turning his gaze briefly from the road. "Don't worry. I made sure it wasn't turned on before we left."

"Really? Thanks. Wow, I'm glad you thought to do that." Avery leans back in his seat, relieved. He likes Malin's car, and he likes watching Malin drive it. It makes him feel kind of guilty because it's not a hybrid. He'll buy some carbon credits or whatever. It'll be fine.

"I didn't," Malin says, and Avery can tell he's trying not to laugh. "It wasn't plugged in."

That would be why his apartment never smelled like delicious chicken, then. At least he can tell his mom he tried.

Chapter 14

Malin has a radio in the Jaguar, and it's tuned to NPR. Which is fine with Avery, as he likes NPR quite a bit. But he does have a tendency to talk to the newscast as if he is actually on the program.

Which he wouldn't be, because journalists should be "unbiased" or, at the very least, not have as many opinions as Avery does.

He's trying not to be annoying, but he ends up muttering louder and louder until finally he just gives up and keeps talking. This is who he is. And maybe if Malin wants him to be quiet, he should say something.

Malin turns the radio off when the program is over, and Avery looks at him a little guiltily. "Sorry. I should have warned you that I talk to the radio."

"It would be easier to let me know the things you don't talk to, wouldn't it?"

"You, for two minutes," Avery informs him. He's teasing, but things still feel weird between them. Maybe because he doesn't know where they're going. "Seriously, though. If you want to listen to something, I can try to be quiet."

"That's not why I turned the radio off, but thank you for the offer."

Avery gets the feeling that there's a reason, but he doesn't press for it. He's made it clear he wants to know things. If that's why Malin's brought him into the wilderness of rural Massachusetts, then that's really all Avery can ask for, isn't it?

He's watching the scenery flash by outside of the car window, but it's dark and mostly comprised of bare trees, so it's not all that interesting. Avery considers taking another nap. Hopefully he's going to be up late, so he should get some rest, right?

Except he doesn't take a nap, because out of the blue, Malin starts to talk.

"I didn't start out in commercial design. I don't know if you knew that."

Avery isn't sure if he's supposed to say anything. But he does so Malin will know he's listening. "No."

Malin is staring straight ahead. Avery can see his hands on the steering wheel are white-knuckled. He really doesn't seem like he wants to do this, which makes Avery want to kiss him. Except that's a bad idea, considering Malin's driving.

"I had no thought of going into either commercial *or* into project management. My focus was on residential design from the very beginning, throughout school, graduate school, and when I took my first position."

Avery nods. "I knew you were a designer, and it makes more sense that you'd do residential."

"Does it?"

"Yeah." Avery feels bad suddenly, like he's interrupting. "Sorry. Go on. See why I'm impossible? I want you to tell me things, and then I can't even let you."

"It's all right. I'm interested in why you'd say that."

"Well, project management... no offense, Malin. But you're not the most, ah, people-centric person I've ever met. But I love people, and the idea of being someone's boss freaks me the fuck out. So you know. Maybe that doesn't matter."

"You don't have a sense of authority, that's why."

"Thanks. But yeah. The reason I said that is... I love commercial design because of that whole people thing. I really like serving the needs of communities through shared spaces." Avery clears his throat. "If that sounds familiar, it's because it was in my portfolio as often as I could put it in there."

"Yes. Well, that's a good reason to want to do it."

"So I can see you'd probably like working with a single client or two, rather than deal with committees and zoning boards. Damn. Why *are* you doing this, anyway?"

"We're getting to that part. But yes, I thought perhaps I could learn to relate to people a bit better if I was doing so through architecture. And I've always loved houses. I understood them much better than the people inside of them. So when I graduated from McGill, I took a position at a small, exclusive firm in Boston."

"McGill?"

"It's in Montreal."

"Oh, I know that. It's just... you went to Canada for graduate school?" There's something he definitely didn't know about Malin. "Why?"

"Because I'm Canadian." He looks over and laughs at the embarrassed look of surprise on Avery's face. "Quebecois. That's why I speak French. Did you really think I was from France?"

"I don't hear you speak French all that often," Avery says honestly. He feels stupid he didn't realize before. "You hardly do, and you hide your accent unless you're... y'know. Worked up. Or relaxed. But wow. Yeah. I can't believe I didn't put that together."

"It's all right. I don't like people to ask me about it, so I try and hide my accent, if possible. And I've lived in the United States for twenty years."

"You're not a Republican sympathizer, are you?"

Malin looks briefly confused. Avery would apologize, but Malin is going to have to get used to his rapid subject switches at some point. "No. I might not have your rabid allegiance to sustainability—"

"Hey, Canuck, watch it."

"—but that doesn't make me a conservative," he finishes. And then, "Avery, I am not... telling you this story is very difficult for me. If you would just listen, I will try and answer whatever questions you have when I'm finished, oui?"

Malin is clearly making an effort, which makes something warm and sappy and dumb swirl around and cause Avery's heart to do a flippy thing. "Sure. But just so you know. I like your accent, so you can use it around me."

Malin acknowledges that with a slight nod. "I would have stayed in Montreal, but I got married, and my family was not... entirely welcoming to my wife." Malin's voice goes very quiet. "My first wife, I should clarify."

And that's when Avery knows this story isn't going to end well.

"I'D KNOWN Claudia since I was twelve years old. I grew up in a very wealthy household, and Claudia's mother was a gardener. In the summer, she would bring Claudia to the house with her. She was ten

160

when I met her, and I'm not certain why, but I think I knew I was going to marry her that very first day. She found me drawing a house in my notebook and demanded to know what it was. When she saw it, she said one day she wanted me to grow up and design a house for her because it looked like a happy house, and hers wasn't. And mine wasn't either. I promised her that I would. Every day after that, she would find me and sit next to me when I was drawing. She was—"

He pauses and is quiet for a long time, like he can't think through what he wants to say.

Avery, enthralled by the story, has to tell himself to wait for Malin to finish. Of everything he could have imagined hearing, this story is definitely not it.

"She was a lot like you," Malin says very carefully, as if it's hard for him to say. "As in, she would talk constantly. I used to hate when people tried to talk to me when I was drawing. Somehow when it was her, it didn't matter. And that's when I realized I would marry her. And I did, when I was twenty-two and she was twenty. And my family was furious at me. They cut me off for a time, right when I started graduate school. I couldn't even give her a ring. So I gave her a sketch of a house, instead, and told her, that one I'd build for her.

"We lived in a tiny student apartment in Montreal. The heat never worked, it was miserably hot in the summer, and our walls were thin. We both worked part-time jobs to afford it, even with my stipend. We would drink cheap wine, and she'd put the pictures I drew of our house on the wall. 'You told me you'd build me a happy house, and you will.' But that apartment, as miserable as it was, it was happier than either of our homes before that. And any of mine since."

Avery closes his eyes briefly. Malin is quiet for a long time, but he starts talking again as he turns onto a dark road. Dead trees flash like bones in the light of his headlights.

"I had a job offer in Quebec, one in Toronto, and one in Boston. I took the one in Boston, because Claudia liked the city, and the hockey tickets to watch the Habs play the Bruins were cheaper in Boston than Montreal." He smiles briefly. "She was a fanatic about hockey. I had to carry her—literally—out of a bar in Boston because she was taunting Bruins fans. Not because they were threatening her, but because they kept buying her drinks to encourage her."

Avery laughs at that, charmed. He likes Claudia already.

"When I'd been there a year, something happened that made my family rethink their decision to disown me."

Malin falls into silence again, but Avery doesn't mind. He wants to keep the image of Malin with a pretty French-Canadian girl in a Boston bar, or in an apartment decorated with sketches of houses and cheap wine-bottle candles, as long as possible. It's good to hear he was happy once.

"Claudia and I had decided not to have children until I was a bit more established, and she had decided to go to school. She never really had a firm answer when I asked her what she wanted to study. So when we found out she was pregnant, I was worried she would be angry at postponing her schooling. But she wasn't angry. She was thrilled. Later she told me she only wanted to go to school because she didn't want to embarrass me in front of all the other *smart architects* and didn't want me to be ashamed of her because she only finished high school."

Avery remembers yelling at Malin—was that just yesterday?—and accusing him of being ashamed of him. He stares down at his hands and takes a deep breath, because it's hard not to apologize for that. But he didn't know, and now he does.

"My family came around, and they were happy about the baby. They wrote me back in the will, which she said she didn't care about. But I cared because I remembered all those nights in that freezing apartment and her telling me it would all be worth it one day. And I wanted it to be one day for her, so very badly. She didn't want to take any of my parents' money, even though she was happy they changed their mind about disowning us. But I did take money from my trust fund account, and I bought something so that one day would be sooner rather than later."

Malin turns the car onto another dark, unmarked road, and Avery's heart starts to slam in his chest because he hears the pain, the regret Malin can't hide. He knows they must have arrived where they're going, and that means the story has to end.

"I told her I had my first client and was working on a design that was very proud of. And that the client was very important, of course because it was my very first one. I worked long hours, and she was busy getting ready for the baby. For her birthday, I gave her a diamond ring because I could finally buy her one. And then I told her that I was going to buy some land for our house, and I'd used money from my trust fund to buy it. She was furious at me for buying land with my family's money. Furious. And when a Quebecois woman is furious, she throws things. She picked up the first thing she could find and threatened to hurl it at my head for lying to her. I think she only put it down because I reminded her it was a graduation gift, and she'd spent a lot of hours making crepes in Montreal to buy it for me."

It's a graduation gift, so please leave it alone.

For a brief moment, Avery is so horrified he almost throws himself out of the car. He has to remind himself the paperweight is still safe on Malin's desk in his office.

Avery is still processing this when he realizes the car's stopped. Malin is staring straight ahead, not speaking. Avery turns to look at the house, gently lit from within, and the simple beauty of it takes his breath away. He gets out of the car silently and walks toward it. It's too dark to see it in its entirety, but he can see enough.

The house is made of classic lines and elegant curves. Traditional but with enough touches of unexpected whimsy to be charming. Where there are squares and sharp angles, there are round windows to soften the severity. Where there are several curves rushing together, there are sudden straight sections to keep it from being too busy or overwhelming.

"I didn't tell her that I was having the house built, because I wanted it to be a surprise. She knew we had the land. But we had a baby, and that was a lot of work too. So she thought it was just sitting and waiting for the house I would one day build her. But I wasn't building houses for other people until I built hers. Because if it hadn't been for her, I wouldn't be building them at all."

Avery steps closer to him, but he keeps his distance. His heart is in his throat. It's freezing outside, but the house looks warm despite the stark-white exterior, the dead trees, and the dry, brown grass dotted with snow.

"She was on her way to meet me here, thinking we were going to do a land survey and then spend the weekend at a resort a few miles away. It was raining, and her car was hit by a semi just outside of Boston. She and our son were killed on impact. He was six months old. I waited for her, standing right here, until the sun set. And then I heard a car, the crunch of

163

gravel, and I—" Here Malin falters just a little. "I knew before I saw that it was a policeman's car that she was dead. I knew because the lights were wrong. They didn't look the way they were supposed to."

Avery takes a very deep breath and exhales slowly through his teeth.

"For a few months after the accident, I tried to go back to work. But when I sat down with my paper and my pencil, it didn't matter what ideas I had or what image was in my head when I started. It didn't matter if it was a sketch or a blueprint. I could only draw one design, and it was this one. There weren't any others." Malin puts his hands in his pockets and tilts his head to look at the sky. "This was the only house I was ever meant to build."

Avery doesn't know what to say. He didn't know, so he can't apologize for anything. That wouldn't sound genuine. He can't say he's sorry because that's not even close to how he feels. He badly wants to touch Malin, but he doesn't. But he can't just not say anything, and saying "I love you" seems like pressure he doesn't want to create. He doesn't know what that pain must be like, when everything that means the world to you is taken away in a single, horrible moment.

Surprisingly Malin isn't finished. "You're trying to think of what to say, aren't you? It's all right. You don't have to say anything. I almost didn't keep this house. I thought it would hurt too badly, but the thought of anyone else living in it enraged me. So I kept it. You ask me why there's nothing in my apartment, why it's quiet, why I don't change the décor, and why I keep things I don't like. Because I have one house, and this is it. This is where I wear my heart, Avery, and for a long time, this is where I wanted it to stay."

"It's… it's beautiful," Avery says. That's inadequate, but it's all he's got. "I can see the parts that are you, and I didn't know her, but this house makes me feel like I do. And I can see that the two of you were perfect together, because this house is perfect." He looks down, feeling stupid and awkward. He—who always has something to say—is struck dumb at the depth of emotion and love he's seeing before him. "Thank you. For showing me. And for telling me about her. I know it's hard for you, and I… thanks. I wish I could have known her. I bet we'd get along."

"Yes, I think you would. She would appreciate, I think, that you tried to throw the same paperweight at me." Malin starts walking back to the car. "I'll get your things. The door should be open. It's freezing out here, and it's late."

Avery didn't think they were actually going inside. Which is stupid, maybe, but he feels like it's trespassing. He goes in, and the house is so warm and inviting—and nothing at all like Malin's apartment—that it's almost hard to believe he lives here. *Hi. I do love him. I hope that's all right.* Avery thinks Claudia might hear him. Calm settles over him, although that could just be warmth after standing outside.

Avery is quiet when Malin comes in, and he follows him through the house, uncertain how he feels. He smiles at the Montreal Canadiens flag in the entertainment room and gives Malin a pointed look at the television. There are movies too. A lot of them have French titles. He watches Malin move around the house, comfortable and at home in a way he never is in Manhattan.

In the kitchen there are a lot more than four plates and two bowls. Something from Malin's story comes back to him, and he watches Malin looking through the pantry for something to eat. "Hey. You said your wife made you crepes?"

"Well, yes and no. She and I both worked at a crepe restaurant in Montreal. I made them. She served them. That's where I learned how to smoke and make them at the same time. And we would have them a lot because we would make extras and hide them during our shifts, and then bring them home."

"That's why you never eat any, isn't it?"

"Oui. But it's not because they make me sad. It's just that I never want to eat another one ever again."

Avery laughs, and that feels good. Malin pours them both a Scotch, and he starts to make them something to eat. There's music playing, and Avery isn't sure if this is the same man or what he's supposed to do with all of this new information.

What if this is who I am, Avery?

"Why did you bring me here?"

Malin looks at him while he's slicing something into tiny pieces, and he seems to be thinking about how to answer. "I need... some time... before I can tell you."

"All right." Avery sips his Scotch. He usually drinks beer, but this is making him feel worldly and also like a kid kicking his heels against a barstool. Because he's actually doing that. Oh. "What about Marie? I mean, you fell in love with her. Right?"

"No. I thought I could, maybe. I'd known her family since I was very young, and she came to New York a few years after I did. At first we would have a drink and talk about people we knew. She never asked about Claudia or Julien, and she didn't seem to expect anything from me. And I had to attend all of these functions, as you know, and she was a good date because other women I'd tried to take all wanted something I couldn't give them. And Marie didn't seem to have any interest in me at all."

Avery immediately dislikes Marie, which could be because he's now totally on Team Claudia. And also because that's stupid. How could Malin think that? "You believed her?"

"You are maybe a bit biased, oui?"

"Maybe. But obviously she wanted you because she married you. I'm more curious...." Avery lets the thought hang there, because maybe it's not a nice thing to ask.

"Avery, you can say it," Malin drawls. Despite the sharing of emotional baggage, he seems relatively relaxed.

"Why you married her," Avery finishes and pushes his empty glass toward Malin. "Can I have some more Scotch?"

"No," Malin says, and gives him some water. "And I thought it might be a good idea to have someone, only if it kept other people from wanting things from me that I couldn't give them. We did get along. We liked similar cultural events, and we spoke the same language."

"So she's like an escort and a pen pal, kind of?"

"I had no intention of sleeping with her, but she came on to me one night, told me it was so strange and that she didn't mean to be attracted to me. It was all very—I should have seen through it, and maybe I did. I took her to bed, and she seemed to enjoy herself. I'd been... concerned about that, because it was hard for me to be engaged... ah... in the act, if you know what I mean."

"It was hard for you to fuck them. Is that what you're saying?" Avery finishes his water. "Now can I have some more Scotch?"

Malin takes his glass but brings it back with water again. And some bread and cheese. So that's good. "Yes. That's what I'm saying. I would check out, emotionally and often physically. It would not endear me to whoever I was with, certainly."

"Well, that's what you wanted," Avery says, shrugging. "I mean, you didn't want to feel anything for them. Right?"

"Oui, I suppose. Marie made me feel better about that and told me that she would be happy to be my wife without my undying devotion. And so, against my better judgment, I married her. It was fine for a few years, but then she, of course, became dissatisfied and distant and found what she needed elsewhere. Which I admit was more of a relief than anything. Eventually she left me for someone, and they were married two months after our divorce was final."

"So it was always bad... like, every time?"

Malin's eyebrows raise at that. "Such strange things you want to know about, cher."

The endearment makes Avery warm again. He still wants more Scotch, though. "Well?"

"Not bad. No. But she was right. I was emotionally distant and physically incapable of showing her any affection. It would have been all right, but I did try at first because I.... It was fine in theory. But when she was living with me, I couldn't help remember how it was with Claudia, and I suppose I thought I should try to have that again. It didn't work." Malin smiles in a very self-satisfied way. "There was one time I was angry at her, and it was very good. She told me maybe she should just make me angry all the time, but it never worked again."

"What'd she do to make you angry at her?"

"I had a framed print on our wall. It was the one thing I brought with me to our apartment, the one I have now. It was gone one day, and I asked where it was. She told me it was for my own good that she'd removed it."

Avery suddenly can't swallow his piece of bread. "What was it?"

"A sketch."

"Malin," Avery says, eyes narrowed. "Tell me. I'm already mad at her."

"A sketch I'd drawn for Claudia, of this house. She'd framed it for me, for my office, when I got my job in Boston."

"And that bitch threw it away?" Avery slams his glass down. What the actual fuck. Who does that? "I can't—how did you—were you trying to strangle her, and she just got off on it? I mean, that happens. And I don't want to share anything with her, but why would you fuck her if she destroyed your one keepsake of your dead wife. That is the saddest fucking thing I have ever heard." Avery's voice is raised, and he's angry. How could anyone hear that story of Malin's and do something like that?

"Avery—"

"No. Don't make excuses for her. Had she ever been here? That is the most—I've heard some terrible things, but I'm serious, that's maybe the worst. Not, like, Holocaust-worst, but on an individual level? Definitely up there. Ugh, Malin, how could you fuck her after that? And okay, I'm on Team Claudia here, and I was the second you told me she got drunk in bars and threw things at you and made you crepes, but I could have been okay with Marie if you didn't tell me that."

"*Avery.*"

"What?"

"I appreciate the sentiment, but she took it *down*. She didn't destroy it."

"Oh." Avery clears his throat. "I guess that's better. Yeah, okay. I can get behind some angry sex for that. What did you do with it?"

"It's in the hallway upstairs." Malin looks at him strangely. "Team Claudia?"

"Sorry. Wow. That was totally disrespectful." Avery looks down, embarrassed. "It's just I can tell that her and I would have been friends. Even if I'm a Pens fan, and she was a Habs fan, which is like the hockey equivalent of being a Yankees fan. Which I am *not* despite living in New York. But I guess it's okay, since you lived in Montreal," he says to the house at large. "And who doesn't hate the Bruins?"

"Who are you talking to?"

Malin's voice sounds a little choked, and Avery hopes he's not furious. "Umm. Claudia? She spoke English too. Right?"

"She's—Avery, she never set foot in this house."

God, hearing that makes his heart ache a little. "It's still her house, though. You built it for her, so." He clears his throat. "Marie. Right. So you two divorced. She remarried... and what, divorced him too? And took your last name back?" Avery's eyes narrowed. "That seems suspicious. I'm suspicious."

"I see that," Malin says dryly. "And no, she's still married."

"Why'd she keep your name, then?"

"She didn't. She married my brother, Augustin, two years ago. He's a financier on Wall Street. As far as I know, they are very happy."

"Then why was she at your house that morning?" Avery gets up and pours himself a Scotch. Fuck water. He's a goddamn adult.

"She wants me to come to dinner with her and Augustin."

"So you can forgive her for taking down mementos of people you loved?" Avery is really, really angry about that.

"No. So I can forgive my brother."

"For marrying her?"

"Avery, my ex-wife and I are not friendly, but I assure you I am not blameless in the disaster that was our marriage."

"Oh, I know. I haven't gotten around to yelling at you yet."

Malin sighs. "My brother refused to come to Claudia and Julien's funeral. We were not close as children, and he never approved of our family reinstating me. And she says he's very sorry and as stubborn as I am, which is a Lacroix trait. Which she knows, since she's been married to both of us."

Avery is horrified to feel his lips twitch at that. "Okay. That's funny."

"She, ah—she did say something about you." Malin smirks. "She said she would have been open to the idea of sexual experimentation, but not with an escort, as you don't know where they've been."

"What?" Avery starts laughing. "Okay, fine. You have a fucking type, and it's not just brunettes. It's snarky brunettes. Was Claudia a brunette? I bet she was, huh."

"Oui, she was."

"Fine. I'm still Team Claudia. But I mean, we both know I'll get over it. And also calling me a rent boy is pretty fucking funny." Avery looks at him hopefully. "Is there more to dinner than bread and my ire...?"

Malin finishes their dinner, which is rice and vegetables. They are fresh, because he had someone stock the house before they got here. "You were going to come up here for Thanksgiving, then?" Avery asks, mostly because he's hungry and trying to shovel food in his mouth. And wow. It's two in the morning, and will they ever, ever eat a meal at a decent time?

"No. I called this morning, before I came to your apartment, to have someone stock the house." Malin gestures to his plate. "Are you done?"

"Yeah. I think so. Fuck, that was good. Are you going to cook all week, because I can't really make anything, as you've seen with my Crock-Pot experiment."

"Oui."

"And not just crepes? I mean, I like them, but you need to eat too."

"Oui."

"And—"

"Avery? We're going to bed now." Malin walks out of the kitchen, just like he would do at his apartment. The boring apartment Avery hates even *more* now that he's seen Malin does have the capacity for a personality.

Avery follows him, and they go into the master bedroom, which is a-fucking-mazing. There's a skylight on the ceiling and beautiful floor-to-ceiling windows Malin tells him look onto the lake and the swimming pool. Which is heated, if he wants to go swimming.

Of course he wants to go swimming in a heated pool. Who wouldn't? But Avery is confused by the windows without curtains and the skylight. Doesn't Malin need it to be dark? "I thought you couldn't sleep if there was too much light?" Avery asks.

"Only if it's the wrong light," he answers slowly, like he isn't sure that makes sense. "I can always sleep here."

Fuck. This whole time Avery's thought Malin has no emotions, when really he just has no idea how to deal with having them. People who repress things. Goddammit. "You want me to sleep here with you. Right?"

Malin walks to him, takes his face between his hands, and gives him a look Avery's never seen before. Then he kisses him, and there's no hesitation at all in Malin's embrace. "Yes, Avery. I want you to sleep here with me."

Avery strips and gets into bed. He has shared a bed with Malin before, but this feels different, like it means something more than just sleeping. As he closes his eyes, comfortable despite the potential weirdness, he feels the briefest touch of fingers sliding through the back of his hair.

Just that, and Malin retains his usual measure of space. But Avery doesn't mind. Not in the least.

CHAPTER 15

WHEN HE wakes up, the bedroom is flooded with light, and he's alone in the bed.

The view from the windows is beautiful—the lake sparkling in the morning sunlight. It's coming through the skylight too. And the bedroom is placed where it won't be in-your-face sun, just a gradual, warm light that wakes you up naturally.

Avery thinks about how Malin must have designed that for Claudia, and his heart flips in his chest again. He gets dressed, and he finds Malin in the kitchen, sitting at a table built into a little alcove and drinking coffee. "Morning."

Malin nods toward the kitchen. "There's coffee, if you want."

"Awesome." Avery gets some and sits down, smiles at Malin, and gets the usual stare in return. Well, no matter how at home he is here, it's still Malin. "Thanks again. For bringing me here. I know I maybe could have asked nicer. Um. Or not been so dramatic."

"Yes, well." Malin sips his coffee. "It is *you*, Avery."

Avery drums his fingers on the table. "And you could have told me sooner, you know. Then I wouldn't have had to slam doors and yell and end up with a killer hangover."

Malin meets his eyes steadily. "No. I don't think I could have." Before Avery can say anything, he slides something across the table. A photograph.

It's Malin—looking younger but still impossibly handsome and with those same sharp cheekbones and pale eyes—and a gorgeous, *gorgeous* woman next to him. The two of them are smiling at each other. They're each holding one small hand of a tiny, adorable blond child with fat cheeks. They're swinging him between them. The baby has his mother's bright, happy grin.

"This was taken two weeks or so before they were killed."

Avery looks up at Malin and smiles. "She's a fox. So are you."
His smile fades a little when he looks at the baby. It's horrible to think
about his life ending before it really began. Avery traces his little cheek
with his finger. "I'm so sorry, Malin," he says quietly, because now it
seems like it's all right to say it. "They're both beautiful, and I'm sorry
that you lost them."

Malin nods very stiffly, rigid as ever. "Merci, cher."

"You should bring this back with you," Avery says, because
that's just how he is.

"Oui. There are many things in this house I should bring back
with me." Malin looks at the picture. He shifts his attention again and
pins Avery with his intense, hawklike eyes. "This is what I was
drawing on Saturday, before you left my apartment." Malin pushes
another piece of paper across the table. "There are other sketches with
the same design. On meeting notes, contracts and schematics, the back
of a takeout menu."

Avery takes it, flips it over, and sees the rough outlines of a house.

*It didn't matter if it was a sketch or on a blueprint. I could only
draw one design, and it was always this one. There weren't any others.
This is the only house I would ever build.*

The house on the paper is nothing like the one Malin built for
Claudia. The design is too bold. Sharp angles meet impossibly to form
a graceful and yet forceful exterior, with a roof that's high-pitched but
fully anchored. On the back of the house, a full wall of windows are
boldly bared to the world. Less noticeable are the skylights, half hidden
in the more dramatic lines of the design, allowing for plenty of light in
the most intimate of places.

*The skylight in the bedroom. It isn't Claudia. It's Malin. Letting
in the light only because something holds it together and makes it safe.*

Malin's voice is very quiet. "I've always tried to make this my
home, with the memory of those who were supposed to share it with
me. But somehow that apartment has become my home, even though I
didn't want it to. And it wasn't until you left on Saturday that I realized
why. A house is meant to be shared with the living, not the dead. If all
you have inside of it is memories, it is nothing but a tomb."

Avery doesn't know what to say. He isn't sure if he understands
what he's hearing. He doesn't want to ask, and he's terrified of ruining

the moment by saying the wrong thing. So he goes to Malin and carefully puts his arms around him from behind. He feels the slight tremble in the body pressed against his own and says, "Does this mean we can have a television?"

There's a pause, and then Malin laughs. It's quiet and far from boisterous, but it's a laugh all the same. He leans his head back against Avery's chest. "Oui, I suppose. I miss watching hockey."

Avery notices he isn't the only one shaking. They should probably hurry up and move past this whole "moment" thing. Avery hasn't even finished his coffee yet. He taps the design on the paper with a finger. "Did you design this house to be only one level so you don't have to go up and down stairs in your old age?"

"Non. I didn't want to come home one day and find a passive solar coil on the staircase."

"I hope you don't want to build it anywhere in New York," Avery says. "Because you've pissed off so many people, the sun will have exploded before you get all the necessary permits."

Malin's laugh is sudden and bright—and maybe just a little bit evil.

"HEY, MOM."

"Avery. How was your Thanksgiving? Did you get the Crock-Pot?"

"It was nice, and yes, I did." Avery decides the less he mentions his failure with cookware, the better. "How was the cruise?"

He listens to his mother and father's adventures, and it makes him smile to hear how she made friends with practically everyone on the boat. Of course she did.

"Did you end up staying at home for Thanksgiving? If you ate takeout instead of using the Crock-Pot, I'll cry, Avery. It's practically foolproof."

As long as you plug it in. Avery clears his throat. "I didn't. I went to the Berkshires."

"Oh, I see. Less Midwestern Thanksgiving, more F. Scott Fitzgerald?"

Avery grins, delighted. His mom is so cool. "Something like that. Yeah. Hey, Mom?"

"Yes, son?"

"I... ah. I'm seeing someone. And I went with... with him to the Berkshires." Telling his mother he's having an adult relationship for the first time in his life is a lot harder than he thought it would be. Now she's going to have expectations. And probably want to meet Malin. God help them all.

There's the slightest hesitation on the other end of the phone before his mother responds. "Oh, darling, that's wonderful. What's his name?"

"Umm. You don't mind it's a him, right?" Avery knows she doesn't. He's totally stalling.

"Of course not," she assures him. "Your grandfather always said sometimes a man needs another man to keep him in line."

Avery gapes for a minute. Because seriously, what? "Grandad said that?"

"Your generation thinks they invented everything," his mother says, sighing.

"Grandad was *gay?*"

"No. He was just very open-minded. And no offense, son, but no woman would ever put up with you."

"Hey," Avery protests. "I'm just like you, you know. What's that say? Huh?"

"That no woman would put up with me either," she answers immediately. "Now stop avoiding the question. Tell me what his name is."

"If you're going to type his name into Google, don't," Avery threatens. "Or that other one that checks criminal backgrounds."

"Does that mean you're dating an infamous serial killer? Avery, I don't want to be on a Lifetime movie." She pauses for a moment "Unless Julianne Moore would play me. That might be all right."

"I love you, Mom," Avery says, overwhelmed momentarily a how he lucked out when it came to parents. And grandparents, it woulc seem. "But he's not a serial killer. He is, however, kind of my... boss."

That's when his mother sounds disapproving, of course. "Avery you've worked very hard to get where you are. I would hate you to mess up things because of this. You didn't... you're not doing thi because he had your building built. Right? I believe in using your skill to get ahead, but... Avery?"

Avery is laughing so hard he can't breathe. "Mom, *no.*"

"Well. All right." She sighs. "No Lifetime movie, then, is what you're saying?"

He almost suggests the Spice Channel would be more appropriate, but if his mother knows what that is, Avery wants to remain forever in the dark. "Don't count your chickens just yet, on that one. I'm still young. And his name is Malin Lacroix."

Avery tells her a little about him—that he's older and an architect. She asks if he's been in a relationship before, clearly trying to make sure Avery isn't his experimental gay sex fling. Avery appreciates her not using those words, because he might die. He tells her that he was married twice.

"Twice? Well, third time's a charm, I always say," his mother says breezily. She's always optimistic. And as his father says, good at avoidance. "Is he still friends with his exes? That's important."

"Ah." Avery thinks about how to answer that. "I don't—well, his ex-wife married his brother, but they're not close."

"Why?"

"Umm. Because... it's kind of a long story? And his first wife was killed in a car accident." His mother gives a little exclamation, and Avery keeps going, not quite ready to rehash all of it right now. "But it's... he's kind of... well. It takes him a while to open up, and he's very intense and quiet."

"Well, those are the only people who keep our attention," his mother informs him, and Avery doesn't want to think that he's maybe, possibly dating his father. "Will we meet him soon, do you think?"

Avery has no idea how to answer. "I don't know. We're taking things kind of slow for now."

The noise his mother makes suggests she doesn't believe that. Before they get off the phone, she tells him to use condoms and not to drink and drive and then hands the phone to his father.

Avery gives a much more abbreviated version of the story to his dad. Who, as he's done since Avery was a teenager heading off to college, couches his concern for his son in questions about car maintenance.

"Well. All right, then. You tell this young man we'll expect to meet him soon. You keeping the oil changed on that car of yours?"

Avery's father is suspicious of his hybrid. Avery is sometimes convinced his dad thinks the Prius is nearly the same vehicle as Fred

Flintstone's. "Yeah. Of course." Actually he needs to check that. Maybe it does need to be changed.

"Good. Any problems with that engine?"

"Running great so far, Dad," Avery tells him and smiles. His father is a college professor. At some point he learned enough about cars to use them as very obvious metaphors for his son. "Also Malin drives a Jaguar. The kind that uses all gas and has a standard transmission."

"Well. That's good to hear." His dad sounds pleased. "I'll look forward to meeting him, then."

Before his father hangs up, he tells him to look on Jiffy Lube's website to find an oil change coupon—which is vaguely confusing to Avery, because that's not metaphorical enough for him. But now his parents know, and he's told his friends, who did not provide him embarrassing advice about condoms or car metaphors. So this isn't some hidden thing he can't be proud of or that he needs to be ashamed about.

Who has Malin told? Avery shushes that little voice and tells it to stop acting like a fifth grader. Malin is free to do whatever he wants, as long as he doesn't expect Avery to keep it a secret. And it's a lot more complicated for him than Avery.

"You're aware you're ignoring basically everything about this. Right?" Harlan asks. Avery responds that he needs an oil change, and does Harlan know where the nearest Jiffy Lube is, because Avery has a coupon, and it's going to expire before Christmas.

CHAPTER 16

MALIN HANGS up some photographs and the sketch of the Berkshire house and organizes all of the movies and CDs Avery packed for him. He puts the Canadiens flag in the bedroom, right above the bed, which makes Avery roll his eyes a lot and make jokes like, "They don't give out Stanley Cups for blowjobs"—which make no sense.

They watch the Habs versus Penguins hockey game together, because Malin finally has a television. At the first intermission, Malin fucks him over the couch with his hand over Avery's mouth while biting him on the neck. Yet another reason to be happy the Habs are losing, as far as Avery's concerned. But then the Habs come back and start winning, and Malin is so insufferably smug about it Avery threatens to burn his stupid flag, and Malin starts doing that horrible, horrible "Ole, Ole, Ole" chant in response.

Avery wonders, in a vaguely horrified way, just how much *worse* Claudia was about hockey than Malin. Because the first time Malin raises his voice during a Habs game, Avery is so startled, he almost drops his beer. Nothing makes Malin lose his shit like the Habs. But one of the pictures he brought back from the Berkshires house is of Claudia in a Habs jersey, outside of what is obviously the Bruins arena, held aloft by a Bruins fan who is twice her size.

"I have no idea who that is," Malin says, but there is a fond smile on his face that makes Avery punch him in the arm—hard—in the guy version of sympathy.

Work remains mostly the same. Malin is busy doing project-y things, and Avery is trying to beat his highest score on *Candy Crush Saga* and taking long lunch breaks with Brandon. He's not working on a design, at the moment, and the Knight Performing Arts Center folks are all vacationing in St. Moritz or wherever rich people who build performing arts centers spend the entirety of the winter holidays. He and Justin meet for drinks after work, and Justin shows off his badass ring and tells him, with the cutest, most disgustingly happy smile ever, about how it's made of dinosaur bones and meteorites. But he laughs at Avery's pun about being boned out of this world, even though it's really lame—only because he's happy and engaged and shit.

No one asks him about Malin, so he doesn't say anything. For Christmas, he gets him tickets to the Habs versus the Rangers at Madison Square Garden, and something else he's not sure he wants to give Malin but keeps hidden under the bed in his apartment.

The separation between his friends and his boyfriend is making Avery nervous. He hates that they can't just meet people out for drinks or watch the game, even though he has *no* friends who are hockey fans—Harlan likes baseball, and that's the closest Avery's got.

The only time he even interacts with Malin around them is when Brandon, a nervous wreck, shows up at his house when Avery is supposed to be on his way to Malin's apartment. Brandon is going to tell his parents about Justin over Christmas, and he keeps trying to practice with Avery. Which is a bad idea, because Avery tries to be helpful by saying, "You're no son of ours!" dramatically, or "Your mother and I have gay lovers too, son. It's perfectly fine."

This is not helpful, so Avery isn't sure why Brandon keeps at it. Justin finally tells him it makes Brandon feel proactive, so Avery lets him do it, even though he's worried he's causing more harm than good.

Avery calls Malin and says he'll be about an hour or two late, and can he bring dinner? He can feel Brandon's eyes on him while he makes his phone call, and Malin is still *Malin* so this phone call consists of him saying two things in response to Avery—"all right" and "no." It's not a very long call, but it never is. Still Avery feels like Brandon is going to think it's like before, when it isn't.

When the office closes for Christmas, Avery packs his stuff and goes to Malin's for the week. He still has the gift he's not sure about giving wrapped up in his bag. While he's deciding whether or not he should give it to him, Malin shocks the hell out of him by asking him to go to dinner at his brother's.

"Your brother, as in, the one who doesn't talk to you?"

"That would be him." Malin is watching him string up lights on the edge of the glass coffee table. Avery needs somewhere to put presents, doesn't he? "My ex-wife will be there."

178

"This sounds fun. What are we doing for New Year's, going to dinner with everyone who doesn't like *me*?" Avery finishes with his lights and gives Malin an "I dare you to say something about it" look.

"Are there people who don't like you?" Malin asks, sounding curious.

"Besides O'Keefe and you during hockey games? Probably." Avery shrugs. "But seriously, you want me to go with you?"

Malin sighs and sips his Scotch. "I don't want to go at all, but yes."

"What are you going to tell them about why I'm there?"

Malin smiles at him, his pale eyes glittering. "That it was cheaper to pay for the week," he answers. Avery laughs and then tries to punch him in the arm. Not because of feelings this time, but because Malin's a jerk.

It isn't until later, when he's half-asleep, that he realizes Malin never answered the question.

AUGUSTIN LACROIX is older than Malin by four years and so stuffy he makes Malin seem like the carefree, fun-loving one of the family. They live in a brownstone on the Upper East Side, and it's obvious his brother doesn't share Malin's love of modernism, because it's completely traditional. It's a gorgeous historic home, and Marie Lacroix is clearly gifted at decorating, but it makes Avery think he's in a museum. He likes modern designs because they're open and bright, and it looks like this is the kind of place where it's too easy to hide.

Dinner reminds Avery of that scene in Tim Burton's *Batman*, where Vicki Vale and Bruce Wayne eat dinner at opposite ends of a long, formal table. Augustin and Malin barely speak, Malin and Marie barely speak, and Avery doesn't speak French, so he doesn't say anything either.

After dinner, Malin and his brother stand around looking uncomfortable and sip brandy like they're on the *Titanic*. Avery, at a loss, starts looking at the house. He's surprised when Marie Lacroix comes up to him, all perfectly put together and coiffed. She smells nice, like some kind of flower Avery doesn't know the name of. A stuffy flower. Definitely an expensive one.

"You don't seem to like me, Mr. Hextall, and I am not sure I know why."

Whoa. He was not expecting that at all. Avery blinks and looks at her, thinks about lying, and finally settles on, "I don't know you, ma'am," which makes her smile in a way that suggests he is not at all funny.

"No, you don't," Marie says very bluntly. "And yet Malin tells me you are his...." She waves a hand. "You know."

"Rent boy?" Avery asks, and he sees the slightest hint of a smile on her face. "I don't know how to say that in French."

"Would you like to?" she asks, looking briefly mischievous, and Avery thinks maybe he's being unfair to Malin's ex-wife. Before he can say anything, she surprises him by saying bluntly, "I'm aware you must not have the best opinion of me, and I am not going to apologize for my past with Malin. I made mistakes, and so did he."

"It's really not my business," Avery says cautiously, because he doesn't really care if it's unfair, he's still biased toward Malin.

"It must be, at least a little," Marie says slowly. "You're here. And I think maybe you are the reason *he* is here. Hmm? I have asked many times, but he has always refused."

Maybe because if this were any more depressing, it'd be an Ingmar Bergman film. "Why do you keep asking, then?"

They're looking at a painting on the wall, some traditional thing with a man in a ridiculous hat and velvet coat, with one hand up in a wait-a-minute gesture and the other holding a quill. There's a dog at his feet. It's a boring picture. Why would anyone want this thing in their house?

"Because when you love someone, you want them to be happy. Oui?" Marie gives him a sideways look. "Sometimes you have to push a little. Yes?"

"I guess you do," Avery agrees. "And if his brother is like Malin, you have to push hard enough to get their attention."

"Oui," Marie says. She's not smiling, but it's there in her voice, which is something. "Do you know in that picture, the dog's head is on incorrectly? And if you look closer, there is a reflection of a naked woman in the mirror, behind him."

Avery peers at the portrait, and does indeed notice both of these things. "Yeah. Wow. And is that a pack of cigarettes on the table thing, there?"

"Oui. There's a bottle of wine somewhere. Augustin's business associates ask me if this is an original Vermeer." She looks very pleased with herself. "I found this painting on eBay for ten dollars, including shipping."

"Ha." Avery grins. "That's awesome. I want one of these for my office. Good catch."

"Merci." She nods and turns away from the painting. "We do not need to be friends, Mr. Hextall. But I would like my husband and your... Malin... to remember they are family. Or have the chance to be, even if they decide not to take it. Sometimes you can only push so far."

Fuck it. He can't hate her. She's actually kind of sneaky and puts deliberately tricky art up on her walls. "It's Avery," he says, and smiles a lot more genuinely. "Can we be friends, though? And are you interested in faux pop art, because I can get you a sweet picture of a sandwich."

She looks like maybe that confuses her, but he can see something relax in her posture. "If I want to see soup cans, I will open the pantry. But I appreciate the offer."

"No problem," Avery says, and then, "Will you teach me how to say rent boy now, because I really want to know. Also did you think I was expensive—or more the twenty-five-dollar blowjob type?"

"Perhaps somewhere in the middle," she answers, completely serious. Avery might be on Team Claudia, but Marie's a lot different than he thought.

When they leave Augustin gives Malin the world's stiffest handshake, and then bestows the same upon Avery. Marie kisses Malin on both cheeks, and also Avery, who gallantly returns the gesture as best he can.

On the way home, Malin looks at him and says with a raised brow, "It would seem you have befriended my ex-wife." Avery shrugs and says they bonded over art.

CHAPTER 17

CHRISTMAS MORNING Avery thinks about what Marie said, about having to push sometimes. He gives Malin the package he wrapped. His heart does weird things, and he's saying something like "It's okay if you don't like it" and "You can let me keep it if you want" and "You don't have to put it up if you don't want to" while Malin opens it.

It's the sketch of the house Malin gave him, framed like the one he framed of Claudia's house. Malin looks at it for a long time. Then he stands up, grabs Avery's arm, and takes him back to bed. Later he hangs it on the wall next to the one of Claudia's and kisses Avery until he's dizzy with it.

Right after the first of the year, Avery's at home and in the middle of a *Call of Duty* marathon with Brandon—whose parents were shocked, vaguely upset, and are now calling about wedding venues and asking to meet Justin's family—when there's a knock on his door. Avery detonates a few explosives and goes to see who it is, because no one ever comes to his place, given he's rarely there.

It's Malin—only the second time he's ever been to Avery's apartment.

"Is everything okay?" Avery asks, and to his shock, Malin walks in and pulls him in against him. Not to kiss him, but just so he's there, warm and close.

"I put the Berkshire house on the market," Malin murmurs, his voice unsteady, accented so it sounds like "'ouse" instead of "house."

Avery pushes the door closed. They stand quietly, with the sounds of video game mayhem playing loudly in the background. Avery runs his hands down Malin's back—once, twice—until Malin moves away.

"I want you to fuck me," Malin tells him right there, and Avery goes from feeling a mixture of concern, pride, and sorrow to "oh my fucking God are you kidding me" in seconds.

"You're sure—"

"Don't—don't speak, Avery," Malin says roughly, and Avery pulls him in and kisses him hotly.

"You know how you told me sometimes you give me what I need, which isn't always what I think I want?" Avery asks, pulling him back into the bedroom. Fuck. His bedroom is a mess, and he hasn't made his bed since... ever.

"Oui?"

"Mmm." Avery bites at his ear. "Same thing for you, babe."

"I asked you to fuck me," Malin tells him, which makes Avery almost moan, because fuck yes. He wants that. "Are you saying I don't need that?"

"Oh no. You definitely need that, and I really, really need to do it too. So that's great." Avery pushes him on the bed. He's all over him, pulling at clothes and kissing him. "But I'm not going to be quiet, because you don't need that."

Malin sighs, even though his breath is hitching, and he's moving beneath Avery. Not a lot, but enough to make it clear he wants this. "Non?"

"Non," Avery says. He kisses at Malin's neck and bites him a little too hard. He can't help it. He's all keyed up, and this is something he's wanted but hasn't known how to ask for. He's glad he didn't and Malin asked first. "I want you to stay with me. That's all."

He pulls back, and Malin looks... not quite scared but something else, apprehensive or anxious maybe. Avery knows exactly how to deal with that.

He kisses him and gets his clothes off, murmuring and telling him "This'll be good, don't worry" and "Fuck. You know how badly I wanted this?" while he settles between his legs. He sucks Malin until he's gasping and muttering in French, grabbing at Avery's sheets and twisting hard.

When Avery gently presses his fingers inside, Malin tenses up because that's just what happens. It's different and new, but Avery hits him just right, and he nearly comes at how Malin almost shouts and arches up off the bed.

I hope Brandon's not waiting for me for that game anymore, and I wonder how far the range on that headset mic goes?

Avery fucks Malin with his fingers and kisses him, shifting so he can get into place. He grabs for the lube in his bedside table... and then he has to search through about six bags until he finds the one he took to the Berkshires, goddammit, because that was the last time he saw his. Malin leans up on his elbows and watches him, breathing hard, idly stroking his cock with one hand while he waits.

That's so hot it distracts Avery for a minute, but he finally finds the lube and goes back to what he was doing. They're both reduced to moans and half phrases like "fuck. Yes, just" and "do you like" and "oui, allés." It's always extra hot when Malin speaks in French like he doesn't know he's doing it. Avery gets on top of him, and he's practically shaking. He tells himself to get it together. He said he was really good at this, and now he's dropping the lube he took sixteen minutes to find in the first place. And that's not good, that's "nineteen-year-old who hasn't done this before." He's getting a little annoyed and worried when Malin grabs the back of his neck and makes Avery look at him.

"Avery, it's good. I want it," he says, voice heavy with lust. His eyes are so bright they're like fire—the whitest part of a flame, where it burns the hottest. "Now."

Avery gets momentarily lost in how that makes him feel—happy and safe and really goddamned hot for it. He's not as careful as he should be when he presses in, but he bites at Malin's ear and tells him to breathe, to relax—all that stuff he should say. He's telling himself too, so he doesn't end this before it's started. He fucks Malin slowly at first, and it feels so good he wants to slam his hips forward and fuck him through the goddamn mattress. But he loves Malin. He wants Malin to like this, because he absolutely does not want this to be the one and only chance he gets.

Malin doesn't look like he's in the throes of ecstasy, but he does look totally fucking out of it. That's hot, but Avery really wants the throes of ecstasy, so he tries to move slowly and steadily. Like he's observed in more than one video on the Internet. Like Malin's done with him sometimes when he makes Avery fucking wild for it, thrashing and asking for things in a way that sounds a lot like he's begging, even if Avery would never call it that.

Except maybe that's not what he should be doing. He's trying to make this what Malin needs and also justify not going slow anymore, because fuck it, it's impossible. So he starts doing it harder, and Malin's eyes flash and meet Avery's almost in surprise. His fingers dig hard into Avery's muscles, and Avery grins, fierce and pleased. He gives up trying to be in control and just fucks him like he wants to, hard and rough and barely in control. They're both moaning, and Avery puts a hand on the wall for leverage. He's close. His hips stutter, and he loses any sense of rhythm. He reaches for Malin's cock with his other hand and jacks him roughly.

Malin grabs Avery's hair, twists, and pulls hard. Avery shifts so he can throw a forearm across Malin's throat. He thinks about that first time in his office when he choked and how good it had felt—that weird release of control. He holds his forearm and watches Malin. When he finally lets him catch his breath, Malin comes over his fist, and Avery follows a few seconds later, blood pounding in his ears.

After it's over, they lie there for a long time, until Malin gently pushes his shoulder and says, "The music from that video game is making me angry, *amour*." Avery grins all dopey and then kisses him and gets up to turn it off. He comes back and takes Malin to the shower. It's not as awesome as Malin's, but they still manage to get clean.

He gives Malin a pair of cotton pajama pants and a T-shirt, and then teaches him how to play *Call of Duty*. Malin is terrible and doesn't like it. Later Avery flips on the Spice Channel and they make out watching girls do the same. They go to bed, and Avery's cat hops up to join them when it's obvious they're sleeping and not doing people gymnastics or whatever the cat thinks they were doing earlier.

They never mention the house, because Avery's learning there's more than one way to say the things that need to be said. It's great when those include really good sex and waking up in the morning with Malin's mouth on his cock. Relationships are a lot better than he thought.

AVERY'S THIRTY-SECOND birthday falls on a Saturday. On Friday night, he makes plans to go out with Brandon, Justin, Harlan, and a few other pals for some drinks after work.

On Wednesday, Malin asks him if he wants to go to the Rangers game because they're playing the Penguins. Avery says he'd love to, but he's going out for his birthday after work on Friday, since he figured they'd do something together on Saturday.

"Something like... oh... sex," Avery tells him cheerfully. But he's starting to recognize Malin's expressions, and he sees Malin's eyes go cold when he nods and says it's fine, they'll go another time.

Avery doesn't know what that means, and he has no idea why Malin would be mad. He's never said anything about Avery's plans with his friends, and it's not like Avery's not going to see him on his actual birthday. This part of relationships is annoying, and he doesn't like it.

Thursday Malin walks into Avery's aquarium office at work and tells him, "Come over tonight." Then he walks out without waiting for him to answer. Avery gets all hot and bothered by professional Malin, and how he's kind of bossy. But there's something about the way Malin looks at him that makes Avery nervous. He feels like he's done something wrong.

When he gets there, Malin's waiting with a glass of Scotch. There's a box on the glass table. When Avery walks in, Malin points and says, "Open that."

"Is it a bomb?" Avery asks, shaking it. It's not wrapped. It's just a box that's plain and unmarked, and he opens it with no idea what's in it. And when he sees what it is, he stares at it without a word.

"Do you know what that is?"

"Yeah," Avery answers and looks up at him. His eyes are very wide. "I know what it is."

"And what is it?"

Avery's having a strange reaction, like he does when Malin uses the belt on him or wraps it around his neck or ties his wrists and makes him kneel—the things he does when he wants Avery to be quiet and calm. "It's a collar," he says, running his fingers gently over the leather.

It's a plain collar, black leather with a simple round loop. They have never discussed this, ever, not even once. Avery likes the idea, but it also feels a little silly—like next Malin's going to be in latex, and Avery will have to wear a gimp suit.

"Bring that to me, then go into the bedroom and strip. Wait for me."

Malin does this whole "I will tell you what to do and you will do it" thing in a way that is completely different from normal—Malin saying things like "Avery, would you please stop leaving your shoes in the middle of the room" and "must you have your phone announce every text message? And who is sending you so many? Can't they just call you?"

Avery takes the collar, and it feels cool in his hand, likely because his skin is overheated. He hands it to Malin without saying anything. He feels that stir of nerves in his stomach and doesn't understand why, but he goes into the bedroom and strips off his clothes—everything but his boxer briefs, because he's figured out what "strip" means. Malin likes him in those.

Malin comes in and puts the collar on the dresser. He takes his time with his tie and his cufflinks, takes the collar, and comes to stand by Avery. He strokes his fingers down Avery's jaw and shoves them in his mouth, which he does when he wants Avery to be quiet and when he's feeling particularly in the mood to be dominant and wants to be obeyed.

Avery usually obeys him when he's like this, but not always. He does this time, though. He can't stop looking at the collar in Malin's hand.

"Stand up," Malin says. He unbuckles it, and Avery stands. His face is flushed, and he sees Malin's eyes run over him and linger at the bulge in Avery's boxers. He goes behind him and pushes Avery so he's in front of the dresser and can see himself in the mirror. "Good. Watch, Avery."

Malin is taller than Avery by a few inches, enough that he can easily slide the leather around Avery's neck and buckle it securely. It's a little too tight, but it doesn't matter. Avery doesn't care. His breathing is fucked-up in seconds, and he can't stop looking at himself. The collar is really hot.

"Do you know why I got this for you?"

Avery shakes his head. He remembers the rules.

Malin leans in and kisses his neck. "Good. Good, Avery. You never asked me for this. You do know that. Yes? Just nod for me. That's it."

Avery nods. He turns a little, wanting to kiss Malin, who is standing behind Avery but not really touching him.

Malin takes two fingers and presses Avery's face away from him. "No. Not now. I did read some things, you know, after the night you came here, and I finally understood what it was you wanted from me. I don't think you understand how confused I was about that, Avery." He leans in and kisses the back of Avery's neck again, and then straightens and hooks his fingers in the loop of the collar.

"I have told you that I was not attracted to men, before you. But the truth is, after Claudia, I was not attracted to much of anything. And you gave that back to me. Did you know that?"

Avery smiles and shakes his head almost shyly. That's a nice thing to hear.

"Oui, you did. And I found myself looking at websites—images of men in collars like this one." He tugs on it, making Avery's breath catch. "And I found it... very arousing. Very attractive. When you weren't here, I would think of you in one and get off on it. I put my belt around your neck because I wanted to put this there, instead."

Holy fuck. This is one of those times when Malin shares things in his head, and Avery thinks he's on to something with the whole "saving those for an opportune moment" thing.

"I ordered this. Not for you, but for me. It was not something I understood, at first. I was never like this with Claudia, and certainly not Marie."

Avery privately thinks Marie would have been into it a lot more, but he doesn't share that. He wonders where this is going, though, because Malin's voice is getting that cruel edge to it, the one that means he's going to hurt Avery—and not necessarily in the way Avery likes.

"This is not something I want to put on you all the time, though it is harder than I can tell you not to throw you down and fuck you right here, right now. I've been waiting a long time to see you in that."

Avery makes a small, small noise. It doesn't count as talking, but he almost wishes it did because he wants Malin to smack him. He wants something. Instead, Malin turns him so Avery's facing him, and Malin is still holding the loop but not touching him. "I want you to trust me enough to give me what I want when I put you in this. Can you do that for me?"

As if he's going to say no? Avery nods, and Malin stares at him for a long moment, eyes consuming. He really does seem distracted by the collar on Avery's neck. Which makes Avery tilt his chin up a little like he's showing off. Malin smiles and smacks him gently on the side of the face.

"Pay attention. You, Avery, if you need something from me, you will bring me this, and I will put it on you. Not the things you usually need, oui? Things like... the night I fucked you the first time. You remember? You know that was different. Hmm?"

He does, but it's getting really hard to stay focused. Avery nods, and he's swaying a little on his feet.

Malin pulls him in with the loop and kisses him. "Bon, Avery. Now I am going to tell you what I want. Are you ready?"

Like ten minutes ago. Avery nods.

"Look at me." He uses the collar to keep Avery's gaze locked with his. "What do you want for your birthday? Tell me."

That's the absolute last thing Avery expects to hear. It takes him a few seconds to answer. "Umm. This?"

Malin smacks him, harder this time. "Don't tell me what you think I want to hear."

"But you asked," Avery says, and gets smacked again, which he expects. "No, I really... don't understand." He feels suddenly frantic, like he's doing wrong or not meeting expectations. Goddammit. He hates that Malin knows that.

"All right. Shhh." Malin kisses him again. "Calm down. Let me try another way. I want to ask you something, and I want you to answer me honestly. That's all you have to do. Do you understand? Do not think about what I want to hear or what you should say. Do not think about anything but telling me the answer. If you do that, I will be very happy with you. I think you are afraid to ask me for something because you are afraid not to have it."

That's a lot of words from Malin—hot words—and ones that make Avery nervous as fuck.

"Do you understand? Let me hear you say that you do."

"I understand."

"You will tell me the truth? You don't have to worry. Nothing you say will make me leave you. Do you know that?"

He didn't actually. But Malin just tightens his fingers on the loop and tells him to be quiet—not to worry—and kisses him again.

"Why didn't you ask me to come with you on Friday? For your birthday."

Avery blinks. He knits his brow, lowers his eyes carefully, and takes a breath. "I didn't think you'd want to come."

"Why didn't you ask me?"

Oh, fuck this. "I didn't want you to say no or to think maybe you'd be there and then have you not show up."

Fuck, fuck, fuck.

"Do you want me to be there? It's all right if you don't."

"Of course I want you to be there." Avery swallows hard and looks up, eyes searching Malin's. "I love you." He says it quietly, shivering like he's freezing, even though it isn't cold. "You're my boyfriend. But I know you've got work considerations, and I'm not going to make you out yourself or—"

"Shhh," Malin murmurs, pulling on the loop. "You are very good for me, Avery. Do you know that? You are. I am not ashamed of you. I am a private person by nature, and I've never had a lot of friends, even before Claudia and Julien's death. And I meant what I said. If you don't want me to be there, I won't be. But if you do, I want you to ask me. Why do you think, after everything you've done for me, I wouldn't do this for you?"

"I hate when you point out how stuff makes me look bad, when I thought I was just being nice," Avery mutters, cranky.

Malin makes a noise that might be a laugh. "Do you know why I had to put this collar on you to ask you this?"

"Because you wanted to hurt me for being a moron?" Avery asks, smiling a bit wryly.

"Because I couldn't ask you. Do you know why? I didn't want to hear you say no either."

"Oh." Avery looks at him solemnly and then smiles wider. "So we're both morons." He was afraid to ask Malin to come, and Malin was afraid to ask Avery if he wanted him to, both afraid the other would say no.

"Oui. It would seem we are."

They stand for a moment, and then Avery says, "Malin, will you come to my birthday dinner and drinks thing after work on Friday? I want to tell everyone you're my boyfriend and make out inappropriately and shock the hipsters. Because we'll both be in suits. They'll be like, 'Check it out. The man is getting hot man lovin' and—'"

190

Malin smacks him—hard. At Avery's affronted look, he smiles evilly. "I did tell you the first time, didn't I, that I don't want the commentary?"

"Or you just want to smack me," Avery mutters. He winks when Malin smacks him again. He never does it hard enough to leave a mark or bruise, just enough to get Avery's attention. Which, of course, is why Avery likes it so much.

"Yes. I will come to your party. And Avery, after that, we will figure out what to do about work, because it is going to be a problem."

That is true. And it isn't because they're guys, as the reaction to Brandon's announcement of his engagement to a man was "How did you even have time to date anybody, run a marathon, and design a building? I hate you." But everyone would think Avery sucked his way into that contract for the Knight Performing Arts Center. Though, wow. It would be flattering to his blowjob skills, at least, if they *did* think that.

"Can I ask you something else?" Avery asks, moving closer.

"Oui?"

"Can I make that party on Saturday, instead, so we can go to the hockey game?" He looks up through his lashes at Malin.

Malin leans in and kisses him. "Oui. Now I want to fuck you with this collar around your neck."

"That's excellent, because I want you to do that too," Avery says and pauses. "Can I touch you? Are we done…?"

"I don't think we are. I like this collar, and I like how you look when you have to ask for things." Malin starts pushing him back toward the bed. "Yes, you may touch me."

Excellent. "I thought this was my birthday present, so shouldn't—ow," he says dramatically, narrowing his eyes. He's still pulling at Malin's clothes, sliding his hands underneath his dress shirt.

"It's not. It's *mine*."

"Your birthday is in June," Avery reminds him, suspicious. This time when Malin smacks him, he moans.

Malin really does like that collar. He fucks Avery on the bed and then drags him into the shower and just stares at him in it. He tells Avery how he wants to put Avery on his knees and have him suck him off while wearing it.

Even Avery is sad when Malin takes it off and puts it away. But then he's allowed to be obnoxious, so he does. He tackles Malin onto the bed and asks him to tell him all about those websites he visited.

"If you had a membership to kink.com, I'm going to laugh because I did too."

"Had?" Malin asks, pulling gently at Avery's hair. "I still have it."

"You do? What? What's the username?" Avery glares at him playfully. "If you're teasing, I'm stealing your credit card and signing you up for one. With an obnoxious name, like Master Hab or something." Avery gives him a horrified look. "That's not your name, is it...?"

"No, it isn't. But a decent suggestion. Maybe I'll change it." Malin pulls him down to kiss him. "Avery?"

"What?" Avery bites him on the mouth. "I'm not calling you Master Hab. I'm not calling you Master anything—ever."

"Please don't."

There's a moment of silence, and then he says, "I love you."

Avery kisses him and says, "I know," which is a thing he's always wanted to say because Han Solo was pretty cool and also because, hey, he does know.

CHAPTER 18

AVERY'S BIRTHDAY party is on Saturday, and his friends are all at the bar waiting at a table with a pitcher, a frosty glass, and a bow they make him wear on his head.

Malin shows up a few minutes after Avery does. He was parking the car, and Avery pretended he bought that and didn't think that Malin was stalling. For a minute, there's a strained silence, because Malin apparently thinks "party" means "wear a suit."

If these people only saw him last night, in the Habs jersey. Even though they were at a Rangers game, and they were playing the *Penguins*. They won, because Avery's birthday was a charmed day, and nothing could go wrong. Even the Pens' goaltending.

"Who invited the boss?" James Santana, one of the other junior associates, murmurs. He looks at Avery with raised eyebrows. "I thought you hated him."

"Well. I do sometimes. When he's the boss," Avery says and shrugs. He's acting a lot more nonchalant about this than he feels. He's nervous, and he also had no idea James would be here. He invited the whole office, because he was that kid who invited the whole class to his birthday parties in school and gave all of them Valentines—even the creepy kids who didn't wash their hair. "I like him a lot better when he's my boyfriend, though."

It's actually kind of worth the nerves to see the look on everyone's faces when he says that.

Malin is clearly out of place and not enjoying himself, but he's giving it an effort even if that means standing around in a suit and awkwardly holding a drink and staring a lot. Avery is good at drawing people into the conversation, but his friends are being dicks, and Avery knows it's just going to take some time.

He realizes Malin is checking his phone at one point, which he only does for two reasons—he's at work or there's a Habs game on.

193

Grinning, Avery excuses himself, goes to the bar, and asks the guy to put the game on. It's also a Devils versus Habs game, which means there are a few Devils fans in the bar, and that's excellent.

Nothing will prove to his friends Malin is socially awkward and uncomfortable around crowds like watching him be a weirdo about something. Malin actually glares at him when Avery slides back into his seat, grinning in triumph.

"Look, you're already losing your scary cred by dating me," Avery informs him. "You might as well just go ahead and yell at the hockey game in French. Come on." Then he kisses him, right there, in front of everybody.

It's New York, and it's a bar on a Saturday night, so no one notices except his friends. After that, they seem a bit more willing to try to get to know Malin. Baby steps.

He's not doing so bad for thirty-two, he realizes when his friends sing a horrible version of "Happy Birthday," after more than a few pitchers. He's got a building going up, he's going to be in a wedding, he's got friends and some fantastic parents, a Crock-Pot, and a hot boyfriend with a collar fetish.

Next up—an energy-efficient dishwasher. And he still really needs that oil change.

AVON GALE wrote her first story at the age of seven, about a "Space Hat" hanging on a rack and waiting for that special person to come along and purchase it—even if it was a bit weirder than the other, more normal hats. Like all of Avon's characters, the space hat did get its happily ever after—though she's pretty sure it was with a unicorn. She likes to think her vocabulary has improved since then, but the theme of quirky people waiting for their perfect match is still one of her favorites.

Avon grew up in the southern United States, and now lives with her very patient husband in a liberal Midwestern college town. By day, Avon is a hair stylist who loves her job, her clients, and the opportunity to spend her time being creative and making people happy and look fabulous.

When she's not writing, she's either doing some kind of craft project that makes a huge mess, reading, watching horror movies, listening to music, or yelling at her favorite hockey team to get it together already. Avon is always up for a road trip, adores Kentucky bourbon, thinks nothing is as stress relieving as a good rock concert, and will never say no to candy.

At one point, Avon was the mayor of both Jazzercise and Lollicup on Foursquare. This tells you basically all you need to know about her as a person.

Website: www.avongalewrites.com
Email: avongalewrites@gmail.com
Twitter: @avongalewrites
Facebook: www.facebook.com/avongalewrites
Pinterest: www.pinterest.com/avongalewrites

Bound TO FALL

JAIME SAMMS

www.dreamspinnerpress.com

The CAGE

Catt Ford

CAGED
SANCTUARY
Tempeste O'Riley

www.dreamspinnerpress.com

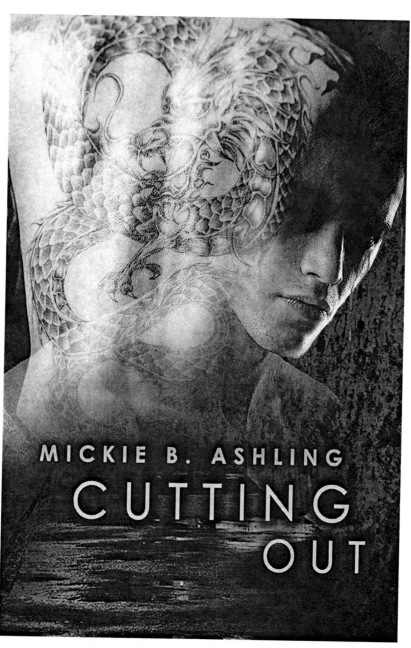

MICKIE B. ASHLING

CUTTING
OUT

www.dreamspinnerpress.com

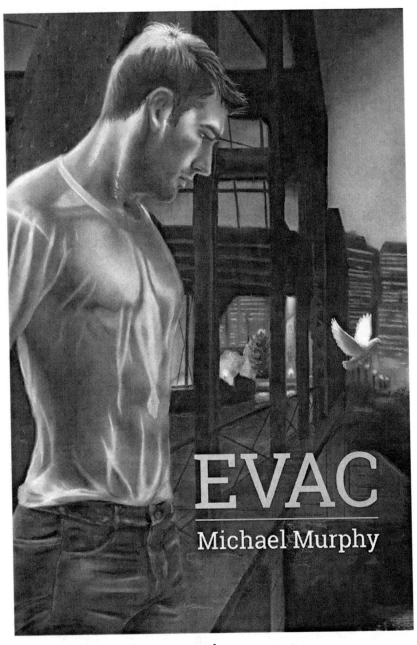

EVAC

Michael Murphy

www.dreamspinnerpress.com

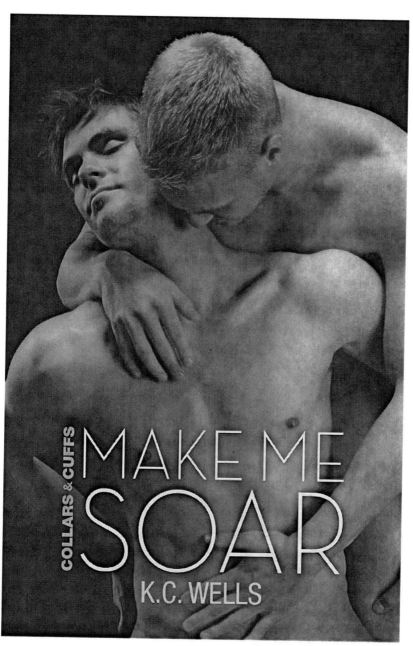

COLLARS & CUFFS

MAKE ME
SOAR

K.C. WELLS

www.dreamspinnerpress.com

www.dreamspinnerpress.com

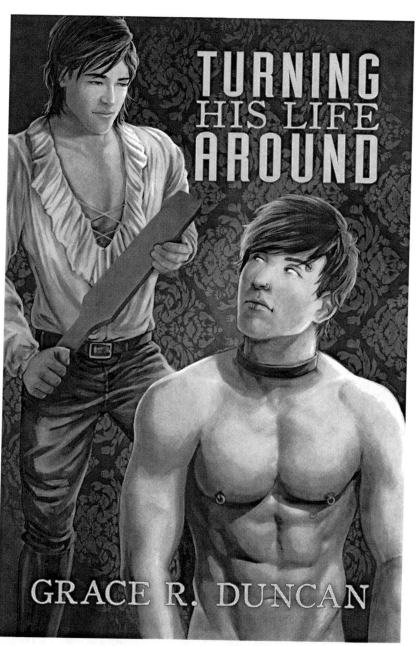

TURNING
HIS LIFE
AROUND

GRACE R. DUNCAN

CPSIA information can be obtained at www.ICGtesting.com
Printed in the USA
LVOW10s1354230616

493831LV00015B/137/P